Miss Dimple Suspects

Center Point
Large Print

Also by Mignon F. Ballard and available from
Center Point Large Print:

Miss Dimple Disappears
Miss Dimple Rallies to the Cause

Miss Dimple Suspects

MIGNON F. BALLARD

CENTER POINT LARGE PRINT
THORNDIKE, MAINE

This Center Point Large Print edition
is published in the year 2013 by arrangement with
St. Martin's Press.

This is a work of fiction.
All of the characters, organizations, and events
portrayed in this novel are either products of the
author's imagination or are used fictitiously.

The text of this Large Print edition is unabridged.
In other aspects, this book may vary
from the original edition.
Printed in the United States of America
on permanent paper.
Set in 16-point Times New Roman type.

ISBN: 978-1-61173-659-5

Library of Congress Cataloging-in-Publication Data

Ballard, Mignon Franklin.
 Miss Dimple suspects / Mignon F. Ballard.
 pages ; cm.
 ISBN 978-1-61173-659-5 (library binding : alk. paper)
 1. Elementary school teachers—Fiction.
   2. Older women—Crimes against—Fiction.
   3. Japanese Americans—Fiction.
   4. World War, 1939–1945—Georgia—Fiction.
   5. Large type books. I. Title.
 PS3552.A466M593 2013b
 813′.54—dc23
                                                    2012043055

For our wonderful family and friends,
with love and appreciation

 CHAPTER ONE

H ey, look, Miss Dimple! Watch me! Watch me! I'll bet I can jump "hot pepper" to 'bout a hundred!*

While her classmates counted, Peggy Ashcroft, cheeks flushed and pigtails flying, became the undisputed jump-rope champion of Miss Dimple Kilpatrick's first grade class at Elderberry Grammar School. Her new blue jacket with the fuzzy lining, along with its matching tam, had been tossed in a heap at the foot of the school steps with an assortment of other wraps, and their teacher knew from long experience it would be useless to urge her small charges not to shed them.

That had been yesterday. A million years ago, it seemed. Now Dimple Kilpatrick carefully searched the bare December landscape for a sign—any sign—of a round little face and a glimpse of bright blue. A scurrying in the dry leaves just ahead lured her forward, her breath coming faster.

"Peggy! Peggy, where are you?" She drew up short when a squirrel scampered into a tree and out of sight.

"Dimple, are you sure we're looking in the right

direction? Chief Tinsley didn't seem to think a child Peggy's age would be able to wander so far in this length of time." Dimple's friend Virginia paused to catch her breath, clinging to a sapling to steady her progress on a hill slippery with pine needles.

But Dimple knew that Peggy Ashcroft could run faster, climb higher, and race farther than almost any boy in her class. "Bobby Tinsley obviously doesn't know our Peggy," she said, shoving aside the limb of a large cedar as she continued up the hill. The fragrant evergreen reminded her that Christmas was only a few weeks away and the children in her class were already wild in anticipation, although gifts would be limited again this year. Bicycles, tricycles, roller skates, and anything else made of metal or rubber would have to wait until after the war.

Sighing, Virginia plodded along behind her. "Didn't her mother say the child had a fever? Might be coming down with the flu—it's going around, you know."

However, Dimple Kilpatrick also knew how much the little girl loved her calico, Peaches, and doubted if a fever would hinder her search for the missing cat. Peggy had confided in her teacher about her special place on what she called Bent Tree Hill. Before that bad thing happened to her mama and she'd come to live with Kate and Mathew, she said, she'd had picnics there with dolls made of acorns, sticks, and leaves, built tiny houses of twigs and moss.

And Dimple Kilpatrick had listened with understanding because she, too, had been raised in the country with only her brother to play with, and Henry Kilpatrick wanted nothing to do with creating dolls and houses of sticks and grass. If it didn't have wheels or wings, it wasn't worth his time.

How long had she been missing? Dimple didn't stop to look at the watch pinned to her dress under the worn purple coat because she didn't want to know. She did know it was getting late and the days were much too short. Night would soon be upon them, making it almost impossible to look for a small six-year-old girl alone in the cold and dark.

Below them on an adjacent hill, searchers spread out in all directions in a frantic endeavor to find her. The little house on Fox Grape Hill, where Peggy had lived less than two years before, had been demolished after the fire that claimed her mother. Now a tangle of underbrush and honeysuckle obscured the blackened remains.

"If Peggy thinks her cat has roamed back to the place where they lived before, it only makes sense she'd try to find her there," Oscar Faulkenberry reasoned as he organized a group of townspeople to help look for the child. As principal of Elderberry Grammar School, he was accustomed to giving orders, and several teachers, as well as others, willingly scattered to cover that area while Chief Bobby Tinsley led volunteers in a search around Etowah Pond.

Of course she would go there first, Miss Dimple thought, but she didn't believe Peggy would linger when faced with the ruins of her former home. She would probably return to that other place, her happy place, she'd called it, on Bent Tree Hill. But the other searchers remained unconvinced, and now she and her friend Virginia Balliew were determined to cover the area together—or at least Dimple was determined. Virginia wasn't as physically fit as her friend. As town librarian, she spent much of her time behind a desk, while Dimple, with her lively charges, rarely had a chance to sit down, and her brisk early-morning walks only increased her stamina.

"Ah!" Virginia collapsed on a moss-covered stump and pulled her coat snugly about her. "Have to sit just for a minute." She shivered. "I believe it's turning colder, Dimple. I hope somebody finds her soon."

Dimple looked through the bare trees to the faraway figures on the next hill. The whole town, it seemed, had turned out to look for Peggy Ashcroft. The child's father had died when she was barely three, and her mother supported the two of them on the little she earned as a waitress at the Dixie Belle Diner. The fire was believed to have started from a spark from a kerosene heater, and a passerby, seeing the flames, pulled the sleeping child from the house but couldn't awaken her mother in time.

Kate Ashcroft, who taught music and piano at Miss Dimple's school, and her husband, Mathew, had long wanted a child of their own. The couple welcomed five-year-old Peggy into their home and made the arrangement permanent by legally adopting her. Some people found it disrespectful that Peggy was allowed to address her new parents by their given names, but Kate insisted, saying that Peggy once had a mother who loved her very much and although she and Mathew couldn't take her place, they could do the next best thing. That seemed to suit all concerned.

"Tell me again what we're looking for," Virginia said, brushing leaves from her coat as she stood. The wind had picked up and she sneezed, fumbling in her pocket for a hand-kerchief.

"It's a tree bent horizontal to the ground. There was one on the farm where I grew up and I've seen pictures of others. They were made to grow that way and used as trail markers by the Indians. They usually indicated graves or campsites—sometimes water." She frowned. "Virginia, you have no business out here in this cold. I don't know why you insisted on coming after that bad bout of bronchitis. You don't want to come down with pneumonia."

"It's only a sneeze, Dimple, and I want to be a part of this. I won't be able to sleep tonight not knowing what happened to that little girl."

It wouldn't help Peggy Ashcroft if Virginia got sick, Dimple thought, but she didn't say it aloud because she knew how important it was to aid in the search. She paused to look around at the oatmeal-colored woods. Except for an occasional brush-stroke of green where cedars and pines lent a smear of color to an otherwise drab landscape, the only other relief was in the dark winter branches of oak, sweet gum, sycamore, and hickory. Under ordinary circumstances, Dimple embraced the starkness of the season, the sharp, cold air, even the piercing wind, just as she relished the distinctive differences in spring, summer, and fall. Not today.

Dimple ducked under the swaying limb of a shortleaf pine and held it back for Virginia. "Peggy! Peggy, can you hear me?" she called again, and Virginia joined her in shouting. If the little girl were near, she would certainly have heard them.

"I can't help thinking about little Cassie Greeson," Virginia said, sneezing again. "Remember, Dimple? They dragged Etowah Pond, scoured the countryside for miles around, but never did find her."

Dimple remembered. In fact, she had been thinking about the same thing but had tried to dismiss it from her mind. The child had disappeared about a quarter of a century before and no one ever had a clue about what happened to her. It was almost as if she'd vanished off the face of the earth.

"We weren't living here then," Virginia continued, pausing to cough. "Albert was preaching at the Methodist church in Eatonton and I remember his coming here to help look for the little girl. It upset him terribly—upset everyone."

"Eugenia Greeson was pregnant with Jesse Dean," Dimple said. "Poor woman died soon after he was born. I don't know if Cassie's disappearance had anything to do with her death, but it certainly didn't help."

"What ever happened to Jesse Dean's father?" Virginia asked. "I don't remember him ever being in the picture."

"He left not too long after that—supposedly to find work, but I don't think anybody ever heard from him again." Dimple paused to untangle herself from a clutch of briars. "Some say Sanford Greeson never was right after he came back from the war," she explained. "The war to end all wars, they said, which, as we all know, it didn't."

Jesse Dean's sister, Cassie, was about four when

she wandered away from her parents during a Sunday school picnic at Etowah Pond. Her father, caught up in a lively game of horseshoes, paid her little attention, and her mother dozed off for a minute while Cassie played with children nearby. It was a scorching July afternoon and Eugenia Greeson was well past her sixth month of a difficult pregnancy, but she never forgave herself. Upon her death, Jesse Dean was raised by his maternal grandmother, Addie Montgomery, who, in an effort to "bring back" her missing granddaughter, dressed him as a girl and attempted to raise him as such until the little boy finally rebelled.

Through a tangle of underbrush, Dimple thought she saw a tree bent in the manner Peggy had described and used a stout stick to clear a pathway but was disappointed to find it was only a fallen limb. "Peggy?" she shouted again. "Peggy!" Her only answer was the soft thud of a pinecone dropping to the ground and the sound of her own breathing. Surprised to find herself a bit winded from the climb, she rested a minute, watching each breath disappear in a puff of vapor in the frigid air. From here she couldn't see or hear the searchers in the distance, and it suddenly occurred to her that she couldn't see Virginia, either. Dimple started back the way she had come, calling her friend's name, and found her seated on the ground some distance away, her head resting against the scrawny trunk of a redbud tree.

"I'm afraid my knees gave out on me," Virginia said, struggling to stand. "I'll be all right in a minute."

"Your knees aren't what concern me. I don't like the sound of that cough." Dimple pulled off a glove to touch her friend's cheek. "Your face is flushed and you feel warm to me. I'm afraid you might have a fever, Virginia."

"Oh, come now! I'm not one of your first graders, Dimple! I'm just not accustomed to all this climbing." Virginia's laughter turned into a rattling cough and she clung to the tree until the spasm passed.

"That does it. Back you go!" This time Virginia didn't protest when Dimple supported her part of the way down the steep hill until they reached the area dotted with scrub pine and cedar with a clear vista ahead. From there they could see cars parked below and hear other searchers calling from the adjacent hillside.

"I'm fine, really, Dimple. I can see my car from here, but how will you get back?" Virginia hesitated, bracing herself on the hillside. "You aren't going back up there alone, are you? There's not much daylight left."

Dimple Kilpatrick was very well aware of that and that was exactly why she was in a great hurry to search more of the hill before it got too dark to see. "I can get a ride back with Bessie Jenkins or with Lou and Ed Willingham if I need to," she said. And my goodness, she could walk home if she had to! Didn't she walk this far or farther almost every day?

Dimple stood and watched her friend make her way down the hillside before turning to go back the way she had come. Virginia had promised to drink hot lemonade, take two aspirins, and go to bed. And yes, Dimple in turn said she would call her when she got home.

It didn't take as long to find her way back to the place where Virginia had rested against the tree, and Dimple explored the undulating terrain above it, using her stick to help keep her footing on treacherous ground where hidden hollows and stump holes might bring about a broken ankle, or roots a harmful fall. Faced with a steep gully, she chose to sit and slide down, as the bank was slick with pine needles and the bottom soft with fallen leaves. If she weren't on such a grave mission, Dimple thought, she might enjoy the experience, as it brought to mind happy memories of a time long past when she and her brother played follow the leader through the woods on their farm, splashing through streams and swinging on vines before racing home across familiar fields. After their mother died when she was fourteen and Henry, eight, Dimple's carefree hours were limited, as she had to help with much of the housework as well as look after Henry. Dimple Kilpatrick took mothering seriously, as she did later with her teaching. Her father had hired a cook to take care of their meals, but Dimple saw that her little brother didn't skip his baths, had clean clothes, did his homework, and went to bed on time. And she loved him with all her heart. At the present, Henry was working at the Bell Bomber plant in Marietta on a top secret project that might help them win the war against Germany and Japan, and Dimple liked to think that her parents, if alive, would be as proud as she was of the man he had become.

Having no children of her own, Dimple Kilpatrick discovered that she had plenty of leftover love to share and knew she had found her mission in life when she first faced a classroom filled with squirming five- and six-year-olds, some of who clung to their mothers in tearful desperation.

Peggy Ashcroft had seemed a happy child since she walked into her classroom on the very first day of school in her shiny new brown shoes and a red plaid dress sewed painstakingly by Kate, who admitted she'd had a little help from Mary Edna Sizemore, who taught home economics at the high school. Apart from a normal period of grief and questions about what had happened to her mother, the little girl appeared to have become adjusted to school and to her new family, and Kate and Mathew—Well, it made Dimple happy just to look at them.

Now she tugged her lavender knit hat snugly about her ears and turned up the collar of her coat as a stiff wind sent brown leaves skyward. It was already cold and would soon become colder. Was a frightened little girl lost and shivering somewhere on this wooded hill? Dimple stood still and listened. Again she called, but only the wind answered. She was too far away to hear or see the other searchers, and the bare trees seemed to stand in judgment around her. Dimple Kilpatrick pulled a handkerchief from her coat pocket to blot her eyes, as the wind had caused them to water. Of course it was the wind. Not that there was anything wrong with crying, but it wouldn't help anyone now.

She thought of red-eyed Kate Ashcroft earlier at the school where they had gathered to organize the search and how she had stood at the top of the steps to tell everyone about her little girl: what she looked like, what she wore, how she sang "Santa Claus Is Coming to Town" to her calico cat, Peaches, and wanted a red scooter for Christmas but knew she would have to wait until after the war. That was okay with Peggy. Although her hair was naturally curly, she preferred to wear it in pigtails but the ribbons tended to get lost. She had one tooth missing right in front and loved chocolate ice cream just about better than anything—except maybe watermelon . . .

Seeing his wife about a breath away from melting into tears, Mathew Ashcroft stepped up to thank everyone for their help, and arm in arm, the two moved aside for Bobby Tinsley, who would direct the search.

Mathew had joined the group combing the area around Fox Grape Hill, where the charred remains of Peggy's former home lay buried beneath a jungle of honeysuckle vines. Although Kate begged to go with them, on the advice of Chief Tinsley and others, and accompanied by several friends, she reluctantly went back to the house to wait and hope for Peggy's return.

The stricken look on the young mother's face would stay with Dimple Kilpatrick for years to come, and she yearned to comfort her and tell her everything would be all right, but she wanted even more to help find that child and bring her safely home.

Was everything going to be all right? When she and Virginia had first set out to look for Peggy's "happy place" on Bent Tree Hill, she was almost certain she would find her there, but now . . .

Daylight was slipping away quickly, and in spite of her warm wool gloves, Miss Dimple's hands were numb from the cold, and she could scarcely feel her feet. How far had she come? If she didn't start back down soon, it would be too dark to see. In her coat pocket she was comforted to feel the cylindrical shape of the small flashlight she had thought to bring along at the last minute. It didn't give much light, but it was better than nothing and might prevent her from taking a serious fall. Except for members of the Home Guard and a few hardy others who intended to search through the night, most volunteers would soon be leaving, and Virginia was the only person who knew where she was. Her friend Phoebe Chadwick, who owned the boardinghouse where she lived, was visiting a relative in Macon, and her fellow roomers were usually on their own on Saturday nights, having a quick sandwich in the kitchen before going to their rooms to read, write letters, or listen to the radio. Those who chose to gather in the parlor would probably think she was either in her room or sharing supper with Virginia. Miss Dimple sighed and surveyed the spreading gloom around her. It was time to make a decision. A practical decision. And Dimple Kilpatrick had always prided herself on her practical sense. She would walk as far as the large rock up ahead, and if she found nothing there, although heartsick, she would begin to make her descent.

At first she thought it was a leaf, dangling as it was on the end of a twig, but autumn was far past and this was much too bright for a leaf. Too red. Dimple pulled the ribbon from the waist-high branches of a bush, and after years of having young children cluster about her, Dimple Kilpatrick knew it was just the right height to snag a ribbon from a little girl's hair.

CHAPTER TWO

I don't want to read about Snow White anymore!" Peggy Ashcroft shoved the storybook aside. "She must've known that old woman with the apple was the wicked queen! Couldn't she *see?* I want to look for Peaches and I bet I know just where she is. Why can't we go and find her?"

Violet Kirby set the book on the table and flipped Peggy's pillow to the cool side. She was usually an easygoing child, content to play go fish, color pictures, or attempt to dress her cat, Peaches, in doll clothes, but today she was ill and feverish and nothing seemed to please her.

"Honey, I've hollered all up and down this street for Peaches. That cat will come home when she's good and ready, you can count on it." According to her mama, once you feed a cat, you ain't never gonna get rid of it, but she wasn't going to tell Peggy that. "You want some more ginger ale? It'll make your throat feel better."

But Peggy turned her face away. "Peaches will

make me feel better, and I think you're mean not to let me go find her!"

Although Violet was only sixteen, she knew when she was being manipulated. "Sticks and stones may break my bones, but words will never hurt me," she quoted. "Your mama and daddy should be home from that wedding before long, and if Peaches isn't back by then, I'll bet one of them will go and hunt for her." She tucked Peggy's rag doll, Lucy, under the covers beside her. Violet's aunt Odessa had made the doll for Peggy two years before when she'd lost her mother and everything she'd owned in that awful fire. "And what if Peaches came home and found us gone?" she said. "What would she think then? I'll bet if you close your eyes and take a little nap, that cat will be back by the time you wake up. . . . And I'm not supposed to tell, but I happen to know your mama's bringing you a piece of wedding cake from the reception, and if you put it under your pillow tonight, you're supposed to dream about the man you're going to marry."

"Won't it get smushed?"

Violet smiled. "Well, I reckon they'll wrap it up real good in wax paper."

Peggy made a face. "Shoot, I'd lots rather eat it! What if I dreamed about Willie Elrod?"

A half hour later, having listened to *The Green Hornet* on the radio, Violet quietly opened

Peggy's bedroom door and tiptoed in to check on her. She hadn't heard one peep from Peggy since she'd tucked her into bed and assumed the little girl had dropped off to sleep.

Not only was the bed empty, but six-year-old Peggy Ashcroft was nowhere to be found and neither were her hat, coat, or mittens. Her neatly folded pajamas had been left on the chair, and a dress she had worn the day before no longer hung on the back of the door.

Not even stopping to put on a wrap, Violet started on a run for the Methodist church where Kate Ashcroft was to play the piano for the wedding. The ceremony should have been over by now, but guests were probably lingering over punch and cake at the reception. She had almost reached the corner when Violet saw nine-year-old Willie Elrod racing toward her on his bicycle.

"Willie! I need you to ride over to that wedding reception at the church and tell Mr. and Mrs. Ashcroft Peggy's done taken off to find that cat, and I think I know where she's gone! Hurry, now! You can get there faster than I can!"

Violet Kirby watched the child wheel about and pedal for dear life for the Methodist church a few blocks away. Only after she saw him safely across the street did she allow herself to cry.

Dimple Kilpatrick felt herself go weak as she reached for the flashlight in her pocket, and only then did she realize she had been holding her breath. The ribbon was red, the same color as the dress Peggy Ashcroft had been wearing when she disappeared that afternoon. She must be somewhere close by! Dimple felt a peculiar emptiness in the pit of her stomach. What if she had turned around earlier without looking further? Clutching the ribbon as if it could somehow lead her to Peggy, Miss Dimple called the child's name. Still no answer.

Well, she certainly wasn't going to turn back now. Standing there in the semidarkness, Dimple Kilpatrick devised a plan. She would take twenty steps forward and call again; then twenty more, and twenty more. After that time, if she still hadn't found Peggy, there should be barely enough light to go back for help. Miss Dimple tied the ribbon to the bush where she had found it to mark the spot and plunged forward. Underbrush clawed her legs, and overhanging limbs raked her so that she had to hold her hat on with one hand to keep from losing it. She tucked the little flashlight back into her pocket to use later and pulled herself along by low-hanging branches, pausing now and then to shout the little girl's name and listen for a response.

But branches and bushes weren't the only things that grabbed at Dimple Kilpatrick as she made her way along uncertain ground. The smothering threat of fear hovered so near she could almost smell it, and it stank of rotten peaches. It was waiting and she knew it, sensed it closing in to make her heart race, her breath come fast, her reasoning take leave of her.

Do get a hold of yourself, Dimple. You are not eight years old and you know very well where you are! If it gets too dark to see, all you have to do is make your way down this hill a few feet at a time. Still, she couldn't erase the memory of her frenzied mission to find help for her two-year-old brother struggling to breathe with diphtheria.

It was the last of August and the day was born muggy and oppressive even before sunlight slanted through the slits in the bedroom shutters. And it was as humid inside as out because her mama kept a steaming kettle next to Henry's little bed with a tent made of bedsheets over his face. Dimple's papa had gone to Milledgeville the day before with corn to be ground into meal and the last of the okra and green beans to sell at the market. He was staying with relatives there and didn't plan to come home until tomorrow, so when Henry woke with fever and chills and his breathing began to make that terrible squeaking sound by late afternoon, Dimple and her mother knew they had to get help fast.

"Minerva will know what to do," her mother said, pacing from Henry's cot to the window for about the tenth time. Their neighbor lived almost five miles away if you went by the road, and in the absence of a doctor, Minerva Sayre had ministered to just about everybody around at one time or another. Why, she'd even stitched up her father's leg when he cut it open chopping wood, and you could hardly see the scar.

"I'll go, Mama! Let me!" Dimple covered her ears to block out the sound of her little brother's labored breathing. She could hardly bear to hear it. Her father had taken the horses and she knew she wouldn't be able to control either of the two mules. "Please! I can run. I'll run as fast as I can!"

Her mother held her close and kissed her, smoothing the soft brown hair from her face. "Go by the road and take Bear with you. Minerva will bring you back in the buggy.

"Be careful, and God go with you!"

Calling to her dog, Dimple ran down the path to the road, glancing back to see her mother watching from the doorway. Once she reached the road, now thick with red dust, she turned toward their neighbor's as her mother had directed, but Dimple Kilpatrick knew a shorter way, and as soon as she was out of sight, she veered off, skirting her father's field where cotton would soon be picked and carried to the gin on the big wagon drawn by mules. Bear, a mixed breed dog of part collie and part who-knew-what, trotted obediently along by her side, although he seemed hesitant about leaving the road.

"It's all right, I know a better way!" Dimple called to him, running ahead. The familiar pathway through the woods was much cooler and the shade welcome after the choking dust of the road and Dimple had played there often, setting up housekeeping for her dolls under the trees, serving them tea in acorn cups. She knew how the big cedar, so old her father referred to it as "Granddaddy," spread its pungent branches like a ceiling, surrounding her with its calming green. She knew how the roots of the water oak made perfect little elf houses, and although she'd never seen them, Dimple knew they were there. She knew that beyond the woods she would have to duck under the pasture fence and cross the grassy meadow where her father's cattle grazed. It felt good to wade through the shallow creek where Bear drank noisily and sprinkled her when he shook himself, but today she couldn't take time to splash and make "frog houses" in the mud or pick a bouquet of buttercups and daisies for the supper table. Trying not to think of what she might find when she reached home, Dimple raced across the pasture and climbed the fence to the other side, where rows of corn taller than she were already beginning to wither and turn brown. They rustled, whispering, "Hurry! Hurry!" as she ran, stumbling over the uneven ground, her breath coming in gasps. Dimple had never been on the other side of the cornfield, but she was sure it wouldn't be far now to where their neighbor lived. Well . . . maybe not too sure.

Picking her way through waist-high weeds where blackberry briars snagged her dress and scratched her legs above the tops of her shoes, Dimple wished she had stayed on the road as her mother had told her. It would take much too long to get through the thick tangle of grass, and she didn't even want to think about snakes. Bear, who had bounded ahead, looked back at her as if to ask why she'd gotten them into such a fix. His shaggy black-and-white coat was matted with beggar lice, and it would take forever to get them all out, but that didn't matter now.

Dimple turned and went back to the edge of the cornfield, following it to the cooler woods. It was easier to walk here, and she was sure to come out in the same place, wasn't she? The sun had dipped lower in the sky and mosquitoes and gnats seemed to follow her every step. Dimple swatted at them with her skirt, wishing she'd thought to wear her sunbonnet. She swallowed a lump in her throat and felt it lodge like a rock in her chest. Stinging tears blurred her vision and she wiped them away impatiently. *Dimple Kilpatrick had no idea where she was!*

What would her mother say if she didn't come home with help? If Henry died, it would be all her fault! Mr. Sayre's big vegetable garden should be just up ahead. Once when she went there with her papa, he had given her a sweet, juicy watermelon. Dimple's mouth was dry but she took a deep breath and ran faster. Soon she would see it.

But she didn't. Instead she came out on a hillside dotted with trees. The crop had been harvested and the peaches left on the trees had fallen to the ground, where wasps buzzed about the sour, rotting fruit. Dimple held her nose as she ran, not even taking time to be careful where she stepped. This wasn't where she was supposed to be, but somebody had to own the orchard and somebody had to pick the peaches. It wasn't until she reached the bottom of the hill that she saw the shiny tin roof of the Sayres' barn and the big vegetable patch beyond it.

Dimple Kilpatrick barely remembered holding tight to Bear during the furious buggy ride home, but she did remember the July flies sawing away with their summer song as they pulled up to the house and her mother running out to meet them.

Minerva Sayre dosed Henry with a tonic made of sage with a pinch of alum and rubbed his chest with a salve of warmed lard mixed with turpentine and loose quinine, and the two women sat with him all night. By morning her brother's fever was down and he was able to swallow a few spoons of beef tea. Dimple never knew if it was the continuous use of steam, the primitive medicine, or both that saved her brother's life, but only she, Bear, and God Himself knew the route she had taken to find help.

". . . seventeen . . . eighteen . . . nineteen . . . twenty!" In the twilight of the woods, Miss Dimple paused to listen. This was the second time she had counted and she hesitated before calling Peggy's name because she thought she heard a rustle in the underbrush ahead. Somewhere nearby a dry twig fell as the wind picked up. "Peggy!" Dimple shouted, louder this time. "Peggy, where are you?" And from just over the low knoll ahead came the distinctive sound of a bark.

Again: sharper and more clamorous as she hurried closer—a dog—*someone's* dog! But where had it come from? "Here, boy!" Miss Dimple answered. "It's all right!"

But the dog wasn't sure it was all right. It wasn't sure at all, and it greeted her baring its teeth with a growl low in the throat. "It's all right," Miss Dimple said again in a soft, soothing voice. "I'm not going to hurt you." Taking a step closer, she held out a hand and stood still, allowing the animal to sniff its approval. It was a short-haired dog, a German shepherd, she thought, with a brown-and-black coat and white throat, and it seemed to be attempting to block her way. It was getting so dark now Dimple could barely see more than a few feet ahead, but she was sure the dog was guarding something—or someone. *Don't show alarm, Dimple! Keep your voice calm.* "Peggy?" she called. "Peggy, it's Miss Dimple!" This time she heard a low but very human whimper. Stepping into a small clearing, Dimple could barely distinguish the tree Peggy had told her about. It looked to be an ancient white oak bent to form a benchlike seat. And nearby, there in the darkness beneath the spreading branches of a large hemlock tree, she saw a tiny huddled shape. "Peggy, are you able to walk? It's dark now, and cold. It's time to go home."

This time Dimple stepped past the dog, who still hadn't seemed to have made up its mind. "Bite me if you must," she said in her stern, schoolroom voice, "but I'm taking care of this child." The dog must have recognized the authority in her voice because it backed away to let her pass but made a point to stay close by.

The little girl lay curled, knees to chest. Her pigtails had come loose and the blue tam lay beside her. Miss Dimple stooped and touched the child's face and found her burning with fever. Peggy began to shake with chills as Dimple crouched beside her and she quickly took off her coat to cover her. "Mama," Peggy cried, and reached up her arms to be held. Was she calling for her birth mother or for the mother she called

Kate? Miss Dimple only knew she had to get her out of the cold as quickly as possible.

Dimple Kilpatrick, in all her years of teaching, had held many a child, and tiny Peggy Ashcroft couldn't have weighed a lot more than the heavy leather handbag she usually carried, but the ground was uneven and night had descended upon them. How was she going to get this sick little girl down the treacherous hillside? Dimple stood, cradling Peggy to her chest as the wind whipped about them, and tried not to think about being cold. She would probably be able to get down by herself, but there was no way she was going to leave this child alone while she went for help. She would just have to take it a few steps at a time and hope she didn't have an accident along the way.

She had promised Virginia she would let her know when she got home and if she didn't telephone in a certain amount of time, her friend would be sure to find out she hadn't returned. Or perhaps others at the boardinghouse would become concerned and come looking for her when they learned she wasn't in her room. Meanwhile, she couldn't wait. Locking her arms around Peggy, Miss Dimple was trying to decide on the best way to begin her descent when the dog's frenzied barking caught her attention and it became obvious the animal objected to her plans.

Dimple clenched her teeth to keep them from

chattering as the dog raced back and forth between her and a spot a few feet away. Was he trying to lead her somewhere? Miss Dimple shifted her small burden; the little girl's cheek felt scorching next to her own and she could hear a distinctive rattle in her chest. She thought again of the long-ago neighbor who had helped to save her little brother. *Minerva, where are you when I need you?*

Again, the German shepherd demanded her attention, urging her farther up the hill. Miss Dimple sighed. "Maybe you know something I don't know," she said, stumbling along behind him. Using her flashlight, she walked cautiously, the pale beam probing the way a few feet at a time. She didn't know anything about this dog except that it was protective of Peggy, but from her own early experiences with Bear, Dimple was aware that sometimes animals had keener instincts than humans, and several minutes later she realized she had made the right decision. At the top of the next hill, a welcoming yellow light beckoned to them from the window of a cottage only a few yards away.

CHAPTER THREE

T he door of the house opened and Miss Dimple squinted through dirt-streaked glasses to see the silhouette of a woman framed in the light. "What do you have there, Max? Come here, boy!"

The dog bounded across the clearing and up the steps to the wide porch to jump with abandon about the woman's feet. "What is it, Max? Who's out there?"

Dimple Kilpatrick, her arms aching from carrying Peggy, sank to her knees at the edge of the clearing. She tried to call out but she was so winded and cold from the climb she could scarcely make a sound. What if this woman had a gun? It wasn't unusual for people who lived in the country to keep one on hand to protect themselves and their property. She bent her body over that of the child as the dog Max raced toward them, barking. At the same time another person joined the woman on the porch.

"Please, we need help!" Miss Dimple gasped, hoping they could hear her.

"I believe there's someone out there." Another woman spoke, sounding younger than the first. "You stay here, Miss Mae Martha. I'll see what's going on."

"Wait! Take the lantern, Suzy, and be careful, you hear?"

The flashlight! What had she done with the flashlight? She must've dropped it when she fell to her knees. Clutching Peggy closer, Dimple glanced over her shoulder to see a glimmer of light in the leaves behind her. If she could turn it on her face, it should let these people know she was in no shape to harm them, but it was too far out of reach. Max, obviously proud of himself for bringing home such a prize, remained close by, demanding attention with an occasional bark, and Dimple was glad to have him there. As long as the dog stayed between them and the two on the porch, they would be less likely to shoot them. She closed her eyes against the glare of the lantern as footsteps approached. "Please," Miss Dimple repeated. "The child is sick."

"Oh!" A young woman knelt beside them. "We have to get you inside." Setting aside the lantern, she called to the older woman, who had started down the steps. "We need blankets! Quickly!" She held out her arms. "Here, let me have the child. Are you able to walk?"

"I think so." Miss Dimple stumbled to her feet. She thought she still had feet, although she couldn't feel them anymore. Numbly she followed the woman who carried Peggy. The other one had already disappeared inside.

My goodness! How many stairs were there? What in the world was wrong with her? She had never been this out of shape! Grasping the railing, Miss Dimple paused a few steps from the top. Each breath brought in razor-sharp air.

Suddenly a soft blanket enveloped her and an arm encircled her waist. "Only a few more steps," someone said. "Let's get you inside by a warm fire."

Warm fire. Surely those were the most beautiful words she had ever heard. Miss Dimple hoped they would allow her to keep the blanket around her for at least a little while longer. The room was larger than she'd expected, rectangular with a stone fireplace at one end, and it reminded her a bit of the rustic log cabin that served as their town's library where her friend Virginia worked. The older woman led her over heart of pine floors and a colorful braided rug to a comfortable chair by the fire and, kneeling, began to remove Dimple's shoes.

Dimple Kilpatrick hadn't had anyone take off her shoes since she was . . . well . . . it had been so long she couldn't even remember. "Please," she began, "you don't have—"

"Nonsense! You don't want frostbite, do you?" Miss Dimple realized for the first time that the woman looking up at her was probably even older than she was. She was tall but seemed rather frail and wore her gray hair pulled into a bun at the back. Her face, however, was surprisingly unlined and her cheeks, pink from the cold.

She winced in spite of herself when her icy feet and hands met the warmth of the fire, and the woman named Mae Martha gave her shoulder a comforting pat. "You'll feel better after you soak your feet in warm water. I'll put on the kettle."

Miss Dimple started to rise. "Peggy?"

"She's right here. I'm afraid she's very sick." Miss Dimple turned to find the younger woman on the settee behind her, stripping off the little girl's clothing. "Her fever's high and we have to get it down or she could go into convulsions." Peggy shivered as the woman laid her gently on the couch and covered her with a light blanket.

"What can I do to help?" Dimple asked.

"Just watch her while I heat some water in the tank. We'll start her off in warm water and gradually add cool. It would be too much of a shock to immerse her in cold right away."

The young woman, whose name Dimple assumed was Suzy, certainly seemed to know what she was doing. She was small and lovely with straight black hair worn in a short bob styled just below her ears and there was no doubt she was of Asian descent.

While Dimple obediently soaked her feet in a pan of warm water, she heard her moving about the next room, which she assumed was a bedroom, and she soon emerged carrying a large tin tub much like the kind Dimple had bathed in as a child. "We have a tub in the bathroom, but it might be more comfortable here by the fire," she said.

Sitting with Peggy while the water heated, Miss Dimple sang to her the songs her mother had sung so many years before: a Stephen Foster favorite, "Oh! Susanna," and the one she always loved best, "The Riddle Song" her mother claimed came from the Kentucky mountains, although she learned later it probably originated in fifteenth-century England.

Peggy's face was flushed and her eyes puffy with fever. Dimple touched the child's neck and found her glands hard and swollen. Could Peggy have scarlet fever? Usually the rash began on the abdomen, and she folded back the blanket to look but, although Peggy's skin was hot and dry, she didn't see redness there. Yet.

Dimple looked up to see Suzy standing over her. "It looks like tonsillitis," Suzy said. "With your help, I'd like to get a better look at her throat."

Using a flashlight and the flat handle of a spoon as a tongue depressor, Suzy managed to get a brief look at the child's throat while Dimple held the light. Peggy gagged and cried and Miss Dimple wished more than ever they could pick up the telephone and call Ben Morrison, the local doctor. She had noticed him earlier with the group who went to search the area around Etowah Pond.

"I couldn't get a good look," Suzy said, "but there's a lot of inflammation in there. Has she had trouble with her tonsils before?"

Of course Miss Dimple couldn't give her a definite answer, but she did remember Peggy's being absent from school several days the month before.

While Suzy filled the tin tub with warm water, Dimple explained to the two women how she and Peggy happened to follow Max into their dooryard. "We were most fortunate to find you," she added, "as I really don't know if I would've been able to make it all the way back carrying Peggy. I just wish we could get in touch with her parents, as I know they must be frantic."

Mae Martha frowned. "It fretted my grandson—God bless him—that I don't have a telephone, but I told him I've done all right without one so far. My nephews live a couple of miles away and Bill's around more often than not—he does errands and odd jobs for me."

Dimple noticed Mae Martha didn't mention the reason for Suzy's presence. Perhaps, she thought, she was there as a companion or nurse to the older woman, as it was plain to see that she had some kind of medical training. She watched as Suzy lowered Peggy into the warm water. They had placed the tub by the fire, and Miss Dimple spoke softly to the little girl as Suzy gradually added cold water. When Peggy cried and begged to get out, Dimple told her stories about Brer Rabbit, Brer Bear, and Brer Fox that had always been favorites of hers as well as of the children she taught. Later, with Peggy wearing one of Suzy's pajama tops that came to just below the child's knees, they made a bed for her on the settee and Suzy fed her half an aspirin dissolved in honey and water a spoonful at a time.

"That should help to bring the fever down," she told them, "and as soon as it's light, I'll go down to Esau's and use his phone."

Suzy's voice was calm, but Miss Dimple could see the distress in her eyes. What if Peggy became worse? Outside the wind wailed in a pitch-black night and Max, who slept on a rug by the door, would now and then pick up his ears and pace to the window. Dimple wanted more than anything to grab her flashlight and try to make her way back down. She was warm now and her coat, gloves, and shoes had been toasting by the fireside, but she knew it would be a reckless and foolhardy errand. What good would it do Peggy if she sprained an ankle or, worse, broke a leg?

"You must be about ready for something to eat," Mae Martha said, and served them generous bowls of chicken stew with hot biscuits and spicy apple butter. Miss Dimple cleaned her bowl and tucked away two of the biscuits, washing it down with strong steaming tea. Dimple noticed Mae Martha walked with a slight limp and sometimes used a cane, and Suzy insisted that both of them rest while she took care of the supper dishes.

"Miss Mae Martha took a tumble awhile back and got a pretty bad sprain," Suzy explained. "Her ankle's much better now, but I try to get her to stay off it as much as possible." She smiled at the older woman. "Of course, she doesn't pay a bit of attention to me!"

"Blasted hickernuts!" Mae Martha sputtered. "Went outside to get me some sage from that bed by the front steps and my feet went right out from under me!"

"Now I check to make sure those steps are clear of hickory nuts," Suzy added. "They're as hard as marbles and can trip you in a minute but I haven't seen any since—thank goodness! It's a wonder you weren't hurt worse than you were."

Suzy's speech was clear and her English, perfect, Dimple noticed. She didn't speak with the soft Southern accent like most of the people she knew. "It looks as if you did a good job nursing her back to health," she told her.

"Oh, my Suzy's been here with me since I came down so poorly with pneumonia last spring," Mae Martha said, smiling. "Reckon I'd be lying out there in Damascus Church Graveyard if Madison—that's my grandson—hadn't talked her into coming here to look after me.

41

"My Madison . . . he . . ." Her voice broke and she turned away. Miss Dimple noticed that Suzy quickly reached out to the older woman and gently touched her shoulder. "He was with the Seventh Infantry Division," Mae Martha continued, "but I lost him back in May—killed in the Aleutians. Madison was gonna be a doctor when he came home," she said proudly. "He was already learning how when this war started. That's how come he got to know Suzy. She's come all the way from China, you know."

"Emory." Suzy spoke softly, referring to the large university in Atlanta.

Miss Dimple nodded. She was familiar, of course, with the medical facility that turned out many excellent physicians and nurses.

Mae Martha dozed by the fire while Suzy washed the dishes in an enamel pan and Dimple pulled up a rocking chair beside Peggy's makeshift bed and was relieved to find she didn't feel as feverish as before. Later, Suzy checked her temperature by putting a thermometer under the little girl's arm. "A hundred and one and a half," she reported, shaking the mercury down. "Of course it would probably read a bit higher if we took it by mouth, but she's definitely cooler than before."

Dimple refused Suzy's offer of a bed in order to stay close to Peggy, and she was glad she did because the child woke during the night crying for Kate. Her teacher calmed her by assuring her she would be going home to her parents in the morning and even managed to persuade the little girl to take a few sips of water.

Mae Martha had turned in soon after supper and Suzy made herself comfortable with a pallet on the rug. Growing weary of sitting, Dimple walked about the room, noticing for the first time the colorful paintings that hung on the walls. Most were landscapes painted in oils as well as scenes of everyday life on a farm, and the longer she looked, the more she began to feel she had seen this style of painting before. Although the room was darkened now, there was enough light from the fire for her to see the initials M.M.H. in the corner of a painting of an apple orchard that hung over the mantel. Where had she seen a similar picture before? And often . . . why was it so familiar? Why, the library, of course! It was a painting of two children feeding a calf that Virginia had bought to hang in the tiny room where she shelved the books for small children. And Mae Martha must be the artist who painted it!

The clock on the mantel struck two before Dimple sat again in the cane-bottom rocking chair next to Peggy's bed. Had Virginia tried to call her earlier? If so, her friends at Phoebe Chadwick's boardinghouse must be wondering what had happened to her. Would searchers be combing the hills for her as well as for Peggy? Maybe she should have gone for help as soon as she found the ribbon, but she would have had to take a chance on finding her way back down in the dark. Miss Dimple pulled one of Mae Martha's soft knitted coverlets all the way to her chin. She knew she needed to sleep, but she didn't think she would be able to catch a wink before morning.

Dimple woke to the sound of whimpering and the gray light of dawn outside the windows. Peggy was fretful and feverish and refused to drink when Suzy held a cup to her lips.

"Her temperature's over a hundred and three," Suzy told her, frowning. "Do you think you might be able to get her to take that other half of an aspirin? She seems to do better for you."

Dimple kissed the child on her forehead, and her lips were sensitive to the heat of her skin. Tears came to her eyes in spite of her resolve not to show how worried she was, but her heart ached for this little girl and she would give anything to make things right for her.

After several attempts, the two of them managed to get down not only most of the dissolved aspirin, but a little water as well, and Suzy made a compress from a piece of torn flannel dipped in cold water, which she applied to Peggy's forehead. "Keep changing this every few minutes," she instructed Miss Dimple. "I'm going on down to Esau's to use the telephone."

"Better take a flashlight," Dimple suggested. "It's not much help, but it's better than nothing."

"Thank you, but I believe I might be better off with the lantern," Suzy said. "I'll take Max along for company."

But the dog had to be persuaded to leave Peggy. He had made a point, Dimple noticed, to check on her during the night, padding back and forth from his rug to keep watch over the sleeping child.

"It's all right, Max. Your little friend will be just fine, and you can come back and tell her good-bye," Miss Dimple assured him.

Bundled in coat and scarf, Suzy turned at the door. "What number should I call?" she asked.

Miss Dimple shook her head and smiled. "All you have to do is call the operator. Florence McCrary will notify the Ashcrofts and everybody else in town before you can hang up the receiver."

CHAPTER FOUR

Young Willie Elrod slapped globs of peanut butter on his pinecone, pausing to lick his fingers one at a time. "Peggy's gonna be all right now, isn't she, Miss Charlie? I tried to tell old Froggie she might've gone to that special place she talks about, but nobody would listen."

"Well, she's at home now, and Doc Morrison's

45

taking good care of her—thanks to Miss Dimple. And it's disrespectful to call our principal Froggie. He's *Mr. Faulkenberry* to you." Charlie made a point not to look at her friend Annie because, due to the poor man's resemblance, the two often referred to him in the same way.

"Go easy on that peanut butter, Willie," she added. "You have enough on there for two. . . . Now, spread it around good and you can roll it in the birdseed."

Charlie Carr and her fellow teacher, Annie Gardner, had been coerced into helping Alma Owens's fourth-grade Sunday school class with their "Christmas presents for the birds" when they arrived at the church earlier to assist in the search for Peggy Ashcroft.

Although coffee was no longer rationed, it was not always available, and Charlie's mother, Jo, her aunt Lou, and several others had pooled their supply to make enough for the volunteers braving the cold. Instead, they were greeted by their minister with the joyful news that the little girl was safe. Of course the coffee was put to good use, as were the doughnuts and cookies that seemed to appear miraculously, for the impromptu prayer service that followed.

"Didn't *anybody* worry when Miss Dimple didn't come home yesterday?" Annie asked, tying a red ribbon around a pinecone for Junior Henderson. Later the children would hang their sticky offerings on the large cedar in front of the Methodist church.

"I guess everybody thought she'd gone to bed early," Charlie explained. "The last time I saw her, she was with Virginia Balliew."

Alma sighed. "Poor Virginia! She must feel terrible! I understand she went to bed with a fever last night and was practically beside herself with worry this morning when she realized Dimple hadn't called."

"My mama said the woman who lives out there on that hill—you know, where Miss Dimple and Peggy spent the night—well, she didn't have a telephone." Willie held up his finished pinecone for approval, scattering birdseed all over the floor. "Somebody had to walk all the way to a neighbor's house this morning to call."

"A bit of a recluse, I believe," Alma said, shrugging. "I'm not familiar with the people at all, but I'm grateful they were there to help. Why, I shudder to think what might have happened if Miss Dimple and Peggy hadn't found shelter when they did."

Junior giggled and said he reckoned Miss Dimple would've turned into a grape Popsicle, referring to her custom of favoring purple.

"That's not funny! You take that back!" Willie, who had shared a frightening experience with Dimple Kilpatrick the year before, smacked his friend in the shoulder with a grubby fist.

Separating the two, Charlie gave one child a broom and the other a dustpan. "That was a callous thing to say, Junior, but I'm sure you didn't mean it. Now, let's get this mess cleaned up and I imagine Miss Alma will let you all go outside and hang your pinecones on the tree."

"I'm sure you didn't mean it!" Annie said, mocking Charlie as the two walked to Charlie's aunt Lou's for dinner after church. "You can bet your boots Junior Henderson meant every word." As fourth-grade teacher at Elderberry, Georgia, Grammar School, she had no illusions.

"Oh, you mean that comment about Miss Dimple being a purple Popsicle? Of course he did!" Charlie, who had taught the class as third graders the year before, had no doubts about the child's intentions. "I said that more for Willie's benefit to avoid bloodshed on church property."

"Miss Dimple wasn't at church today," Annie said, buttoning her coat against the cold. "Of course, I didn't expect her after yesterday's excitement. I don't imagine she got a wink of sleep."

"We'll probably get all the details from Aunt Lou," Charlie told her. "I don't know how she does it, but she's just like that motto for the *Atlanta Journal*. She 'covers Dixie like the dew!' "

"That woman's name sounds familiar," Jo Carr said later as she helped herself to *just a tiny bit more* of her sister's chicken pie. Charlie's mother was rail thin and, much to Lou's disgust, could eat all she wanted without gaining a pound. "Mae Martha Hawthorne . . . now, where have I heard that before?"

Charlie's younger sister, Delia, frowned. "I've heard it somewhere, too. She must not have lived here long, though. I don't remember ever meeting her." She spooned applesauce into Tommy, her eight-month-old son she called "Pooh Bear," as he struggled to get down from his chair.

Charlie's uncle Ed looked at his empty plate and flapped his arms. "Am I clucking yet? We've eaten so much chicken I swear I expect to grow feathers. Fried chicken, stewed chicken, chicken salad, baked chicken . . . What else can you do with that bird?"

"Oh, hush, and count your blessings! We're lucky to have it," his wife told him. "Keep on clucking and you might just lay an egg!"

Charlie laughed. "You know just about everybody around here, Uncle Ed," she said, passing her mother the rice. "Willie Elrod said somebody telephoned the Ashcrofts from a neighbor's house."

"That would probably be the Ingrams—or one of them," her uncle said. "They're brothers, Esau and Isaac. One's married, but I can't remember which, and the other lives close by."

"That would be Esau," his wife announced.

"Ida Ellerby—she's in the choir with me, you know—well, she has a cousin who lives out that way, and Ida said there's some kind of nurse— Chinese, I think—who lives with the Hawthorne woman, and she was the one who made the call this morning. From what Ida said, this Mae Martha has only lived there since sometime last winter. Seems her grandson wanted her to be close to kin when he enlisted in the service."

"*Mae Martha Hawthorne* . . . now I know where I saw that name," Jo said. "There was an article about her in the *Atlanta Constitution* not too long ago. She's an artist, paints a lot of rural scenes in what I guess you'd call a primitive style. I think there's one in the library."

Lou made a face. "I don't know why people make such a big fuss over that kind of art. Now, when Mama painted a picture of a vase of flowers, it *looked* like a vase of flowers! You remember the one she did of the hydrangeas, Jo? It's hanging in our bedroom."

Jo nodded. Their mother's watercolor of pansies was her favorite, and the still life she painted in oils hung over the mantel in their dining room, but it was such fun baiting her sister! "You'll have to admit, they're restful to look at, and this article said she seemed to have a way with colors."

"Oh, good! Maybe she'll have an exhibit," Delia said, wiping Tommy's face.

"If you're all that eager to see that kind of thing, maybe Charlie and Annie will let you come look at the bulletin boards over at the grammar school," their aunt said. "Now, where are those cookies you brought for dessert, Delia?"

Delia and Charlie had baked a batch of the spicy molasses cookies called "crybabies" to send to their brother Fain and Delia's young husband, Ned, who were on the other side of the world, both fighting somewhere in Italy. The cookies didn't require much sugar, which was rationed, and were especially good for shipping. They had sent packages meant for Christmas as early as October so these might not reach them for several weeks—if at all.

"I hope little Peggy Ashcroft will be all right," Charlie said as she helped clear the table after dinner. "From what I heard, she was one sick little girl."

"Had a real high fever, but between the nurse and Miss Dimple, they managed to keep it under control," Lou said. "Funny, though," she added, frowning. "When the Ashcrofts and Doc Morrison drove up there to bring her home this morning, the nurse wasn't even around."

"Maybe she was asleep," Delia suggested. "If she was looking after a sick child all night, she probably didn't get much rest."

Lou Willingham shrugged. "All I know is Amanda Morrison said the doc told her they wanted to thank the woman, but Dimple said she hadn't seen her since she went to make the telephone call."

"And guess who turned up on the Ashcrofts' doorstep last night?" Annie said. "Peggy's cat, Peaches!"

"All this trouble over a cat!" Ed muttered. "And I'll bet it was under the house sleeping the whole time."

"I do believe if it weren't for the dog, Max, I might've been stumbling about on that hill all night," Dimple told her friend Virginia as they sat in Phoebe Chadwick's front parlor later that afternoon. A fire burned low in the grate and a tray of ginger mint tea and some of Odessa Kirby's applesauce muffins sat on a small table in front of them.

"Remind me to get him a bone the next time I go to Shorty Skinner's," Virginia said. "If anything had happened to you or that child, I'd never forgive myself. I can't believe I slept the whole night through!"

Dimple took a sip of her favorite tea, and then another. Had it ever tasted this good? "That's because you were sick and needed the rest, Virginia. I hope you're feeling better now."

"Much better, thank you. Now, tell me all about your adventure. I hear from Doc Morrison that Peggy has a bad case of tonsillitis. I don't even want to think of what might've happened if you hadn't found her when you did."

"Wait! I want to hear every word." The home's owner, Phoebe Chadwick, stuck her head in the doorway. "And by the way, I want you to know Odessa brought those muffins by for you today as soon as she heard what happened.

"She usually doesn't cook for us on Sundays," she said aside to Virginia, who, of course, knew that already. Phoebe pulled up a hassock and made herself comfortable. The rug was threadbare and the loveseat needed re-covering, but every time she mentioned it, her guests protested that they liked the room as it was. Well, so did she.

"I'm afraid to leave town anymore if you're going to disappear on us again," she said to Dimple, who seemed to have done exactly that the year before. "Maybe we should sign in and out like the girls do now in college to keep up with our comings and goings."

"I don't think I have to tell you how grateful I am to be back," Dimple said with the faintest hint of a sigh. "But the people there were so kind to us. I'd love for you to meet them."

"I hear the woman who lives there is an artist," Phoebe said.

Dimple nodded. "I think you'd both enjoy her paintings. In fact, I believe you have one at the library, Virginia, the one with the children and the calf. They remind me of my early days growing up on a farm. I'd love to purchase one for Henry for Christmas."

"Mae Martha Hawthorne." Virginia smiled. "Oh, I do like her work. I didn't know she lived anywhere around here."

"Her companion, Suzy, told me Mae Martha's grandson moved her there back in the winter to be closer to her nephews, and it was probably a good thing as he was killed last May in the Aleutians," Dimple explained. "She's a pleasant person but seems to be extremely shy, and from what Suzy tells me, keeps to herself most of the time. Her nephews and a hired man take care of errands for her. She doesn't have a telephone or a car."

"My goodness, you'd think they'd get lonely way out there on that hill," Virginia said, choosing a muffin.

"I suppose it suits her," Dimple said, "but I feel a bit sorry for Suzy. She seems sad to me somehow, but such a capable nurse! It was grand how she stepped in and took care of Peggy. I'm afraid my energy was exhausted by then and it was a relief to have a responsible person take matters into her own hands."

"Someone told me she's from China," Phoebe said. "I wonder if she's homesick."

"She speaks perfect English, and Mae Martha said her grandson met her at Emory, so I expect she's been over here a good while," Dimple told her. "I'd like to go out and visit them sometime soon, thank them for their kindness. Perhaps I'll take along some of my Victory Muffins."

Phoebe and Virginia exchanged brief glances at this suggestion as everyone but Miss Dimple was aware that the muffins she claimed would help to keep you healthy, and regular as well as patriotic, tasted like sawdust and could probably be used as a building material should the need arise.

"Odessa's baking this week," Phoebe said quickly. "I'm sure she'll want to send along a loaf of her yeast bread."

"I suppose you plan to be at school tomorrow as usual," Virginia said to Dimple, knowing full well what her answer would be.

"Of course. There's no reason why I shouldn't, and there's quite a lot to do before school lets out for the holidays."

"Only two more weeks," Phoebe reminded her. "I don't know what they'll do about the Christmas assembly program now that Kate Ashcroft's taking a leave of absence to look after Peggy. Doc thinks she should have those tonsils out as soon as she gets better."

"They'll have to find someone fast," Dimple said, frowning.

"Someone who's able to play the piano and sing," Virginia added.

"And has experience with children," Phoebe pointed out.

But please not Alma Owens! Dimple thought, and she could tell by their expressions the other two were thinking the same thing. But nobody said it out loud.

"I believe we might be in luck," Geneva Odom announced the next afternoon after the children had been dismissed for the day. Geneva taught the second grade in the classroom across from Charlie's. "Frog—I mean Mr. Faulkenberry—said he'd located someone to take up rehearsals for the Christmas program." Stepping into Charlie's classroom, she saw Miss Dimple had also dropped in and Dimple Kilpatrick *never* addressed the principal as Froggie, nor did she think it was amusing.

"She . . . or he will have her work cut out for her," Annie said, joining them. "I wonder how he found a replacement so quickly."

"I believe this young woman's husband is serving in the navy and she wanted something to keep her busy," Geneva said. "She's from somewhere in north Georgia and is supposed to be here tomorrow."

"Where will she stay?" Annie asked. "I don't think there's an extra bed at Phoebe's."

"Delia and Tommy have taken over the upstairs at our house," Charlie said.

Miss Dimple thought for a minute. "It would be nice if she could have access to a piano."

"Miss Bessie, of course!" Charlie reminded them. "Our neighbor, Bessie Jenkins, has rooms to spare *plus* a piano in the living room, and I think she'd enjoy the company."

"Would you mind asking her?" Miss Dimple said. "I know this is very short notice . . ." She frowned. "Does anyone know her name? I think we should all try to make her feel welcome."

Geneva nodded. "I believe he said Charlotte, and I don't have to *try* to make her feel welcome. You might have noticed I can't carry a tune."

"I wasn't going to mention that," Charlie told her, laughing. "I'll talk with Miss Bessie as soon as she gets home. She works at the munitions plant in Milledgeville three days a week, you know, with Mama and Aunt Lou. And speaking of welcome—I know we've told you this before, but, Miss Dimple, we are all so glad to have you back with us safe and sound.

"I was wondering," she added, "if you would drive with me out to visit Mrs. Hawthorne sometime. I'd like to buy one of her paintings for my sister for Christmas—that is, if I can afford it."

Dimple Kilpatrick's smile lit up her face. "I think that's a lovely idea! Her young nurse, Suzy, doesn't seem a lot older than you and she must be lonely out there. I think it would be nice for her to get to know someone close to her age."

And there was something else that bothered her about Suzy, but Miss Dimple hadn't quite figured out what it was. Oh, well, she thought. It would occur to her in time.

 CHAPTER FIVE

O h, my goodness, the dust in that front bedroom must be an inch thick, and I'll need to put clean sheets on the bed." Charlie's neighbor had barely had time after work to change into comfortable slippers when Charlie showed up at her kitchen door with her request.

"That's what I'm here for. Just toss me a dust rag and tell me where you keep the sheets."

"Oh, honey, you don't have time for that. I expect you'll be wanting to get supper on the table." Miss Bessie peered into her own kitchen cabinet and decided on a can of vegetable soup.

"Now, put that back! You're invited to have supper with us—that is, if you don't mind scrambled eggs and cheese. And I think Delia made banana bread today."

Bessie Jenkins smiled. "You don't have to do that, but I accept anyway. My feet are about to give out on me, and it's dark as sin by the time we get home these days. Too late to go to the store."

Charlie switched on a light in the hallway.

"Wouldn't it be nice to have somebody here to keep you company? You could take time about in the kitchen . . . and she plays the piano, too.

"It will probably only be for a few weeks," she added, noticing her neighbor's hesitation.

"Well, are you going to tell me my new roomer's name?" Bessie asked, rummaging in the closet for furniture polish and a scrap of what used to be flannel pajamas.

"I hear poor little Violet has just about made herself sick over that child running away like she did," Bessie said as they made the bed together with sheets that smelled faintly of mothballs. "I hope Peggy will be all right."

"Miss Dimple checked on her today and said she seemed to be somewhat better," Charlie said, tucking in the bottom sheet. "I can understand how Violet feels, but how was she to know Peggy would slip out the back door the minute her back was turned? We're all relieved that everything turned out the way it did. It could've been much worse."

"I remember how we all grieved over the little Greeson child," Bessie said. "It was before your time, Charlie, but I don't know of anyone it didn't affect. I still think about it sometimes.

"You know," she said later as she looked thoughtfully at the freshly made bed and furniture that now smelled of lemon oil, "I believe I'll have a Christmas tree this year if I can remember where I put the decorations. It could be a difficult Christmas for this young woman—Charlotte—with her husband away in the navy." She smiled. "Don't you think some of those nandina berries would look pretty on the dresser with a little greenery? I'll gather some for a vase tomorrow—give it a holiday look."

Charlie Carr was busy the next afternoon helping the temporary music teacher get settled at her neighbor's house, so the visit with Mae Martha and Suzy would have to be delayed. Dimple Kilpatrick took the opportunity to call on the Ashcrofts with twenty-four laboriously printed and crayon-illustrated get-well messages from Peggy's classmates. She found Peggy propped up with pillows on the living room sofa with her cat, Peaches, at her feet and her rag doll, Lucy, tucked in snugly beside her. Peggy tossed aside a picture book, *Puss in Boots*, to welcome her and at once began reading her friends' greetings.

"She's bored," Kate Ashcroft whispered aside to Miss Dimple, "and that's a good sign. Her fever's not nearly as high as it was yesterday, and she ate most of her oatmeal this morning and a little chicken noodle soup for lunch."

Dimple was glad to see the child's eyes weren't as red and puffy and that she seemed more alert. "I'll have to admit, this young lady gave us quite a scare," she said. "When does the doctor think they'll be able to take out her tonsils?"

"Probably not for another couple of weeks, but before Christmas, we hope." Kate smiled. "We promised her all the ice cream she can eat."

Miss Dimple only nodded. She remembered from her own experience how much it hurt to swallow even ice cream.

"I understand they've hired someone to fill in for me at school," Kate continued, "and I'm relieved they found a replacement on such short notice. I don't like having to leave with the Christmas assembly program only a few weeks away, but, as you can see, I have no choice."

"The young woman dropped by the school for a short time today, but I didn't have a chance to do more than speak to her. Charlotte Nivens, I believe she said her name was, but she prefers we call her Lottie. She'll be staying with Bessie Jenkins, so she'll only have a short walk to the school."

"Good! I'll telephone her tonight to discuss plans for the program." Her hostess offered cake and coffee but Miss Dimple politely declined. She seldom indulged in sweets before supper. "Miss Dimple," Kate began, "Mathew and I don't even know how to thank—"

"You already have, so please don't say any more." Miss Dimple held up a hand. "I'm so very happy things worked out as they did and that I could be a part of it."

"I'd like to thank Mrs. Hawthorne and the other person who took such good care of Peggy, but they don't have a telephone," Kate Ashcroft said. "Of course I plan to write to them, and when Peggy is feeling stronger, she'll be writing to several people as well to thank them for their help and apologize for the trouble she caused—

"No, she *should,* and we know she should," she added before Miss Dimple could reply. "Violet told her we would look for Peaches when we got home and she disobeyed by running off on her own. She should be made to realize how much grief she caused, not just to Mathew and me, but to Violet, and you, and all those who love her and took time to search for her."

Miss Dimple, who had always stressed responsible behavior to her students, agreed silently, although the memory of a very sick little girl huddled alone in the cold almost caused her to protest. "A few of us plan to drive out to see Mrs. Hawthorne after school tomorrow," she told her. "If you'd like to send a message along I'll be happy to deliver it."

"Oh, that would be wonderful! And I'll send more than a message. We just got a crate of fruit from my aunt in Florida. Do you think they might like some oranges and grapefruit?"

Miss Dimple said she was certain that they would, and the next afternoon she climbed in the front seat beside Charlie, and with Annie in the back, the three started out for Mae Martha Hawthorne's with ginger mint tea from Miss Dimple, yeast bread from Odessa, a large bag of citrus fruit and a letter from the Ashcrofts, and a crayon drawing of a smiling little girl in a blue coat from Peggy.

"Do you think we should first stop at the nephew's?" Miss Dimple asked as they came in sight of the weathered farmhouse at the foot of the hill. "I hesitate to just show up on someone's doorstep, but I don't see that we have any choice."

Annie spoke up from the backseat. "I don't think it's necessary. If they're not in the mood for company, I guess they don't have to let us in." She sniffed. "But once they get a good whiff of Odessa's bread, I'll bet they'll welcome us with open arms."

According to Charlie's uncle Ed, Esau Ingram and his wife, Coralee, lived in the old family place and his brother had a small house near his blacksmith shop a little farther down the road.

Charlie drove slowly along the rutted red dirt road that snaked its way up a hill where winter bare trees stood stark against a mottled background of brown. During her search for Peggy, Dimple Kilpatrick had walked a distance of several miles from the other side of those same hills. The rustic cottage where Mae Martha lived, she learned, had belonged to a family from

Atlanta who used it as a weekend getaway, but the people lost interest in it when the father died, and after the place remained empty for several years, Mae Martha's grandson convinced her to buy it to be closer to her relatives while he was away.

"I thought we might see somebody outside when we passed Esau's place," Charlie said, avoiding a hole in the road that looked like it went down to China, "but it seems deserted around here."

"Wait, I believe there's someone up ahead," Miss Dimple said, and Charlie slowed as they came in sight of a stocky grizzled man with a rifle over his shoulder and a burlap sack in his hand.

Charlie rolled down her window. "We're on our way to visit Mrs. Hawthorne," she told him. "Do you know if they're at home?"

The man glanced at them but didn't slow in his walk. "They were there about an hour ago," he said, swinging the sack by his side. "Don't know where else they'd be."

Annie giggled as Charlie thanked him and drove on. "The strong, silent type. Wonder what he has in the sack."

"Probably a squirrel or two, or rabbits perhaps," Miss Dimple answered. "That must be the man who does odd jobs for Mae Martha. I believe she said his name was Bill."

"Ugh! Creepy if you ask me," Annie said. "I don't think I could eat a squirrel, or a rabbit, either."

"You could if you were hungry," Miss Dimple said, and had.

Max greeted them, first with barking, and then with wildly wagging tail when he recognized a friend, and Dimple stooped to pet him, calling him by name. The two women who lived here would surely know they had visitors by now, she thought, and looking up, saw Suzy glance at them from the kitchen window.

"Why, it's Dimple, isn't it? And you've brought company. Come in, come in." Mae Martha Hawthorne stood in the doorway with what looked like a man's shirt over her dress and hugged herself in the cold.

"I'm afraid we've interrupted your painting," Dimple said, noticing splotches of color on the woman's shirt.

"Aw, I was fixing to quit anyhow." Mae Martha paused to rub her right elbow. "These old bones are lettin' me know I'm no spring chicken anymore. Would you all like some coffee? Bill brought me up some from the store just a little while ago and I think Suzy's already put on a pot. Lordy, it's good to have real coffee again!"

Miss Dimple declined, but Charlie and Annie said they would love to have a cup, and would it be all right if they looked at some of her paintings?

"Oh, law, go ahead. I just keep on paintin' 'cause I don't know when to stop," Mae Martha said. "And a good thing, I reckon, because folks keep buyin' 'em."

"Where is Suzy?" Dimple asked. "I was hoping to thank her, as well as you, for coming to our rescue the other night. I've brought some fruit from Peggy's parents as well as a letter and some other things." Miss Dimple looked about for Suzy but didn't see her.

"Oh, she's here somewhere. She's a funny one, that Suzy, but she was in here just a minute or so ago." Mae Martha took the coffeepot from the kitchen stove and poured it into three mugs. It looked to Dimple exactly like the oil she'd seen her brother empty into his car. "Sure you won't join us in a cup?" she asked Dimple. Dimple was sure.

"Suzy!" Mae Martha bellowed. "Suzy! Where've you gotten off to now? We got some friends come to see us!"

Dimple didn't see how such a thundering voice could come from a woman so frail but was happy to see Mae Martha's young companion step quietly from what she assumed was her bedroom. She relayed messages from Peggy's grateful parents to both women, and although Suzy was courteous and thanked her for coming, she seemed uneasy in her presence.

"Miss Dimple, you *have* to come and see these!" Charlie called from a doorway off the kitchen.

"Oh, you must be Suzy," she said, seeing the other woman had joined them. "I'm Charlie, and my friend Annie is in there trying to decide which of those wonderful paintings she likes best. I like all of them, but can only buy one . . . that is, if they're for sale . . ."

Mae Martha flushed and laced her fingers together. "Shoot! You all are gonna give me the big head. My nephew Isaac usually takes care of that kind of thing, but it doesn't matter to me. You go on and pick out whichever ones you want and pay me what you can."

Miss Dimple turned to Suzy. "There must be a price list," she said softly so that Mae Martha couldn't hear, and Suzy smiled and shook her head. "There is one of sorts, but she has no idea of her talent," she whispered. Everyone followed the artist into the room that obviously served as her studio, where several easels stood near the windows and a large table and several chairs took up one side of the room across from shelves cluttered with paints and brushes. Stacks of finished paintings lined the space that was left. The room had originally been used as a dining room, Mae Martha told them, but she chose it to paint in because it got the best light. Charlie had selected an oil painting of a man fishing from the

67

banks of a small stream for her sister. "Our father loved to fish," she explained. "I don't think he ever caught a thing, but he didn't seem to care." She didn't add that the father, for whom she was named, had died several years before.

Miss Dimple chose one of two children picking blackberries. The little boy wore overalls such as her brother, Henry, had worn, and the girl, a purple dress with an apron smeared with berry juice. A sunbonnet much like the one young Dimple had worn hung down her back. The painting was priced at twenty-five dollars, which seemed an enormous amount to her, but over Mae Martha's protests, she wrote a check for the full amount. What fun it would be to watch her brother open his Christmas present!

Annie finally decided on a watercolor of people gathered outside a country church, and Mae Martha flatly refused to take more than ten dollars from either of the young women. "I know how hard it is on you young ones just startin' out, and what Isaac doesn't know won't hurt him," she told them.

Less than five minutes passed, it seemed, before Max began barking and Mae Martha's nephew Esau turned up at the door along with his wife, Coralee.

Coralee and Esau Ingram reminded Dimple of Jack Spratt and his wife of nursery rhyme fame. Wiry and thin, Esau lacked an inch or so of being as tall as his wife, while Coralee bulged in every place one could bulge, Dimple thought, and seemed out of breath from walking the short distance from the car to the door.

"Bill said he saw you folks headed this way, so I thought—well, Coralee and me—we thought you might like some of her sweet potato cake."

His aunt accepted the offering with thanks and introduced her visitors. "Miss Dimple here was the lady who found that poor little girl who got lost, but she tells me she's doing a lot better. Got to have her tonsils out, though.

"Law, Suzy, I'll bet we've done let that fire die down!" Mae Martha turned to lead the way into the living room. "You folks come on in here and sit yourselves down."

"I wish we could, Auntie, but it looks like rain, and I'd better rush home and get the clothes off the line," Coralee said.

"Best be careful on this road coming down," Esau added. "It's hard to see up here after dark."

"I'd offer you some of this cake," their hostess said after the couple had left, "but I doubt if it's fit to eat. Coralee means well, bless her heart, but she either stints on the sugar or doesn't bake it long enough." To demonstrate, she gave the dish a shake. "See there—not even done in the middle!"

"I guess we should be getting back," Charlie said. "I don't want to run off the road in the dark."

"Oh, don't pay any mind to Esau!" Mae Martha poked up the fire. "Sit and visit a spell."

"Miss Dimple tells me you studied at Emory," Annie said, turning to Suzy. "Is that where you got to know Mrs. Hawthorne's grandson?"

Suzy nodded. "Madison and I had several classes together."

"And lucky for me they did!" Mae Martha inched her chair closer to the fire. "I'd have been in a fix without her, especially now that Madison's gone. Esau and Coralee—Isaac, too—they're mighty good to me, but they've farms and a blacksmith shop to run, and when I was so sick last March, Madison didn't like me being here alone. That was right before he shipped out."

"You must be very proud of him," Miss Dimple said, and that was all Mae Martha needed to take a cigar box of letters down from the mantel. "I'd be a whole lot prouder if he was still alive," she said. "His mama and daddy were taken with the typhoid fever when Madison was just a little thing and this is about all I have left."

While Mrs. Hawthorne shared her grandson's correspondence with Dimple, Charlie and Annie had a chance to talk with Suzy, who had seemed reluctant to say much earlier. Now she wanted to know about their lives as teachers and Annie's experience living in a boardinghouse, while they were curious about her life on a large university campus.

70

"Do you ever get homesick?" Annie asked, and Suzy shook her head. She didn't answer for a while, and when she did, her eyes held a faraway expression. "A little, I suppose," she said, "but I was raised here in the States—in California."

Charlie frowned. "Don't you ever have a chance to get out—to town, I mean, to see a picture or do some shopping?"

"Oh, Esau and Coralee, and once in awhile Bill will bring me what I need when they go into town. I really don't mind being here."

"Do you think Mae Martha would care if we came for you some Saturday? We could have lunch at the drugstore, look around in the shops, or just visit." Annie kept her voice low so she wouldn't offend Mae Martha.

"Shoot! You don't have to whisper around me," that lady said. "Suzy knows she's free to go where and when she likes. Max and I will be just fine, but I never learned to drive so I don't have a car, and she has to depend on somebody else to give her a ride."

"I'm going to write down my phone number, and Annie's and Miss Dimple's, too," Charlie said as they were getting ready to leave. "Now promise you'll call one of us when you're ready for the grand tour of Elderberry. And we'd love for *both* of you to come—that is, if you think you can stand the excitement."

Suzy accepted the piece of paper reluctantly. "I don't want to impose—"

"Oh, shush, girl!" Mae Martha told her. "I'm happy here with my paints and my dog, but you're too young to be cooped up all the time.

"She'll be calling," she said aside to Charlie as she followed them to the door. "You can count on it."

"Suzy doesn't seem especially eager to visit us in town," Annie worried as they bumped their way back down the hill in the dark. "I'd think she'd be more than ready for a break."

"I know I would be," Charlie agreed. "I hope she doesn't think we're trying to force her or anything. I like Mae Martha a lot, but I'd go crazy up there all the time."

Dimple Kilpatrick didn't say a word, but she thought she knew what was troubling Suzy. And she'd noticed, too, that they had never heard her last name. Of course she was probably making an issue over nothing. She could almost hear her brother saying, *Oh, for heaven's sake, Dimple, don't invent trouble where none exists!*

Dimple slowly began to relax as they drove into town. There would be salmon croquettes and applesauce for supper, with a good thick slice of Odessa's yeast bread. Suzy was just shy. She would telephone in time and she and her new friends would have a nice time together in town.

72

But when Suzy called a few days later, it wasn't at all what she expected.

"Miss Dimple, can you come? Something terrible has happened, and I don't know what to do! Hurry, *please!* I need your help, and don't—"

And then the line went dead.

CHAPTER SIX

W hy, Miss Dimple, you look like you've just seen a ghost! Is anything wrong?" A blast of cold air followed Annie as she slung her jacket on the coatrack and stood in the hallway, clutching a small bag from Lewellyn's Drug Store.

Miss Dimple replaced the telephone receiver thoughtfully. "It seems that's what we'll have to find out." She hurried past Annie and shoved aside the lace curtain that covered the glass-paneled door. "Is Charlie with you? We'll need a car."

"She stopped at the library, but I had papers to grade . . ." Annie quickly reclaimed her jacket and tossed her package on the hall table. The last time she had seen Dimple Kilpatrick display such urgency was when they learned little Peggy Ashcroft was missing. The papers would have to wait.

While Dimple went upstairs for her wraps, Annie stuck her head in the kitchen to tell Odessa not to hold supper, as the two of them might be late.

Odessa poured corn bread batter in a sizzling iron skillet and shoved it into the oven. "Where you got to go this late in the day?" she demanded. "It's gonna be dark out there before long."

I wish I knew! Annie thought, but she promised they would be careful. "Save us a piece of that corn bread!" she added, hearing the older teacher's rapid footsteps descending the stairs. According to Odessa Kirby, nothing good happened outside after dark because that was when "haints" were on the prowl, and you sure didn't want to run into one of them. Annie didn't think it was a "haint" that caused Miss Dimple's consternation, but it must've been something just as critical.

"Has something happened to Virginia?" Annie's breathing came fast as she struggled to keep up with Dimple's pace.

Miss Dimple gripped her handbag in front of her as if the contents might come flying out as they rushed across Katherine Street on their way to the library. "It's Suzy, Mae Martha's young companion. . . . I just had the strangest call, and I'm very much afraid something's terribly wrong!

"Virginia generally closes at five. I hope we can catch them before they leave for home."

Annie waved to Marjorie Mote, who was hanging an evergreen wreath on her front door. "Is something the matter with Mae Martha? What did Suzy say?"

"It's what she didn't say that alarms me. We were cut off before she could finish and I didn't know how to call her back as they don't have a telephone there."

"She was probably calling from the nephew's house," Annie suggested. "What's his name? Esau? I wonder why she didn't phone again."

"That's why I want to get there as soon as we can. The poor woman was almost hysterical—said something terrible had happened and she needed my help. I tried to call the operator to see if she could reconnect us, but Florence didn't answer."

Probably chatting on another line or listening to someone else's conversation, Annie thought. Florence McCrary, the local operator, admitted to being curious, but everybody knew she was just plain nosy.

"Let's hope Virginia has her car here," Annie said as they crossed the stone bridge in the town park and hurried past the two magnolia trees that bordered the walkway to the library. "Charlie's mother's using theirs. She and Charlie's aunt Lou drove out to visit a cousin somewhere in the country."

Charlie had admitted earlier that the two sisters

had long delayed visiting their cousin Eva. Not only was she a tiresome hypochondriac, they knew she'd insist on sending them home with her awful fruitcake, but as the holidays drew nearer, they couldn't put it off any longer. That afternoon, with a box of chocolates from Lewellyn's and a fruit jar of Lou's sherry-flavored boiled custard, the sisters had resigned themselves to an afternoon of listening to their cousin's list of maladies.

Charlie dropped the book she was holding the instant they stepped inside the building. "What's wrong? Is it Mama and Aunt Lou? They haven't had an accident, have they?" Hurrying to meet them, she reached for Annie's hand and pulled her into the room, still warm from the dying fire and smelling of wood smoke. "You know how Mama gets distracted when those two are togeth—"

Dimple Kilpatrick gave her a look that clearly read: *Settle down at once!* Charlie Carr had seen it often and had been on the receiving end more than once during her own experience in Miss Dimple's first-grade classroom. "As far as I know, your mother is fine," Dimple reassured her, "but I received a frantic telephone call from Mrs. Hawthorne's companion this afternoon and she seems to be in some kind of trouble.

"Virginia, I'm afraid I'll have to ask you to drive if you will." She glanced at her friend, who

76

was already gathering her wraps. "We need to get there as soon as possible."

After banking the embers in the stone fireplace and replenishing the water bowl for Cattus, the library cat, the four of them drove through the darkening December day through the outskirts of town and into the country, dust billowing like russet smoke behind them.

"Should we stop first at Esau's?" Charlie asked as Virginia turned onto the narrow rutted road that led to the hill where the artist lived.

Miss Dimple frowned. "I don't see his truck there, but we might find his wife at home. Maybe she can tell us something."

Annie jumped out and hammered on the door, but no amount of racket brought anyone to answer her. "I guess nobody's home," she said, rejoining Charlie in the backseat. "Suzy must've gone back up the hill to Mae Martha's."

"I wonder why she telephoned you?" Charlie said, addressing Miss Dimple. "If it was an emergency, why not call Doc Morrison or the sheriff?"

"Don't forget, Suzy is a relative stranger in this area," Dimple reminded her. "She probably didn't know who else to call . . . and she had my telephone number. Remember? You gave it to her yourself."

Charlie remembered. "Still, you'd think she'd first go to Esau or his wife, or even that fellow, Bill . . .

"Well, maybe not Bill," she added when Annie shivered and made a face. "He did look kinda like one of Odessa's 'haints.'"

"We'll find out soon enough," Miss Dimple said a few minutes later as they bumped into the clearing behind Hawthorne's rustic house.

A galvanized bucket holding sprays of greenery, still with the strong scent of cedar and pine, sat on the stoop by the door. "Strange, I don't see Max," Miss Dimple said, pausing at the top of the steps.

"Probably inside with Suzy," Annie said. "I can hear him barking.

"Suzy! Mrs. Hawthorne! Anybody home?" she called, and was soon joined by the others. When no amount of knocking or hollering brought a reply, Miss Dimple found the door unlocked and stepped boldly inside.

Max immediately threw himself upon them and began whining and racing frantically back and forth to the door that led to the studio.

Miss Dimple knelt and spoke softly to the animal while calmly stroking his head. "It's all right, Max . . . shh . . . we're here now . . . here to help. What is it, Max? Show us."

With the German shepherd leading the way, the four women walked to the closed door of Mae Martha Hawthorne's studio, where Dimple Kilpatrick wasted no time in turning the knob. "Mae Martha?" The room was in darkness and she called out while switching on the light.

"Oh!" Charlie stumbled backward into Virginia, who reached out for Annie to keep from falling. "Oh! Is she . . ." As if in a daze, Charlie watched Miss Dimple kneel by the woman who lay on the floor, her gray hair dark with blood that had been collected in a pool beneath her head. It didn't take long to see Mae Martha Hawthorne was dead, had probably been dead for some time.

"Someone please get the dog away." Dimple found it an effort to speak calmly as Max attempted to get nearer and began to bark in such a manner it broke her heart to hear him. "Take him outside—hurry."

"Should we phone for the doctor or the police?" Virginia asked, although it was obvious a doctor would be no help here. While Annie coerced the dog out the way they had come in, the others took in their surroundings.

"It looks like the poor thing fell and hit her head," Virginia said as Dimple got to her feet. But Dimple shook her head. "What would she have hit it on? The injury seems to be in the back. There's nothing nearby—and look how she's lying. Look closely."

Do I have to? Charlie thought, but she complied. The woman lay on her back with her arms by her sides as if she had merely lain down for a quick nap. Her eyes were closed and if it weren't for the dark stain congealing beneath her and her mouth had not been open in such a grotesque position, it might appear as if she were asleep. Charlie took a deep breath and looked away. "It doesn't seem natural that she would've fallen like this."

"Someone moved her, arranged her this way," Miss Dimple said. "Possibly her companion."

"But where is she now?" Alarmed, Virginia looked about.

"Surely you don't think Suzy had anything to do with this?" Annie had returned and now stood in the doorway. They could hear Max still barking outside.

"For heaven's sake, why didn't she stay? Call for help?" Charlie said, her voice quaking in spite of her.

"She did," Miss Dimple answered. "She called me. I think she must've found her soon after this happened—probably tried to revive her—and realizing it was useless, left her in this position and went somewhere—probably Esau's—to telephone me."

"But if this wasn't an accident, then *somebody* must have done it," Annie said. "Why? Why would anybody want to do this to Mae Martha?" Her voice rose and her eyes filled with tears. "She was so *nice!*"

"If this companion—this Suzy—didn't do it, then who did?" Virginia asked. "I think we should get out of here *now*."

"And I think you're right!" Annie said, but Miss

Dimple seemed in no hurry, and instead took her time looking over the room. The studio smelled of oil and turpentine, and paintings lined the walls just as they had before. What seemed to be a newly finished scene of two rabbits nibbling near a rustic fence entwined with what appeared to be muscadine vines sat on an easel nearby.

Charlie spoke softly. "Her last painting."

Miss Dimple nodded. The painting was serene and lovely, just as the artist had been. "I don't see anything that might've been used as a weapon . . . at least nothing obvious." She shook her head. "I can't imagine where Suzy has gone."

"Unless . . ." Charlie looked from one to the other. "Unless somebody killed her, too! We haven't even looked in the other rooms."

Annie groaned. "Okay. This is really getting scary. Can we please leave now?"

"But what if Suzy's been hurt?" Charlie pointed out. "What if she's been locked in a closet or something? We have to look."

But the rest of the house proved to be empty and silent except for the ticking of the grandfather clock that stood against the living room wall. Only embers remained of what had been a wood fire in the big fireplace, now mounded with gray ashes. Dimple remembered Suzy telling her she always built the fires as Mae Martha was too frail to lift the heavy logs.

"We can telephone from Esau's," Annie began.

"Surely somebody's home by now. I hate to be the ones to tell them."

"I believe it might be best to report directly to the sheriff in town." Miss Dimple spoke with finality. "Let's leave things as they are for now."

Annie glanced at Charlie who shrugged. She didn't like to argue with Miss Dimple. Besides, she was usually right.

"What about Max?" Virginia asked as they stepped outside to be met with the dog's frenzied capers. "We can't just leave him here. Who would take care of him?"

"I guess we'll have to take him with us," Charlie said, glancing at Virginia. "I'd offer to keep him myself, but you know how much traffic we have on Katherine Street and there's no way to fence him in."

"He could stay in my room tonight if Miss Phoebe wouldn't mind," Annie offered, "but there's really no place for him there."

"Oh, I wish there were! He reminds me of my Bear." Stooping, Dimple again calmed the dog with a few murmured words and offered her hand for him to lick.

"Well, I suppose that leaves me," Virginia said. "He can sleep at my house tonight and have the run of my fenced-in backyard tomorrow, but I'm afraid he'll be lonely with no one there all day."

Charlie agreed. "Poor Max! He needs a family."

Miss Dimple thought she knew of the very one

but, of course, she would have to ask them first.

Max didn't need any coaxing but immediately jumped into the backseat with Annie. Charlie, however, took her time joining them.

"What are you looking for out there?" Annie asked her. "It's too dark to see a thing."

"I thought I might catch a glimpse of Suzy," she said as she climbed into the car. "Do you think she could be somewhere out here in this cold?"

"Well, if she is, she's had plenty of opportunity to show herself." Virginia put the car in second gear as they started down the hill. The yellow glow of the headlights cast eerie shadows in the dark trees ahead. "What makes you so sure that Chinese woman had nothing to do with Mrs. Hawthorne's death?" she said, leaning forward to better see the narrow road in front of them. "Why, she might be just waiting for us to leave."

"Then why call and ask for my help?" Miss Dimple paused as Virginia braked to keep from hitting a small animal, probably a raccoon. "I think I know why the young woman is avoiding anyone with authority, and if I'm correct, she has good reason to be afraid."

Charlie spoke up. "I'd be afraid, too, if I'd been the one to find Mae Martha like that, but I wouldn't waste a minute before calling the police."

"So, *why,* Miss Dimple? Why should Suzy be

afraid?" Annie asked, cuddling closer to Max for warmth.

The older woman hesitated. After all, she couldn't be absolutely sure. "I don't think Suzy's from China," she said at last. "I believe Mrs. Hawthorne's young companion is of Japanese heritage."

CHAPTER SEVEN

T he silence that followed was almost suffocating. Charlie spoke first. "Oh," she said finally. "You mean you think she's . . . but she speaks perfectly good English. And didn't she meet Mrs. Hawthorne's grandson at Emory?"

"I only meant she might be of Japanese *heritage,*" Miss Dimple explained. "I believe she told me she was born in California."

"But to some people—most, I'm afraid—that doesn't matter," Virginia said. "Japanese is Japanese."

"One of my students told me the other day that when the war first started she threw away a whole set of those little china dolls—the kind that came about ten in a box—just because they said *Made in Japan* on the back," Annie said.

Charlie groaned. "Well, that's silly! The dolls couldn't help where they were made."

Miss Dimple smiled. "Just as Suzy had no choice in her family's origin."

"I'm certainly no friend of the Japanese, or the Germans, either," Virginia said. "And with good reason, but I'm afraid most people would be hostile toward anyone they thought might be affiliated with the enemy. If you believe this young woman really is of that heritage I can understand why this would be a problem for her."

"It doesn't help that she seems to have run away," Charlie said. "I honestly don't know what we can do."

"Wait, I suppose," Miss Dimple said. "She phoned once. Maybe she will again, but right now we need to report this to Sheriff Holland, and the sooner, the better."

A light burned in a back window of the house where Esau Ingram and his wife, Coralee, lived at the foot of the meandering road, but Virginia drove past without slowing and everyone seemed relieved when they turned onto the main road to town.

The streets of Elderberry looked deserted, illuminated only by dim lights in some of the stores. "I miss the lighted Christmas tree we used to have on the courthouse lawn," Charlie said sadly.

"And the big blue star over City Hall," Virginia added, "but we wouldn't want to attract attention in case there's an air raid."

They were all familiar with air-raid drills during which everyone turned off their lights and draped their windows with black, but the town was so far inland, Dimple didn't expect enemy planes to be able to reach them. She had read about the dreadful bombings in England and watched accounts of them in the newsreels, and her heart ached for the people there whose homes were being destroyed and their loved ones killed. Some of the children in the larger cities over there were being separated from their families and sent to safer homes in the countryside. How disheartening it would be if the small ones in her care were forced to do the same!

Annie remained in the car with the dog while the other three went in to see the sheriff. They found Sheriff Holland at his desk, finishing a big bowl of ham and bean soup and corn bread his wife had sent over for his supper, and the tantalizing smell of it made Charlie's stomach rumble.

The sheriff washed down his last spoonful with black coffee after offering the women a seat and listened intently as Miss Dimple explained the reason for their visit.

"And you say this woman—this companion— phoned *you?*" he asked after she had related the details of their experience.

"That is correct," Dimple responded, "but she

wasn't there when we arrived. She would've had to go somewhere to use the telephone, possibly the Ingrams since they were the closest neighbors, but no one answered the door there."

"There's no telling where she might be by now." Sheriff Holland reached for the phone. "Can you give me a description?"

Miss Dimple fingered the pin at her throat. "Small, attractive . . . probably in her mid or late twenties with dark hair." She paused. "And Asian. Suzy's Asian."

He relayed that information to someone on the other end of the line. "Suzy?" the sheriff repeated. "What's her last name?"

"I'm afraid I don't know," Miss Dimple said. "She never told me, but I really don't think she had anything to do with what happened to Mrs. Hawthorne, Sheriff. She was confused and terrified at finding her the way she did. Suzy had no reason to kill her."

Excusing himself, the sheriff stood and stuck his head in the door of the room behind him. "Clyde, looks like we've got a homicide over there near Fox Grape Hill. Woman's companion reported it and then took off. I've called in a description but you need to get Mabry in here—Dennis, too, and anybody else you can round up. Chances are pretty slim of finding this woman, dark as it is, but we gotta try.

"I'm heading on out there now, so see if you can

get ahold of Doc Morrison and ask him to meet me there. Peewee will come with me.

"Peewee!" he bellowed, and the man who had been sitting with his feet on the desk eating peanuts in the small reception area lumbered in. "Yessir?" he answered, attempting to tuck in his shirt, although it would be impossible, Dimple thought, for Peewee to see around his huge stomach in order to know what he was doing. The man appeared perfectly capable, she imagined, of balancing a bale of cotton on each shoulder without shedding the first drop of perspiration.

"Grab your jacket. A woman's been killed . . . and for God's sake—er, excuse me, ladies—leave those blasted peanuts behind! Looks like a circus in here."

The sheriff turned to the three women. "I'm sorry to have to ask, but one of you will need to come with us so you can let me know if anything's been moved. And who knows? Maybe you'll think of something else that might help."

Miss Dimple agreed to go, as did Charlie, but Virginia said she needed to get home in order to take care of her overnight guest. "I don't have any dog food," she admitted, "but I reckon he won't turn up his nose at some leftover stew."

"I'm surprised my mother and Miss Phoebe haven't called the police to report our disappearance," Charlie said, and Annie promised to stay behind and explain the situation to both. "But I'll be staying up until you get back," she told Miss Dimple. "Please don't make me wait until tomorrow to hear all the details!"

The Ingrams' house was dark when they drove past and Charlie was glad they had thought to leave a light burning in Mrs. Hawthorne's kitchen. She remembered how kind and welcoming the artist had been when they visited there and took a deep breath to ease the anger rising inside her. Why would anyone do this to her? And what if they had returned?

She was glad they were accompanied by the two policemen as they drew up behind the house. Charlie glanced at Miss Dimple, who sat quietly beside her looking as calm as if she were going to a meeting of the church circle.

She watched Sheriff Holland cautiously draw his gun from his holster as he got out of the car. "The three of you stay here while I check things out," he told them. "And Peewee, you keep an eye out, you hear? Blow the horn if you see anything suspicious."

Charlie felt a little shiver of excitement. Wait until Annie heard what she had missed! *Shame on you, Charlie Carr! A woman lies dead in there— a talented artist who would never be able to share her beautiful work again, and whoever did it is running around free.* She sat up straighter, her hand on the door handle. If she could help find who was responsible for this, she was willing and ready! Beside her, Miss Dimple's stomach rumbled and she coughed to cover the noise. Charlie wanted to giggle. *What was wrong with her?* After all these years she still had trouble accepting the fact that the older teacher had human needs just like everybody else . . . well, maybe not quite like everybody else.

Thank goodness the sheriff stepped outside at that moment to beckon them inside. "I reckon you all left fingerprints all over the place," he grumbled.

Miss Dimple reminded him that when they arrived earlier, they had not been aware they would find a murder victim there.

Mae Martha Hawthorne lay on the floor in her studio just as they had left her and as far as she could tell, Miss Dimple told them, nothing had been moved.

The sheriff knelt by the dead woman and carefully examined her hands. "Doesn't look like she put up a fight. Must've known whoever it was that did this. Doc should be able to tell us more.

"I'm afraid we'll have to get prints from all you ladies who were here before, and her nephew and his wife as well. If you can think of anyone else who might have access to the house, we'll need to get theirs, too."

"I understand there's another nephew, Isaac, who lives around here somewhere," Charlie told him, "and then there's Bill." She explained about the man who worked as a handyman and tried to keep an impartial expression as she described him.

The sheriff frowned. "Bill? Bill who?"

Charlie didn't know but said that Esau or his brother probably would. Miss Dimple showed the two policemen Suzy's room and they took their time going through her belongings. Later, the sheriff said, they would lift her prints from things she would normally use.

The upper half of Peewee's large bulk had disappeared inside an oak wardrobe that stood in the corner as he shoved clothing about and explored the shelves.

"Nothing seems to be missing here. She must not have taken anything with her," Sheriff Holland said, sifting through dresser drawers. He frowned. "What's that on top of the wardrobe?"

Peewee stood on tiptoe and fumbled for what looked to be a folded coverlet. "It's just a quilt. . . . No, wait . . . there's something under it, some kind of box." After straining to reach the object, he handed the sheriff a metal candy box.

"Empty," the sheriff muttered, prying off the lid. "Wonder why she kept that up there."

"My wife uses those for extra buttons, things like that," Peewee offered.

However, Dimple Kilpatrick knew Mae Martha Hawthorne had another purpose for this particular box. It was where she kept the money from her paintings. *This was not looking good for Suzy.* From the expression on Charlie's face, she knew Charlie recognized it, too.

Obviously, this didn't get past Sheriff Holland. "Have either of you ever seen that box before? Do you know what it was used for?" He looked from one to the other. "I'm sure you realize the importance of any information you can give us," he said, using a tone Charlie herself sometimes used to reason with her students. "It's urgent and we need it *now.* If this young woman is guilty, it's imperative that we find her as soon as possible. If she isn't, then she should turn herself in and explain her actions."

Miss Dimple thought that in Suzy's case, that might be easier said than done, but she told him Mae Martha Hawthorne had kept the earnings from the sale of her paintings in a box much like the one he had found.

"Do you know where she kept it?" he asked.

Charlie shook her head. She remembered the artist putting the money they had paid her in such a box but had no idea where it was stored. "Why don't you look in her bedroom?" she suggested. "Isn't it possible there's another like this? After all, they're fairly common—or were before the war."

But no metal box turned up in Mrs. Hawthorne's bedroom or anywhere else in the house, although the two men made a thorough search.

The crunching of gravel outside, followed by the slamming of a car door, signaled Doc Morrison's arrival, and he was soon followed by two men who turned out to be the deputies Clyde had apparently summoned. The sheriff sent two of the new arrivals to talk to Esau and his wife. "Now, go easy, you hear? They probably don't even know what's happened to their aunt up here. And find out if they have any idea where that companion might've gotten to."

Doc disappeared into the studio to examine the victim, who until recently had been a warm, kind, flesh and blood person, and Charlie joined Miss Dimple in the main room of the house, where the formerly cheerful fireplace looked cold and unwelcoming.

"I reckon you ladies are 'bout ready for some supper, aren't you?" Peewee leaned on the mantel to examine a painting hanging there. "Don't see why one of us can't run you home if the sheriff says it's okay."

Charlie was more than ready to leave for home, but the thought of supper made her stomach queasy and she didn't think she would be able to eat one bite.

"Did you say this woman painted all these pictures?" Peewee asked, looking about. "I'll bet my wife would like one of these to go over the sofa in our living room."

Charlie was just about ready to ask him if she

might step outside for a breath of cold air when the man dropped his gaze to the implements on the hearth. "Will you look at those andirons? They look handmade—and the shovel and poker, too."

"They were probably forged by Mrs. Hawthorne's nephew Isaac Ingram," Miss Dimple explained. "I was told he's a blacksmith."

"Mmm . . . nice work." Peewee stooped to examine them closer when a look of alarm crossed his face. "Sheriff!" he called. "Sheriff Holland! Better come here. I think I've just found what might be the murder weapon."

CHAPTER EIGHT

U sing his handkerchief, the sheriff slowly removed the poker from its stand and examined it in the light. "You're right—sure looks like blood on here, and we oughta be able to get some good prints from that brass handle."

Charlie and Miss Dimple watched as he laid it carefully aside to be dusted. Both had seen the wound on the back of the dead woman's head, her hair matted with dried blood. Whoever killed her had planned it in advance, had carried the poker into the studio where she was working and struck her from behind.

Mae Martha Hawthorne had been murdered by a cold-blooded killer.

Miss Dimple shook her head. "I don't believe Mrs. Hawthorne's companion is capable of this," she said aside to Charlie. "I saw how tenderly she cared for her, almost like a daughter. There was genuine affection between those two."

"Maybe that's why she had so much trouble dealing with it," Charlie answered. "But where is she, Miss Dimple? The longer she stays away, the worse it looks."

Suddenly the kitchen door banged open, slamming against the wall, and a man's voice bellowed, "What's going on here?"

"That's what we'd like to know," Sheriff Holland answered. "Who are you?"

"Bill . . . Bill Pitts," the man answered, looking about. "Has something happened to Mrs. Hawthorne? Is anybody going to tell me what's wrong?"

Charlie recognized him as the man they had seen with a rifle over his shoulder on their earlier visit, and in spite of his rough appearance, he looked positively stricken.

The sheriff's voice softened. "When was the last time you saw Mrs. Hawthorne, Bill?"

"Last night about dusk dark, I reckon, when I brought in her firewood. I live just on the other side of the hill." Disregarding the sheriff, who stood in his path, the man pushed his way into the kitchen. "Where is she?" He paused at the table, where a plate of food, probably from breakfast, sat covered with a red-and-white-checkered cloth. "Mrs. Hawthorne! You here?"

Following him, Sheriff Holland put a hand on the man's shoulder and pulled out a chair. "I'm afraid I have some bad news. Here, let's sit down a minute and we'll talk about it. Maybe you can help us out."

Charlie felt the gentle pressure of a hand on her arm, and taking the older teacher's lead, followed Miss Dimple through the living room and out onto the wide front porch. "I don't know about you, but I can use some air," Miss Dimple said, taking a deep breath.

Charlie leaned against the railing. Pale squares of light from the living room checkered the dark porch floor and a rocking chair moved eerily in the wind. She hugged herself and shivered. "That man, that Bill—he kind of scares me, but I felt sorry for him in there. He seems really to care about Mae Martha."

Before Dimple could reply, the door opened behind them and Doc Morrison stepped out to join them. "What are you two doing out here in this freezing cold? Don't I have enough on my hands without you coming down with the galloping gallumption?"

Receiving no answer, he hesitated. "Well, never

mind. I don't blame you for wanting to get away from all that in there. I'm through here for now. Can't do anything more until Harvey comes to pick her up, so . . . barring any objections, how about let's take off for home? You must be about worn out by now."

Charlie had to admit he was right. All she wanted to do was crawl into bed and sleep, and she was sure Miss Dimple was as tired as she was, but if so, she hadn't mentioned it.

Miss Dimple sat up front with the doctor as they drove away, leaving Charlie the backseat all to herself. She watched through the rear window until the light from Mrs. Hawthorne's kitchen window disappeared in the night, and hoped they wouldn't meet Harvey Thompson in his hearse along the way.

"This companion—this Suzy," Doc began after they had driven awhile in silence, "did she come across as somebody who would do this kind of thing? You both met her . . . you must've gotten some kind of impression. I'd like to know what it is."

Dimple spoke softly. "No, she didn't. She seemed capable and caring, and I'm not sure about this, but there's a possibility she might be in some kind of danger herself. I can tell you this: She sounded very much afraid."

"She seemed shy—didn't say much," Charlie said. "And she's small-framed, too. . . . I can't picture her hitting anyone over the head with a poker—especially not Mrs. Hawthorne."

Doc Morrison mulled that over. "Well, the human heart is a curious thing, but I'll say one thing—she made a darn good nurse. If it hadn't been for her, and for you, too, Dimple Kilpatrick, little Peggy Ashcroft probably wouldn't be around to hang her stocking on Christmas Eve."

The news of Mae Martha's murder and the disappearance of her companion was all over town the next day even before Miss Bessie Jenkins opened the ticket booth at the Jewel Theater, where *Tarzan's Desert Mystery* was playing for the regular Saturday crowd.

"My mama says we're gonna keep our doors locked because there's no telling who might be next!" Bobbie Ann Tinsley, whose mother was married to Chief of Police Bobby Tinsley and who should have known better, had staked her place at the head of the line. "That awful woman could be anywhere, you know," she added to anyone who would listen.

"Yeah! I'll bet she's in your basement, Bobbie Ann, just waitin' for you to open the door," Willie Elrod taunted.

"Oh, hush up, Willie! You don't scare me. I don't ever go down there anyway." Bobbie Ann turned her back on him to whisper with Ruthie Phillips in line behind her.

"I heard her head was all bashed in and there was blood everywhere!" Marshall Dodd announced. This was greeted by *ughs, yucks,* and other descriptive commentary.

And that was when Bessie Jenkins opened the ticket window in her little glass booth—but not before she had taken in every word.

Arden Brumlow heard it from Velma Anderson, who had dropped in the store that morning to see if that shipment of rayon stockings had arrived, and Velma had gotten it straight from Annie Gardner over a breakfast of cornflakes at Phoebe Chadwick's.

As for Dimple Kilpatrick, her walk that morning was shorter than usual due to a later start after the demands of a long day before, and the dining room was almost deserted when she sat down for a belated breakfast.

"I've saved you the last of the coffee." Phoebe pulled up a chair beside her and tried not to make a face at her friend's unappetizing Victory Muffin. "Wouldn't you like something to spread on that? There are still some of Odessa's peach preserves on the sideboard.

"This poor woman who was killed," she continued as Dimple helped herself to preserves, "doesn't she have any relatives—other than the nephews, I mean?"

"Other than her grandson, Madison, who was killed in the war, I don't know of any. His grandmother raised him after both of his parents died of typhoid fever." Miss Dimple shook her head. "It's always sad to lose someone we love, but to have her die in such a dreadful manner . . . I feel sorry for her nephews."

Phoebe thought of her own grandson, Harrison, currently undergoing basic training, and was grateful he hadn't yet been shipped off to some foreign land. But she didn't want to think about that. "I wonder if her companion has turned up," she said, offering the margarine. "She had to spend the night somewhere."

Dimple graciously declined the spread. It now came in a disgusting white lump with a blob of red food coloring in the middle that had to be kneaded in in order to make it yellow. Having been raised with the words "Waste not, want not!" framed in needlework in her mother's kitchen, she dutifully finished her muffin, but her appetite had vanished the day before at the sight of that helpless woman's body. And there had still been no word of Suzy. According to the radio, the temperature had dropped during the night to just above freezing. Had Suzy spent the night outside?

Charlie hadn't slept well for thinking of it. She had stayed up well past her usual bedtime writing to her fiancé, Will, who had recently moved on to advanced flight training at Craig Field, and Annie had phoned earlier that morning, waking her with questions she'd neglected to ask Miss Dimple the night before.

Now she found it bracing to be outside in the chill of a December morning, to sweep the wide front porch, which seemed to collect every leaf and twig in the area, and Charlie wielded the broom with gusto, working her way down the walk in front of the house. *Where could Suzy have gone after she telephoned Miss Dimple?* Charlie tried to picture the likeable young woman coming up behind the unsuspecting victim and hitting her with an iron poker—hitting her with enough force to bash in her skull. She shivered. It wasn't from the cold.

"Charlie!" Her sister Delia called to her from the doorway. "Somebody wants you on the phone."

Not Annie, Charlie thought as she hurried inside, or Delia would have named her. Maybe it was their neighbor Bessie's new boarder, Lottie, with a question about school or the upcoming Christmas entertainment. But if that were the case, why wouldn't she call Kate Ashcroft?

The caller spoke so softly at first Charlie thought it was one of her third graders playing a prank. It wouldn't be the first time a small voice had asked if she did washing. *Well, you must be awful dirty!* Or if she was on Katherine Street. *You'd better get off—a car might run over you!*

"Who is this?" Charlie demanded. "Speak up, I can't hear you!"

"Please, I need your help. I know they won't believe me, but I had nothing to do with what happened to Miss Mae Martha! I don't know where to go, who to ask . . ."

"Suzy?" Charlie found herself whispering as well. "Where *are* you? Everybody's looking for you. Why did you leave like that?"

"I was calling from Esau's. No one was there and I was going to wait . . . but then I heard him drive into the yard, and I didn't know what he might do." Her voice stronger now, Suzy hesitated. "Look, I don't know what's going on, but there's wickedness behind it, and I'm frightened."

"Heard *who* drive up? Esau?"

"The man who helps out around there—Bill. I've a feeling he resents me, and I think I know why, but he's wrong. There are things you should know, but I'll have to tell you later." Her words were hurried, breathless. "Your friend, Miss Dimple, I believe she'll understand. Would you contact her for me, *please?* I tried to reach her earlier but was told she was out walking. Is there any way—"

Charlie found herself choking the receiver as her words tumbled out. "Look, Suzy, you really need to turn yourself in. If you didn't do anything wrong, you have nothing to worry about. Now, tell me where you are."

"I-I can't do that. Please, just trust me. I

promise to explain." Now Suzy spoke so softly Charlie had to strain to hear her. "Look, I have to go now—can't stay here."

"Where? Can't stay where?" Charlie shouted.

"You won't bring the police? Come. Just you and Miss Dimple. I'll tell you whatever you want to know. I give you my word, but promise you'll give me that chance. That's all I ask—a chance to explain."

This small woman barely came to her shoulder. What could she possibly do to harm them? Well, her mother always said there was safety in numbers. "I'll see what Miss Dimple advises," Charlie told her, "and Annie will probably be with us, too." If Suzy was wise enough to rely on Dimple Kilpatrick's judgment, it was at least a step in the right direction.

"Good! I found the two of you together!" Charlie usually didn't drive the short distance to Phoebe Chadwick's, but today she didn't have time to waste. Mumbling something to her mother about errands to run, she was out the door and in Phoebe's kitchen in minutes.

There she found her friend Annie and Dimple Kilpatrick seated at the table with a huge bowl of popcorn between them, making fluffy white garlands for the school Christmas tree. Miss Dimple's strand, she noticed, was considerably longer than Annie's.

"It's for the assembly program next week," Annie explained. "Kate Ashcroft usually has her music classes help with it, but with such a late start this year, we decided to step in and give them a hand."

Charlie looked in the hallway to see if anyone else was about before telling them about her phone call from Suzy.

Miss Dimple tidied her place as she spoke, sweeping stray popcorn into the bowl with her hand. "Where is she? Did she say where she spent the night?"

"She called from a little store a couple of miles beyond Fox Grape Hill. Dooley's, I think it's called."

Rising, Miss Dimple nodded. "Of course. I know that place. It's just on the other side of the bridge over Crabapple Creek."

"That's where she wants us to meet her—by the bridge," Charlie told them. "There's a wooded area back there where she said she would wait for us, but I had to promise not to tell the police. She asked for a chance to explain."

"I don't understand." Annie tied off the end of her garland and laid it aside. "I'm not sure that's such a good idea."

This statement was obviously directed to Miss Dimple, who looked gravely from one to the other. "I believe we should give her that chance," she said, heading into the hallway for her coat.

Annie shook her head but followed, and Charlie hurried out in the cold to start the car. It was obvious to both of them that Miss Dimple Kilpatrick wasn't sharing what was on her mind.

CHAPTER NINE

C harlie clutched the cold steering wheel with numb fingers. It was freezing inside the car and she wished she had thought to wear gloves, but she had left the house in such a hurry, she'd only taken time to snatch a jacket. Beside her, Miss Dimple adjusted her purple wool hat, tugging it over her ears, and leaned forward as if she could will the car to go faster.

Few houses dappled the landscape once they left the town behind and fields that had been picked clean of cotton were now plowed over. Only brown stubble remained where alfalfa had been harvested to feed the stock. "There's the store—there's Dooley's!" Annie pointed out later as the road dipped ahead, curving against a hill fringed in green.

Charlie slowed as they crossed the two-lane bridge over Crabapple Creek. Now she could see why Suzy chose this place to meet, as evergreens grew close together near the water, providing a perfect screen for anyone who didn't want to be seen. "I don't see her," she said, scanning the hillside.

"There's a place just up ahead where people who come here to fish park," Miss Dimple directed. "Let's see if she'll come to us."

Maybe Annie was right, Charlie thought as she pulled off to the side of the road. Maybe this wasn't such a good idea. What if the police found out they were helping a suspected murderer? Wasn't there a law against that? The three of them sat in silence as if speaking might frighten the young woman away.

"Doesn't look like she's going to show," Annie said finally.

"I expect she's just being careful," Miss Dimple said. "Let's give her a little while longer."

She wants to be sure we didn't bring the police. Charlie took a deep breath. She was beginning to hope Suzy *wouldn't* come when she noticed a slight movement a few feet up the hillside, and Suzy, dressed in a long dark coat and a gray knitted hat, stepped out from behind a small grove of pine trees and hurried toward the car, looking about her as she ran.

Any doubt Charlie might have experienced about helping Suzy vanished when she saw her face. Her dark eyes pleaded for help, and her expression was unbearably sad as she slipped quickly into the backseat beside Annie.

"Why, you're freezing!" Annie covered both of

her hands in hers. "Where have you been all this time?"

"In some farmer's barn . . ." It was obvious Suzy was making an effort to keep her teeth from chattering as she spoke. "It wasn't so bad. I burrowed in the hay and wrapped myself in burlap sacks—you know, the kind they use for picking cotton." Hugging herself, she glanced about her. "Please . . . we can't stay here!"

"We need to get you somewhere warm," Miss Dimple said as Annie tucked a warm throw around the woman's frail shoulders. "Have you had anything to eat?"

"I bought some cheese crackers and a candy bar at the store back there. The woman let me use the telephone but I could tell she didn't feel comfortable about it," Suzy told them. "I wouldn't be surprised if she has already said something to the police."

"We're on our way!" Pebbles scattered as Charlie backed quickly out of her parking place and turned for town. "Maybe you'd better scoot down in case we meet them," she suggested to Suzy. "And by the way, where *are* we going?" she asked the others. "Our place isn't safe—too many people in and out, and there's no way we can sneak you into Miss Phoebe's."

Miss Dimple was thinking. Eyes straight ahead, lips set in a determined line, she laced her fingers together, clenched them tight. "Virginia should be going home for her noon meal about now, and I know she'll have to see to Max. If you'll let me out there, I'll find out if it's safe."

"Max?" Suzy smiled for the first time. "Oh, I hope he's all right. I had to shut him inside so he wouldn't follow me."

"I wouldn't be surprised to see him welcomed at the Ashcrofts," Miss Dimple said, smiling, "but I haven't had an opportunity to speak with Kate about it. The dog seemed to take quite a liking to Peggy and something tells me the feeling might be mutual."

Stopping in front of Virginia's small gray bungalow, Dimple was relieved to see her friend's car in the driveway and knew she would be at home. If Virginia had walked to work, her car would be parked in the garage behind the house. She hesitated with her hand on the door handle. "I think it might be a good idea if you parked in the back . . . just in case someone comes along." She could only hope she would find her friend in a good mood.

"I guess you've come to check on Max," Virginia said, greeting her at the door. "The dog and I get along just fine. I only wish I could say the same for Emmaline Brumlow! Can you believe she had the nerve to suggest I rearrange all the books in the fiction section? Wants to mix the mysteries in with all the rest. Now, what do you think of that?"

Dimple didn't think much of it at all since mysteries were her favorites and the present method made them easier to find, but that wasn't her concern at the moment.

"Ever since she was elected president of the Woman's Club, she's been like a great big thorn in my side," Virginia went on, "and you know the club pays my salary, so what can I do? How would *she* like it if I tromped into Brumlow's Dry Goods and swapped everything around in her display cases?"

Miss Dimple had found the best way to deal with Emmaline was to agree with her and then go ahead and do as she pleased. She told Virginia that. "I wouldn't waste my time worrying about it," Dimple said. "She'll forget all about it as soon as something else comes along.

"Now," she added, leading the way into the familiar living room. "I'm afraid I have another favor to ask."

"You want to bring that woman in here?" Virginia said when Dimple explained the situation, and immediately ran to the kitchen window to peer at the car parked in back. "Dimple, how do you know she didn't kill that poor soul? I don't want to come back here and find *your* body lying in a pool of blood!"

"Charlie and Annie are with me, so I don't believe she can do away with all of us," Dimple said, not bothering to hide her smile.

"I don't see anything funny about it, Dimple. It didn't take much imagination to see how that Hawthorne woman was killed. Gives me chills to think about it. I can't believe you didn't go straight to the police!"

"Do you really believe that young woman would still be around if she were guilty of murder?" Dimple said. "Suzy spent the night in a *barn,* Virginia, and she's only eaten a few crackers and a candy bar since yesterday—plus, she's chilled to the bone. I'm asking you to look at her—just *look* at her, and if you still feel she's a threat, I promise we'll go somewhere else."

Dimple used the same tone of voice she used when reading *Snow White* or *Cinderella* to her small charges. It never failed to elicit pity for the damsel in distress.

It didn't now. "Oh, well!" Virginia shrugged. "Bring her in, but don't expect me to feel sorry for her."

"Charlie, watch that pan of milk on the stove! And, Annie, there's an enamel tub in that cabinet in the bathroom. If you'll bring it in here, I'll fill it with hot water." Virginia touched Suzy's forehead with the back of her hand. "I'm surprised you don't have a fever. Now, sit right here at the table and let us warm you up."

Max, delighted to be allowed inside after a morning in the fenced backyard, frisked about the

110

small kitchen, obviously happy to see his owner's companion again. From time to time, Suzy stroked the dog's head when at last he had settled beside her.

Virginia frowned as she glanced at the kitchen clock and then at Suzy. "I should be getting back to open the library, but first I have to know what happened. Why on earth did you run away?"

Shedding her wraps, Miss Dimple pulled up a chair as the others gathered around her. "Why don't you start at the beginning?" she encouraged Suzy. "No one's going to bother you here, so take your time."

Her feet immersed in warm water, the young woman held the mug of steaming milk with both hands, sipping it slowly while Charlie kept an eye on the pan of oatmeal simmering on the stove. "First of all," she told them, after taking a deep breath, "I had nothing to do with what happened to Miss Mae Martha." She looked from one to the other. "I can't *make* you believe me, but I promise you I'm telling the truth!"

Suzy sighed and shook her head. "It seems a million years ago. . . . I can't believe it was only yesterday. It was soon after breakfast that Miss Mae Martha decided she wanted some fresh greenery to make an evergreen wreath for the door and to decorate the mantel, so I took some shears and a bucket and walked about a mile or so over that hill on the other side of the house

111

where she told me I'd find some pretty holly, and there's a grove of short leaf pine there, too."

"How long were you gone?" Virginia asked.

Suzy frowned. "An hour at least . . . couldn't have been much longer. It felt good to be out in the cold air, and Max here went with me." She smiled as the dog licked her fingers. "It gave him a chance to run, and he loves to chase sticks. I think we both needed the exercise."

Suzy's face clouded. "Mrs. Hawthorne was in her studio when I left but she said she was going to start some stock to make soup for supper, so I thought I'd smell it simmering on the stove when I got back." She smiled. "When she gets—got— all wrapped up in her painting, she tended to forget about everything else, so I thought about starting it for her . . . but then Max practically went wild barking." Suzy set aside her mug, her eyes filled with tears. "And that was when I found her."

"Did you touch anything?" Annie asked. "Move her?"

"Of course I moved her!" Suzy sat up straighter, her eyes sparked with anger. "She was on her stomach and I turned her over, tried my best to revive her, but it was too late. She'd been struck in the back of the head and there was no way she could've injured herself that way!"

"Are you sure she was dead?" Charlie asked.

Suzy looked at her silently. *"Very sure,"* she said finally.

"And so you telephoned me from Esau's," Miss Dimple said.

Suzy nodded. "No one was there but the door was unlocked. I had your number and didn't know who else to call. I heard a truck drive up while I was talking to you and saw that it was Bill." Suzy paused to dry her feet as Annie removed the tub of water. "Of all the people I might've turned to for help, Bill would be the last one I'd ask! He's made it obvious from the start that he doesn't trust me."

"Why?" Virginia and Annie spoke at the same time.

Suzy spoke softly. "I imagine it's because of my heritage. My parents came here from Japan."

Charlie held back a gasp. Would the silence never end? Although Miss Dimple had mentioned the possibility earlier, she had assumed, as had the others, that Suzy was of Chinese extraction. She and Annie had attended college with a girl from China, but she had never seen anyone from Japan except for the cruel soldiers in the newsreels. How had Suzy come to live among them during a time when most people cursed at the very mention of the name? The people of Japan weren't only disliked; they, like the Germans, were hated by a good portion of the American public, and with good reason.

And there, in Virginia's green-painted kitchen by the heat of the Magic Chef oven, Suzy explained her presence there.

Although Mrs. Hawthorne's grandson, Madison, was a couple of years behind her in medical school, she explained, they had been in some of the same classes at Emory, and the two had become friends while working on a project together. The war was into its seventh month when Suzy had received her medical degree the year before.

She had planned to join her parents in California, where she was raised, Suzy told them, and go into practice there, but they had warned her not to return to the West Coast, as people of Japanese heritage were being moved to war relocation camps as far inland as possible from what the government had designated "military areas."

"They told me to stay where I was until things got better," she said, her voice breaking. "They never got better. My father had to sell their home, and let his business go for practically nothing when my family was relocated to a camp in Utah, where they live with thousands of other people in barracks made of tar paper and wood.

"One of my professors asked me to stay on as his assistant," Suzy continued, "but he left to join the military just before Christmas. Then Madison enlisted soon after that and told me about his grandmother. Miss Mae Martha was suffering that winter from a bad case of bronchitis, which later went into pneumonia." She smiled. "She needed me and I needed her, so it worked out well for both of us. Until now."

"Did you tell her about your background?" Virginia wanted to know.

Suzy shrugged. "I didn't have to. As my friend Mae Martha liked to say, 'I don't allow no cobwebs in my belfry!' "

Miss Dimple laughed. "Now, why doesn't that surprise me?"

Charlie laughed, too, as she rose to spoon up oatmeal for Suzy, but Virginia held up a hand. "Wait! Shh! Someone's coming. What should we do?"

"Miz Balliew? You home? Got a package here from your niece in Knoxville!" A booming voice shouted from the living room.

"Oh, my Lord! It's the postman! Coming, Boyce!" Virginia shouted, and quickly shut the kitchen door behind her.

CHAPTER TEN

W
ell, that was close!" Virginia returned to the kitchen a few minutes later with a square parcel wrapped in brown paper. "I suppose we shouldn't worry too much about Boyce, though. Poor thing's deaf as a post."

"Aren't you going to open your package?" Annie asked as Virginia set it aside.

"Oh, I will eventually, but I know what it is. Carolyn sends me the same thing every Christmas. It's some kind of crocheted atrocity. One year it was dresser scarves, and the year after that, Christmas ornaments—little bells, stars and such. And last year she sent antimacassars—you know, those things people put on the arms of chairs. I do believe if Carolyn had enough thread she would've crocheted her way around the world by now!"

The other women smiled, but Suzy looked up from her bowl of oatmeal with a bleak expression. "Tell me the truth," she said. "Do you think the authorities—or anyone else here—are going to believe me? What am I going to do?"

"I believe you," Miss Dimple assured her, "but I'll admit you might have a problem. If only we had more time!"

"To find out who really killed Mrs. Hawthorne, you mean?" Charlie said.

Suzy frowned. "How are you going to do that?"

"Obviously, you don't know about my friends here," Virginia told her. "Look," she added, gathering her things together, "I have to go, but you're welcome to stay here awhile as long as you keep well out of sight. Be careful about turning on lights and things like that when I'm not here. The Kilgores live just across the street, and what one doesn't know, the other will find out."

After Virginia left, Annie collected Suzy's empty bowl and washed it in the sink. "It doesn't seem right," she said. "If you were born in this country, you're as American as I am. I don't understand why your family was uprooted like that."

"Not just my family, but many others as well. It seems the government doesn't trust us. They're afraid we'll give aid to the enemy."

"I remember when the president signed that order last year," Miss Dimple said. "I believe it might've come about because of what happened when a Japanese pilot landed his disabled plane on a Hawaiian island right after Pearl Harbor was bombed.

"It seems that some of the people of Japanese ancestry who lived on the island went to great lengths to help the downed pilot, but they were

117

outwitted by the natives who were loyal to the United States."

"The island of Niihau," Suzy said. "I read about that, but it had nothing to do with the rest of us."

"Is there anything back at the house—in your room, for instance—that would lead those who are investigating to realize the truth about your heritage?" Dimple asked.

"There's my diploma . . . and medical textbooks—several boxes of them—with my name inside. I've been going by Suzy Amos here, but my given name is Suzu and my family name is Amaya. They won't have to look far to find that out." Suzy started to go to the window but shrugged and changed her mind. "All my correspondence with my family has been going through friends back in California. Miss Mae Martha and I were trying to be careful so that no one here would suspect."

"So, you're a physician," Miss Dimple said. "I'll have to say I'm not surprised after seeing the way you stepped in and took care of our Peggy. Doctor Morrison, by the way, holds you in high esteem."

"She was a very sick little girl," Suzy said. "I can tell you now I was doubtful she would last the night. I don't believe the outcome would have been as positive without your help, Miss Dimple."

"Ah, well . . ." Miss Dimple waved that aside.

"Now, about yesterday morning when you were looking for greenery . . . Do you know if anyone happened to see you leave the house? Did you meet anyone along the way?"

Suzy frowned and shook her head. "There's no one to see unless Bill or one of the nephews makes the trip up the hill, and I don't remember seeing anyone that morning."

"Maybe Mrs. Hawthorne mentioned it to somebody," Annie suggested, but Suzy had no reply.

"I suppose that's something we'll never know," Miss Dimple said.

Suzy carefully smoothed the napkin at her place. "You've all been so kind. . . . I'm afraid I'm putting you in danger. What will happen if anyone finds out I'm here? It might be best if I just go ahead and turn myself in."

"First let's weigh the possibilities, shall we?" Miss Dimple smiled, but there was no doubt she was in charge, and that, in itself, was reassuring to Charlie.

"I think it's safe to assume that you are at present the number one suspect. In fact, I doubt very much if the police are even bothering with further inquiries. There's a chance, I'm afraid, if you turn yourself in now, they might rush to convict you."

Charlie frowned. "You mean she'd be rail-roaded?"

"Something like that," Dimple replied. "Or worse. Oh, I'm confident the sheriff and his staff will do their best to protect you, but unfortunately reasoning doesn't always prevail when emotions run amok—especially now." Pausing, she dug into the handbag she'd hung on the back of her chair and brought out a small notebook and pen. "You'll need a few personal items if you plan to stay here," she announced, tearing out a page of lined paper. "If you'll make a list of the things you'd like, one of us can pick them up in town this afternoon."

"We're probably close to the same size," Annie offered. "I'll bring you a pair of pajamas and a few sweaters." She laughed. "And I'm sure you could wear a couple of skirts I haven't been able to zip since I started eating Odessa's good cooking."

Miss Dimple rose to let the dog outside. "Well, my friend, Max, I'll get in touch with the Ashcrofts later today, but I can't imagine why they wouldn't want to add a fine animal like you to their family."

Charlie laughed. "I can think of one: Peggy's cat Peaches!"

It was obvious that Suzy was trying to put on a brave face as the three of them prepared to leave a few minutes later. Sensing this, Miss Dimple gave her a reassuring smile. "If I were you I'd take advantage of a warm, comfortable bed, as

I'm sure you didn't get much sleep last night. Virginia should be home around five, and I'll drop by soon after.

"Now," Miss Dimple said on parting, "this is what I'd like you to do in our absence: Write down the name of anyone you can think of who might have wanted to kill Mae Martha Hawthorne—*anyone* . . . and even some who might not. It's not much to go on, but right now it's all we have, and we'll just have to work from there."

Later that day while shopping for Suzy at Murphy's Five and Ten, Charlie was browsing at the ladies' underwear counter when she heard a voice that sent a chill dousing her heart like well water.

"*Charlie Carr!* I'm so glad I ran into you!" Emmaline Brumlow's voice boomed across the store, almost drowning out Bing Crosby's crooning of "White Christmas."

I'll bet it's the first *time she's been glad to see me,* Charlie thought.

"And Annie, too! Good, you can help me spread the word!" Emmaline, who rivaled Charlie in height, crossed the distance between them in a few purposeful strides, and Charlie quickly tossed the lace-trimmed panties she was examining back onto the pile. Murphy's selection of lingerie wasn't her style at all and she suspected it wasn't Suzy's, either, but it would have to do in a pinch as Brumlow's was much too expensive, and such a purchase there might cause suspicion.

Annie, who had attempted to escape, darted a look of pure, unadulterated misery at Charlie and dropped the tube of Pepsodent toothpaste and small jar of Mum deodorant onto the cluttered countertop. "Oh, hello, Mrs. Brumlow! I seem to have run out of everything at once," she said lamely.

But Emmaline took no notice of that. "I thought I saw you two come in here from across the street, and you're just the ones I had in mind to pitch in with our search!"

Charlie frowned. "What search?"

"Why, the search for the Japanese spy who killed that poor, unsuspecting Hawthorne woman! Haven't you heard? Peewee Cochran said they found all sorts of incriminating evidence!

"Very incriminating evidence!" Emmaline repeated the words and rolled them around on her tongue as if the taste of them delighted her. "Right here in our midst, she was, pretending to be a friend and passing herself off as some kind of nurse or something, and the longer it takes to find her, the more damage she can do." Emmaline shuddered. "God only knows what else she's been up to!"

"But how do they know she had anything to do

with what happened to Mrs. Hawthorne?" Charlie asked, not daring to glance in Annie's direction.

"Then where is she now, I'd like to know?" Narrowing her eyes, Emmaline folded her arms. "Guilty people don't run away."

Charlie was tempted to ask her if she would've thought her less guilty if she *hadn't* run away, but she didn't want to arouse suspicion.

"We could use your organizational skills," Emmaline continued. "We must all do what we can when the security of our country is at stake, and if we coordinate our efforts, it might help the police flush her out before more harm is done. . . ." Looking about, she waved at Angie Webber, who was gazing longingly at the candy counter on the other side of the store. "Angela Webber! You're just the person I wanted to see. . . ."

By the time Charlie reached home that day, her mother had received a phone call from Emmaline, as had her aunt Lou. Virginia, she learned later, had been paid a similar visit at the library.

"Did she mention anything about reshelving the mysteries?" Miss Dimple asked.

Virginia frowned. "Why no, I don't believe she did."

"You see. I told you she'd be distracted when something else came along," Dimple reminded her.

"I think I'd rather reshelve the books," her friend replied.

Again they had gathered at Virginia's to lend support, as well as other necessities, to Virginia's secret houseguest.

Suzy seemed pleased with the clothing Annie had brought, as well as the purchases from the five and ten, but the prospect of Emmaline's alarming quest disturbed her. "This is going to make it even more difficult for anyone to believe my innocence," she said, turning to Virginia. "And the last thing I want is to get you in trouble."

But Virginia only smiled. "I'll swear if Emmaline Brumlow doesn't sound just like Smiley Burnette trying to round up a posse," she said, referring to a popular character actor in western films. "Anything I can do to thwart Emmaline's outlandish plans will make me a happier person!"

"Still, we must be very careful to keep our friend here under wraps until the proper time," Dimple reminded them.

"And when do you think that might be?" Virginia asked what Charlie was sure the others were probably thinking.

"When we have reliable evidence pointing to the one who's most likely to be guilty, starting with a list of people who were closely associated with Mrs. Hawthorne," Miss Dimple replied with an expectant nod to Suzy.

Suzy left the room and soon returned with a small slip of paper. "I wrote down a few names, but I honestly couldn't think of many," she said, giving the list to Dimple.

"The two nephews, Isaac and Esau; Esau's wife, Coralee, and Bill Pitts . . . That's *all?*" Miss Dimple returned the paper in much the same manner as she would an unsatisfactory assignment to one of her students. "Surely you've met more people than this. What about her art supplies? Food? Someone had to furnish them. And isn't there a little church not too far down the road? Did *no one* ever pay her a visit?"

Suzy folded the paper and folded it again, as if that would make it go away. "Esau and his wife took care of most of the grocery shopping, but now and then she would send Bill on an errand for something." She frowned. "Her other nephew, Isaac, was the one who delivered her art supplies, but she rarely saw him. . . ."

"Anyone else?" Dimple asked, noticing her pause.

"Wait . . . the milk and egg lady—I almost forgot!" Suzy smiled, remembering. "Miss Mae Martha didn't care for pasteurized milk, so now and then she'd buy milk and eggs from a neighbor who had a few cows and some chickens."

"*What* neighbor?" Charlie asked, not having noticed any.

"She lived over a mile away, but I guess that's close as neighbors go out there," Suzy told them. "If the weather was nice, sometimes I'd walk to get them, or once in awhile Bill would buy them for her."

"Do you remember her name?" Virginia asked, and Suzy shook her head. "I think Mrs. Hawthorne called her Becky, but I don't remember for sure. Mostly she just referred to her as the milk and egg lady."

"But you know where she lives, so that's not a problem," Annie said. "How old a person is she? What does she look like?"

"I have no idea," Suzy said, looking from one to the other. "She left the milk and eggs in her springhouse and I was told to leave the money there in a jar. I never saw the woman's face."

They could be meeting to plan a Christmas party, Miss Dimple thought, or to discuss a neighborhood project. To anyone who asked, they were gathering at Virginia's that evening to contribute items to "Bundles for Britain" and suggest ways to decorate the library for the holidays. Now the five of them sat around the gas fire in Virginia's small living room with the shades drawn while Max dozed contentedly by the hearth. Earlier, Dimple had spoken with Kate Ashcroft, who readily agreed to give the dog a home. "After all Mrs. Hawthorne and her companion did for you and Peggy, it's the very least we can do," Kate said, "and from what you've told me about Max, I love him already!

"And, Miss Dimple, is there any truth to that terrible story Emmaline Brumlow is circulating about that young woman who took such good care of Peggy?" she added, lowering her voice in case Florence McCrary was listening in. "I don't understand why she disappeared like this, but whatever the reason, she must be in some kind of trouble."

If only you knew! Miss Dimple thought, and agreed to bring the dog over the next afternoon after church. "Were you able to think of anyone else?" Miss Dimple asked Suzy as they prepared to leave. "Anyone at all?"

"Someone did come a few times to see Miss Mae Martha about her paintings," Suzy told her, "but we felt it best if I didn't meet them, so I stayed in my room. I believe she gave them one of her paintings to hang in their church." Her voice broke with emotion. "She was generous that way."

"Why do you suppose people of Japanese heritage were sent to relocation camps, but not those whose ancestors are from Italy or Germany?" Annie asked as the three walked home together.

A cold wind hit them with full force as they rounded the corner, and they walked faster, hurrying across the street. Charlie thought of the flimsy tarpaper barracks Suzy's family and others were forced to live in and hoped they were keeping warm.

"I suppose they feel the country might be more vulnerable to an attack on the West Coast where many Japanese have settled," Miss Dimple said at last. "And because they look different."

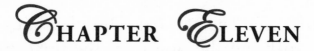

CHAPTER ELEVEN

C harlie thought about what Miss Dimple had said as she walked home alone after leaving the others at Phoebe's. She was aware, as were most Americans, of the brutality and atrocities committed by the Japanese soldiers. They read about them in the news and saw films of their heartless cruelty in newsreels at the picture show. Charlie knew she could come face-to-face with a German or an Italian, and unless they spoke in that language, she wouldn't be aware of their heritage. But the Japanese were different. They looked different, acted differently, thought differently. And *they* had started this war, hadn't they, with the cowardly bombing of Pearl Harbor? Charlie felt hot fury rising within her at the memory of it.

And then there was Suzy, who had been born in

this country, had received her medical degree from a prestigious university right here in the state of Georgia, and had undoubtedly helped to save Peggy Ashcroft's young life. If pressed, Charlie would have had to admit she'd thought differently of Suzy when she believed she was Chinese. Now, although she knew Suzy's people were being treated unfairly, a germ of distrust still lingered, and she wasn't proud of it.

The house was quiet when she reached home and Charlie took advantage of the opportunity to write to Will and Fain. But what could she tell them? For the past few days her life had revolved around the murder of Mae Martha Hawthorne and the frenzied involvement that followed. Charlie took out her note pad and filled her fountain pen in preparation. But how to begin? *Remember the artist I wrote you about? The lady who took in Miss Dimple and Peggy when they couldn't make it home in the dark? Well, guess what happened?*

For heaven's sake, that wouldn't do! Charlie stared at the blank sheet of paper. That kind lady deserved better than this! Maybe a cup of tea would help.

Later, sipping the brew, Charlie wrote to Will and Fain about Suzy's mysterious phone call that led them to discovering the body, and how she had later disappeared. She didn't tell them they were keeping her under cover at Virginia

Balliew's. And she also didn't tell them Suzy's ancestors came from Japan.

The next afternoon, true to her word, Miss Dimple borrowed a leash from her young neighbor Willie Elrod, whose dog Rags seemed to have an aversion to it, and dutifully walked Max to his new home with the Ashcrofts. There they were greeted with unbounded excitement and hugs too many to count. Peaches, as expected, took refuge under the living room sofa. Peggy was scheduled to have her tonsils removed in a few days and the prospect of Max's faithful company on her return from the hospital would make the ordeal easier to face, her mother confided.

Dimple wasn't surprised on her arrival to find Lottie Nivens there, as she would be filling in for Kate during her absence at school and the two were discussing the upcoming Christmas production.

"I hope you've had a chance to settle in at Bessie's," Dimple said. "My friend Charlie tells me how excited her neighbor is to have such good company over the holidays."

"And I'm happy to be there," the young woman said. "It would be a lonely Christmas with my husband so far away with the navy. My aunt, who raised me, died a few years ago and Miss Bessie has gone out of her way to make me feel welcome."

Peggy insisted on taking Max to the kitchen to give him the bone her mother had begged from Shorty Skinner the day before and Dimple spent the next few minutes attempting to answer Lottie's questions about the routine at school. When she rose to go, Kate, leaving Lottie to leaf through suggested plans for the program, walked with her to the door.

"I can't tell you how shocked I was to hear of that terrible thing that happened to Mrs. Hawthorne," she began. "And now her companion seems to have disappeared. She took such good care of our Peggy I find it hard to believe she had anything to do with that awful murder. I know you had a chance to get to know her some, Miss Dimple. Do you have any idea why she's run away? And is it true she's Japanese?"

"Suzy is of Japanese heritage," Dimple said, "but she's an American citizen. She was born in the United States."

"I see," Kate said, although it was obvious that she didn't. Most people who lived in their part of the United States had never seen a person of Japanese descent except in the movies. "Emmaline said she was only pretending to have a medical background, but Doc Morrison seemed to think she knew very well what she was doing."

"I can attest to that," Miss Dimple said. "She has a medical degree from Emory, and if you think about it, you might realize why the young woman has dropped out of sight.

"I can only imagine, of course," she continued, "but she told me earlier that her parents, as well as many others of that heritage who lived on the West Coast, have been moved inland to some kind of relocation camps, and they warned her not to return to California. Suzy might've thought she'd be blamed for Mrs. Hawthorne's death, regardless of guilt, when people learned of her background."

"But you knew . . . ?" Kate Ashcroft let the question hang in the air.

Miss Dimple nodded. "I had an idea, but I wasn't sure until she explained about her background. Naturally, Mrs. Hawthorne knew as well."

Kate stood on her porch and watched Dimple make her way briskly down the walk. "Miss Dimple!" she called after her. "It doesn't look good, does it? For Suzy, I mean. I'm afraid for what might happen."

You have no idea! Dimple thought. Aloud she said, "I'll agree it wasn't a wise decision, but who knows what we might do under the same circumstances. Let's just hope the police will find the person who did this soon."

They wouldn't, of course, because as far as the sheriff was concerned, they already knew who had killed Mae Martha Hawthorne. Tucking her purse under her arm, Dimple Kilpatrick hurried home to Phoebe's, where a warm fire waited in the parlor, perhaps, she hoped, with a small cup of hot spiced apple cider. It seemed they were going to have their work cut out for them.

Does she suspect? Am I giving anything away? Virginia asked herself that question every time someone came into the library. She was sure she had GUILT plastered all over her face in capital letters. Suzy was the perfect guest—or she would've been if she weren't wanted by the police. The kitchen floor had never been as spotless, and the old range gleamed like new.

"Please don't feel you have to clean," Virginia had told her. "You're my guest, and I don't expect you to do anything at all . . . well, except to stay out of sight." However, Suzy had told her she felt she had to do *something* to occupy her time and she really didn't mind cleaning. For lunch that day Suzy had treated her to tempura, a Japanese dish of vegetables dipped in egg batter and fried, which Virginia found delicious.

But what if someone saw her? They kept the shades drawn in the front of the house—to keep the sun from fading the sofa, Virginia explained to her neighbor Mavis Kilgore, although the sofa was at least thirty years old and about as faded as it was going to be. Virginia worried about Mavis, who always seemed to know what was going on in the neighborhood. She wondered if the woman sat up all night keeping watch over the street, and her husband, Jerome, who even worse, could nose out information like a ferret. If only they would find Mae Martha's killer soon!

Suzy had dutifully written the names of all the people she could think of who had even the slightest contact with Mae Martha but couldn't imagine a reason why any of them would benefit from the woman's death.

Mrs. Hawthorne's nephew Isaac, Suzy told them, was responsible for marketing her paintings and saw that the money was regularly deposited to her bank account. She had seen him only on a few occasions and described him as being as robust as his brother was frail. Naturally, as a blacksmith he would have to be muscular, Virginia thought. *And certainly strong enough to kill someone with one blow of an iron poker.*

Dimple took one look at her friend when she dropped by the library later that afternoon, and, glancing about, pulled a chair up close to her desk. Thank goodness there was no one around except Bessie Jenkins, who was searching for a copy of the history of the county in the tiny back room.

"I'm sorry to have put this burden on you." Miss Dimple spoke softly with an eye on the door. "And I promise if things aren't resolved soon, we'll try to find another solution.

"I've done a bit of research," she added, "and Mrs. Hawthorne's paintings are worth a good bit of money. It doesn't seem rational that either of the nephews, who might inherit, would want to do away with the goose that laid the golden eggs."

"She must've had a will." Virginia frowned. "I wonder if Sheriff Holland knows . . . and I haven't heard anything about a funeral service, either."

"You all must be talking about that lady who was killed. . . ."

Neither had heard Bessie enter from the back room. "Bless her heart," Bessie said, "she trusted that Japanese woman and look what happened! Well, I'm locking my doors, I can tell you that, and I warned Lottie to be sure and do the same. You just can't be too careful! Emmaline's having some warning posters printed up and I told her I'd put some up at the picture show."

"That's a bit premature, don't you think? We don't know if this woman had anything to do with what happened to Mrs. Hawthorne." Miss Dimple sighed. She was beginning to sound like a broken record.

"Huh! She's Japanese, isn't she?" Bessie said, offering the history book for Virginia to stamp.

"Reading up on the county, I see." Virginia forced a smile.

"Yes, well, actually it's for Lottie—you know,

the young lady staying with me. She said she wanted to learn a little about the area since it looks like she might be here awhile."

"I understand Peggy's having her tonsils out tomorrow," Dimple said. "I must remember to stop by Murphy's and get her a paper-doll book. I hear they have one now about Princesses Elizabeth and little Margaret Rose."

"Aren't they the bravest people?" Bessie tucked the book under her arm. "I heard that even with all the bombing the king and queen mother refused to move to a safer area away from London."

Dimple readily agreed, grateful for the change of subject. It was getting more and more difficult to steer people away from talking about Suzy Amos—or Suzu Amaya.

"I wish Suzy could come with us," Annie said when they stopped by the library after school the next day to find Virginia momentarily alone. "We thought we might as well start with Mae Martha's closest relatives and see if we can learn anything there."

"Yes, it would seem natural to pay a condolence call on the two nephews," Miss Dimple added, "especially since they would be the ones to benefit the most financially.

"I seem to remember Mrs. Hawthorne mentioning something about spraining her ankle in a fall," she said. "I believe it was because of some hickory nuts. Suzy said they were all over the porch and steps."

"They're good if you have the patience to shell them and pick out those little nut meats, but they can be treacherous underfoot," Virginia agreed.

Miss Dimple didn't say anything but Charlie could tell by the look on her face she wasn't ready to let go of that subject anytime soon.

"We'd better hurry if we want to get back before too late," Charlie reminded them. "Mama and Aunt Lou are working an extra day at the munitions plant in Milledgeville and I want to get home before they do. You know how nosy those two are! Mama's already quizzed me about our meeting at Virginia's so much, and I'm pretty sure she suspects something."

"Oh, dear! That will never do." Miss Dimple started for the door. She knew the two sisters had good intentions, but she also knew the road to a place she didn't care to go was rumored to be paved in that manner.

"I see Esau's truck is here so it looks like we're in luck," Charlie said a short while later as they pulled up beside the small farmhouse. Esau himself, looking subdued and clean-shaven, met them at the door.

"I thought highly of your aunt and I know this must be a difficult time for you and your family,"

Miss Dimple said in a voice that had consoled many a weeping first grader. "We wanted to let you know how very sorry we are for your loss. Mrs. Hawthorne was a lovely person—inside and out."

The other two stood beside her and nodded solemnly until Coralee bustled from the kitchen and led them into the small sitting room where she offered them a seat on a Victorian sofa, covered in burgundy velvet, shiny with use. Charlie thought she smelled coffee brewing and wondered if Coralee had been baking one of her unappetizing cakes to serve with it. The thought provoked a sweet-sad memory of the down-to-earth artist she had known only a short time.

"It just don't seem right without her," their hostess informed them in funereal tones. "Why, I look up on that hill, and for the life of me, I can't believe she's not there! Isn't that right, Esau?"

Her husband nodded silently, his head bowed. He sat on a straight chair across from them, his hands clasped between his knees, and made no move to wipe away the tear that inched slowly down his rugged face.

"The service . . ." Miss Dimple began, but the words caught in her throat. "Have they . . . you . . . decided when that will be?"

Esau Ingram sighed. "I reckon when the sheriff tells us. Right now plans are kinda up in the air. Folks are saying that woman—that Suzy—killed her and went off with the money, but there couldn't have been a whole lot in there . . . not enough to kill for!" He took out a handkerchief and blew his nose. "The folks over at Zion Chapel say they'll take care of the funeral when the time comes."

Coralee reached out and patted her husband's shoulder. "We don't know what makes people do the things they do, but she's with Madison now. Don't guess a few more days are going to matter."

Their leave-taking was interrupted by the arrival of an older couple Esau introduced as Harriet and Stanley Curtis, who came bearing cloth-covered trays of food that smelled delightfully of fried chicken and gingerbread.

Harriet explained they were from the small chapel down the road where Mae Martha had attended when she was able. "We never could talk her into joining," she added with a smile, "but she was a good friend to us just the same."

"If we hurry, we might have just enough time to pay our respects to Isaac," Miss Dimple suggested as Charlie endeavored to back into the road without getting stuck in the mud.

"Esau is either a very good actor or he's genuinely sad," Charlie observed. "Poor thing! I wanted to hug him."

"I'm glad we had a chance to meet the Curtises," Annie said with a backward glance at the house. "I wonder if they were the people Suzy was talking about when she mentioned visitors from the church. Anyway, now that we've met them, it should make it easier to drop in for a visit. They might be able to tell us more about Mae Martha than her relatives would want us to know."

"Maybe they'll have some of that good-smelling chicken," Charlie said, her stomach rumbling. "If they'd offered some, I wouldn't have said no."

Miss Dimple was silent as they drove the few miles to Isaac Ingram's blacksmith shop. "I suppose Mrs. Hawthorne is happy to be with her grandson again as Coralee pointed out, but between you, me, and the gatepost, I'll be willing to bet she would just as soon have put that off awhile longer."

CHAPTER TWELVE

The year was wearing down to the shortest day and the sun would soon be gone from the sky when they wound their way through a grove of pecan trees to the weathered gray building where Isaac Ingram had his blacksmith shop. As they drew nearer they could see the yellow-orange glow of the coal fire in the forge and the dark silhouette of the smithy as he hammered at the anvil. Although the temperature had dipped into the thirties and a chill wind sent brown leaves tumbling, Isaac Ingram worked with his sleeves rolled up in a shop with double doors entirely open on one side. Showers of red sparks rained against the dark grime of the interior.

The blacksmith barely acknowledged the group with a nod as he proceeded to forge what appeared to be a plowshare, and Miss Dimple was reminded of the adage "strike while the iron is hot." Naturally a blacksmith couldn't stop in the middle of this important step. The pounding of the hammer made a musical rhythm when Isaac struck the anvil between beats on the iron being hammered. Dimple smiled, remembering her papa who had referred to that as "tickling the anvil."

They stepped back as the iron sizzled, and steam rose when it was dropped into a tub of water to temper it. The heavy smoke from the coal used in the forge filled the building with an awful smell that made her want to hold her nose and Miss Dimple noticed the two younger women were obviously attempting to ignore it.

Flames flickered low in the forge, leaving the coals to burn away but the blacksmith didn't reach for the bellows that hung nearby. Instead, setting the finished plowshare aside, he wiped his hands and face on a rag as black with soot as he was and finally greeted his visitors. As Suzy had described, Isaac, unlike his slight, fairer-skinned brother, was dark and broad shouldered, and at least four or five inches taller than Esau. Underneath the grime and the beginnings of a beard, he was probably a handsome man, Miss Dimple thought—although a grim one, and one who came right to the point.

"You're here about my aunt," he said, shoving the soiled rag into his back pocket. He didn't smile as he addressed Miss Dimple. "She told me about you and that little girl. She doing all right?"

"As far as I know," Dimple replied. "She was to have had her tonsils out today. If it hadn't been for your aunt and her companion, I doubt if Peggy would be alive." *And I'm not so sure about myself,* she thought. Miss Dimple pulled the muffler from around her neck and unbuttoned her coat as the stifling heat closed around them. "We came to tell you how very sorry we are," she said, introducing the others.

This was met with a stoic silence that seemed to go on forever. "Well, she's gone," he told them, shaking his head. "Shouldn't have happened, but it did." Isaac motioned for them to follow him into an adjoining room. "Not so hot in here," he said as they stepped into an enclosed space lined with shelves filled with the results of his craft. Larger pieces like harrows, cooking vessels, even intricate wrought-iron gates, hung on the walls above them. Dimple saw a beautiful pair of andirons on a table to one side, and Isaac, seeing her notice it, reached out and touched it briefly. "Was going to give it to her for Christmas . . . the ones she had had just about melted through."

Dimple felt a catch in her throat as she searched for words. A kind and talented woman was gone and the grim awareness of it enveloped them as had the dark, suffocating smoke from the forge. She glanced at Charlie, whose eyes filled with tears. Annie's, too. "Oh," Charlie said. Just *oh*. Annie and Dimple said nothing.

"That woman—the nurse who looked after her . . . she turned up yet?" Isaac asked, facing them.

Miss Dimple drew in her breath. *Oh, dear!* "I don't believe so," she told him.

"They say her prints were on the poker," he said.

"What?" Wide-eyed, Annie reached out and grabbed the nearest arm. It was Charlie's.

"The sheriff, he said they found that woman's prints on the poker," Isaac repeated. "The poker that was used to kill her." Slowly he turned away. "I made that poker."

"B-but surely you couldn't have . . . how could you have known somebody would . . . ?" Charlie began.

Miss Dimple spoke softly. "Mr. Ingram, I don't know why anyone would want to harm your aunt, but I do know her companion was the one who regularly tended the fire. It would be natural for her prints to be on that poker."

"Then where is she?" he asked. "And where is the money that was taken? The box she usually kept it in was found in *her* room." Something close to a smile crossed his face. "Of course there couldn't have been much in it. She only kept enough for groceries and other mostly minor expenses. The rest she had me put in the bank."

"I understand you took care of marketing her paintings," Dimple said, and he nodded, pulling at the whiskers on his chin.

"Most of them. Some of them she practically gave away. Nothing I could do about that. Aunt Mae Martha had a heart as big as that old hill she lived on up there, but she didn't have a lot of practical sense. Why, I don't even know where some of her paintings have gotten to. She couldn't have given them *all* away!"

"You mean they're *missing?*" Annie asked.

"A good many, I'm afraid," he said.

"Didn't you keep some kind of record?" Charlie asked.

"Well, for the most part . . . at least I tried to." Isaac sighed. "My aunt was a puzzlin' woman. She loved people, liked being in their company, but she truly relished being alone."

A little twinge of guilt nudged Miss Dimple's noble conscience. "Perhaps I should admit I myself purchased one of Mrs. Hawthorne's paintings. I'm sure she didn't charge me nearly what it was worth."

Charlie and Annie reluctantly confessed they had also bought some of her artwork for a meager fee.

For the first time Isaac Ingram allowed himself to smile and it changed his entire face. "That's good. You enjoy them then—she preferred they go to people she liked, you know."

"Where were most of her paintings sold?" Annie asked.

"Most anywhere—some in galleries and exhibits—but they were displayed in bazaars as well, and a few are even in museums. As soon as the sheriff would let me, I took the ones she had in her studio to a dealer in Atlanta, but they won't go on the market anytime soon." Isaac picked up a hand-forged fire shovel, fingered the edge. "They don't stay for sale long."

"Do you have any idea who might have wanted to kill your aunt?" Miss Dimple asked, and Isaac took the rag from his pocket, squeezed it with two large hands. "I honestly don't," he told her. "But you don't want to be around when I find out."

Bony limbs of the overhanging pecan trees made a tunnel in the darkness for the yellow-washed headlights as they made their way back to the road and Charlie drove carefully to avoid any obstructions. Synthetic rubber tires were a minor sacrifice to the war effort, but she didn't relish having a puncture so far out in the country. "I guess Mama and Aunt Lou have been home awhile by now," she said. "Both trying to figure out what we're up to!"

"Just tell them the truth," Miss Dimple advised, "that we paid a condolence call on—"

"Look out!" Annie yelled from the backseat as a figure stepped from the darkness in front of them right into the path of the car.

Charlie veered to the right to avoid him and threw on the brakes. The person didn't move.

"Be careful! Go around him," Annie said. "Let's get out of here!"

But before Charlie could put the car in gear, the man stepped up and leaned on the driver's window. It was Mae Martha's handyman, Bill Pitts.

"What do you want?" Charlie asked, rolling down her window partway. "Do you realize I almost hit you?"

Miss Dimple leaned toward him. "Don't you know it's dangerous to stand in the middle of the road?" she said in her most authoritative voice. "Is something wrong? Do you need help?"

Bill looked them over silently. "I reckon not," he mumbled.

"Then step back, please, and we'll be on our way," Miss Dimple told him. "I suggest you do the same." She nudged Charlie to remind her to roll up her window and he obediently moved aside. Annie watched him standing there as they drove away. "Well, that was exciting! Did he have too much to drink or is he just crazy?"

"I think he was checking up on us," Dimple said.

"Why? What do you mean?" Charlie asked.

"I believe he was looking for Suzy," Miss Dimple said. "She disappeared the day Mrs. Hawthorne was killed, and we were the ones who discovered her body that same day." She pulled her warm hat snugly about her ears. "I'm afraid we're going to have to be much more careful from now on."

"I hope he doesn't suspect we know anything about her," Annie said. "I don't know what he might do, and Suzy's alone most of the day while Virginia's at the library."

"I can't imagine why he'd think to look there, or to bother with us," Charlie assured her. "It's perfectly natural for us to call on Mae Martha's nephews. I wonder, though, if he followed us from Esau's. For a minute there, I thought he wanted to tell us something. Guess he changed his mind."

"Isaac seems to have genuinely cared for his aunt," Miss Dimple observed. "And Esau as well, although I suppose even the hardest criminal can squeeze out a few tears when necessary. I'd like to know who benefits from Mrs. Hawthorne's will."

"If what I've heard is right, her paintings could be worth a small fortune," Charlie said. "I wonder what happened to the ones that are missing."

"I'll tell you where they *weren't*," Dimple said as they drove into a dark and silent town. "None of them was on Esau Ingram's walls—or at least that I could see."

Annie spoke up from the backseat. "That does seem peculiar, doesn't it? Maybe they weren't to Coralee's taste."

Dimple, having noticed in the Ingrams' hallway a framed picture of a waterfall that looked as if it had been torn from a calendar, thought perhaps the woman's taste in art might be on the same level as her baking skills. But, of course, she didn't say so.

The next afternoon Dimple found little Peggy Ashcroft propped in her hospital bed with her favorite doll in one arm and a brand-new stuffed teddy bear in the other. One of those embroidery kits sold especially for children, although few ever used them, waited on the table beside her, along with a storybook, a coloring book, and a new box of crayons.

"Hurts," Peggy croaked in response to her teacher's greeting, but she managed a weak smile and held up the doll for Dimple to see.

It was obvious the rag doll wasn't new and Dimple cast a puzzled look at Peggy's mother.

"She wants you to notice Lucy's new dress," Kate explained. "Lottie Nivens made it out of scraps from Miss Bessie's ragbag. She said she had a rag doll named Lucy, too."

Dimple praised Lucy's new pink-flowered frock and matching sunbonnet with enthusiasm and gave the little girl the paper-doll book she had bought for her.

"And how are rehearsals coming for the Christmas program tomorrow?" she asked Kate after Peggy turned her face away from a dish of melting ice cream. Dimple remembered how her own throat had hurt after that same surgery.

"Very well, I think," Kate told her. "Lottie . . . Mrs. Nivens has worked hard in the short time she's had to prepare for it. I think she's enjoying her stay here in Elderberry and she seems to adore Bessie."

"We've missed her at Phoebe's noontime dinner for the last few days," Dimple said. "She and Charlie walk to school together most mornings and Charlie tells me Lottie's been having a sandwich at school to have more time to work on the music."

Kate smiled. "It's wonderful not to have to worry about hurrying back full-time until Peggy's stronger. We're lucky to have her step in and help."

"I think that goes both ways," Miss Dimple said.

"I hope you'll feel better soon," she said to Peggy. "And I'll bet Max will be so glad to see you tomorrow, he'll just about wag his tail clean off!" She was rewarded with a smile.

Leaving the hospital, she walked the few blocks to stop by Harris Cooper's grocery for hoop cheese and a small bag of oranges. Virginia had expressed a desire for rarebit and Dimple knew how fond she was of oranges. She had told Phoebe she was having supper at Virginia's that evening, and in addition to helping with the meal, Dimple was eager to talk with Suzy, as she hadn't had an opportunity to see her since their visit to the Ingrams' the day before.

It was almost dark by the time she walked from town to Virginia's cottage on Myrtle Street—but not dark enough.

"Why, Dimple, is that you? It's so dark out here I can hardly see. Seems we've hardly any daylight left!" Mavis Kilgore called to her from across the street as she stooped to pick up what looked like a small piece of litter from the sidewalk.

"Oh, hello, Mavis," Dimple quickened her steps and turned in at Virginia's walkway. She had no intention of prolonging the conversation.

"Virginia's not sick, is she? Seems to be a lot of coming and going lately."

Which is no business of yours! "She's kind enough to help with some research we're doing at school, but I'll tell her you asked," Dimple called over her shoulder.

• • •

"What do you bet she was waiting at that window for you or somebody—anybody—to come along?" Virginia said, overhearing the exchange.

"I expect she's just about worn a trail in the carpet from sentry duty," Dimple said with a worried smile. "Do you think she might suspect?"

Virginia shrugged. "Oh, I'm sure she *suspects!* She probably suspects I'm getting soused every night on bootleg liquor; having an illicit affair with the Baptist preacher; or even worse, dealing in the black market in my basement—if I had a basement—but I doubt if even Mavis could guess what's really going on here!"

Suzy seemed to enjoy the rarebit, although she admitted she had been expecting to be served a supper of the kind Bill Pitts brought home in a burlap sack.

Later, as they cleared away the dishes, Dimple told her of their visit to the nephews the day before, and of meeting the couple from the church.

Suzy filled a dishpan with hot soapy water. "Curtis . . . the name sounds familiar. I believe those are the people who came to the house— came a couple of times if I'm not mistaken. I never met them, of course, but Miss Mae Martha seemed to like them." She put the flatware in to soak. "And how are Esau and Isaac? I suppose they're convinced I killed their aunt."

"I think they just want the truth, as we all do," Miss Dimple said. "And you might as well know the police found your prints on the poker that was used. . . ."

Suzy gripped the side of the sink with both hands and shook her head. "I'm not surprised, since I was the one who used it—to tend the fire."

"By the way," Dimple added, "as we were leaving we received a surprise visit from that fellow Bill Pitts."

Suzy made a face as Dimple told her about how the man stood in front of the car. "I'll have to admit I never felt comfortable around him. Miss Mae Martha seemed to get along fine with Bill, but she liked almost everybody, I guess."

After the dishes were clean, Suzy stacked them in a dishpan and scalded them with boiling water from the kettle. Miss Dimple picked up a dish towel to dry. "You said something earlier about Mrs. Hawthorne injuring her ankle on some hickory nuts that were on the steps. Did that happen often?"

"Only once that I know of." Suzy gave her a questioning look. "I swept the porch and steps clean and that seemed to be the end of it."

"That's odd." Dimple frowned as she tossed the dried silverware into the drawer. "If the branches hung over the porch, I'd think more would eventually fall. It's most unlikely for a tree to shed its harvest all at once, don't you think?"

Suzy met her gaze across the table. "Do you think somebody might have *put them there?*"

"I'm beginning to believe it's possible," Dimple said. "But *who?*"

CHAPTER THIRTEEN

"W hat are you going to do with yourself when the assembly program's over?" Charlie asked Lottie Nivens as they walked to school that last Friday before Christmas vacation began.

"Kate plans to take several weeks off, so I expect I'll be here at least through January," Lottie said as they waited to cross Katherine Street. "That is, if Miss Bessie can put up with me!" she added.

"She loves having you here!" Charlie burrowed her hands deep in her coat pockets, having forgotten her gloves. "I've never seen her so excited about Christmas. Delia and I are bringing you a tree from the country when we get ours."

"She's been so kind to me—everyone has." Lottie smiled as she looked around. "A cousin of ours lived here for a short time when she was growing up and it's every bit as nice as she said it would be. I wish . . . well, when Hal comes home after the war, maybe we . . ."

"I don't see why not," Charlie said. "I'm sure

Miss Bessie would be glad to have both of you until you find a place of your own." Lottie waved to Clarissa Sullivan as she swept her walk across the street and paused to admire the large magnolia in her yard. "I love a magnolia, don't you? They're messy, I know, but there's something kind of sheltering about them—gives me a good kind of feeling."

"They make good Christmas decorations, too," Charlie agreed. Her mother already had a glossy arrangement on the dining room table. Even though the town had to forego its usual colored outside lights because of the threat of bombing, most people managed to display some token of the season. A large evergreen wreath with a red bow hung in Phoebe Chadwick's front window, and on the Elrods' porch next door, a freshly cut cedar waited in a bucket of water to be taken inside; even Marjorie Mote, who had lost a son in the war, had tied a festive wreath of holly on her door.

There would be no lessons today and the children would be wild, but a nice kind of wild, Charlie thought. The assembly program would take up most of the morning, and the afternoon would be filled with parties in the individual classrooms. Even with the rationing of sugar, grade mothers had been baking Christmas goodies for the children and in every classroom mounds of tissue-wrapped gifts surrounded a small cedar or pine brought in from the country-side and decorated with popcorn and colored paper. Earlier Charlie had purchased and wrapped several small gifts from the dime store in case someone didn't receive one from the person who drew his name. It was not a day for tears and disappointments.

And it wasn't a day for worrying, either. Just for today, Charlie decided, she wasn't going to think about what had happened to Mae Martha Hawthorne and the woman they were sheltering from the local police.

That notion lasted until noontime.

"Would it be possible for us to take a short drive to the Hawthorne place tomorrow?" Miss Dimple asked as she, Charlie, and Annie hurried back to school after a hasty pickup lunch at Phoebe's. "Virginia will be at the library most of the day and I don't believe we should delay this any longer than we have to."

"As long as I'm free in the afternoon," Charlie told her. "I promised Delia we'd look for our tree tomorrow."

"Doesn't that family live out that way somewhere?" Annie asked. "The people who're getting the basket?"

"You're right. The Culpeppers," Miss Dimple said. "It shouldn't be too far out of the way. I believe they live a few miles farther on."

For several weeks the first through fourth

grades had been collecting nonperishable food and small gifts for a family that had fallen upon hard times after the father was killed in the war, although only the teachers knew who would receive the basket.

"I'll tell Mr. Faulkenberry we'll collect it in the morning," Miss Dimple said, referring to the school principal. "I have a key if the janitor's not there to let us in."

Charlie laughed. "Good! That'll give me an excuse to take the car. Mama and Aunt Lou don't miss a thing, you know, and they've been asking a lot of questions about our recent outings. I honestly don't know how much longer I can pull the wool over their eyes."

Annie paused on the steps when they reached the brick building with the belfry that housed their respective classrooms. "When shall we three meet again?" she asked with a grin. Charlie laughed and Miss Dimple smiled as well. Both knew she was quoting from the witches' scene by her favorite playwright.

They didn't qualify as witches, Charlie thought, but what they were doing was scary just the same.

"I feel like Santa," Charlie said the next morning after they had delivered the basket to a small unpainted house with a clean-swept yard where a yellow cat sunned itself on the steps and a tire swing hung from the only tree. She was glad they had thought to add fruit and candy to the other contributions when she saw the three small children peering from behind their mother. What would become of them? she wondered. Her sister, Delia, had moved back home after her husband was shipped to the front. If anything happened to Ned, Delia would eventually have to find work while their mother and Charlie helped raise their child. She hoped this woman had family she could rely on as well, but most of all she hoped Ned would come safely home.

"What now?" Charlie asked as they turned back onto the main road.

"Now I'd like to investigate some hickory nuts," Miss Dimple said.

"Some *what?*" Annie laughed, wondering if she'd heard correctly.

Dimple explained why she wanted a look at the trees close to Mrs. Hawthorne's porch. "Most of the leaves have fallen by now, but some of the nuts would still be on the ground and the bark would probably have a shaggy appearance," she added.

"And if we don't find them there . . . ?" Annie sat forward in her seat.

"Then they must have been scattered there on purpose," Miss Dimple said. "A fall from the top of those steps might have injured her badly—or worse. As it was, she only got a bad sprain."

"I guess Suzy will be blamed for that as well,"

Charlie said as they turned into the road that led to Mae Martha's property. "Somebody has made sure there's evidence against her. The empty money box was supposedly *hidden* on top of her wardrobe, and naturally the poker had her prints."

Annie glanced out the window as they made their way slowly up the rutted winding road. "I sure hope we don't meet up with any of Mae Martha's kin. They might wonder what we're doing here."

"And I'd just as soon not run into Bill," Charlie admitted.

It had rained some during the night and it took longer than usual for Charlie to maneuver around pondlike puddles in the road in addition to the usual rocks and ruts. They parked in the graveled area behind the house and walked around to the front, where the wide porch stretched from one side to the other.

"Do you feel as sad as I do?" Charlie said, noticing that someone had turned the rocking chairs against the wall. The war had reminded all of them that life might end abruptly, taking with it a part of those left behind. She didn't know Mae Martha well at all, but felt diminished by her death.

Annie murmured in agreement as they searched the ground for hickory nuts, and Dimple didn't answer because she was having trouble getting past the lump in her throat. The house, once warm and welcoming, was dark and empty and joyless. Mae Martha Hawthorne wouldn't have recognized it.

"Well, I haven't found one hickory nut," Charlie said after the three had been searching for a while.

"That's because there aren't any here. I know they grow around here because I noticed several shagbark hickories the day we searched for Peggy, but they were lower on the hillside. There are several redbud trees up here, as well as a few young oaks and dogwoods, and of course plenty of pines, but I couldn't find even one hickory close to this house."

"I knew they had to grow in this area," Annie said as they made their way back to the car. "The other day in the blacksmith shop I noticed Isaac Ingram had fitted some of his tools with handles and he told me most were made from hickory."

Charlie shivered as they waded through soggy leaves. The place was bleak and gray with a raw chill and smelled of dampness and decay. She flooded the engine in her rush to leave and had to wait to try again. "This place makes me uneasy," she confessed. "I know I'm being silly, but I have a feeling somebody's watching us."

Miss Dimple spoke softly. "Someone is."

"Who? Where?" *Oh, please, God, don't let it flood again!* The engine finally sputtered to life and the old Studebaker rocked forward. Charlie found herself gritting her teeth as they splashed, slipped, and bumped to the bottom of the hill. "It will be fine with me if I never see this place again!" she said. "Miss Dimple, were you able to see who was watching us?"

"I'm afraid not. Whoever it was, was partially obscured by an evergreen. All I could see were legs."

Annie frowned. "A man's legs or a woman's legs?"

"It's hard to say with so many women wearing slacks now. I suppose it could've been either." Miss Dimple looked at the small timepiece pinned to her dress. "We've a good part of the morning left. If you don't mind, I'd like to pay a call."

Annie glanced at her muddy feet and giggled. "I'm afraid I didn't bring my white gloves, Miss Dimple."

Charlie smiled. What a relief to make light of the situation! Yet she knew that Dimple Kilpatrick actually did keep a pair of spotless white gloves in her bottomless handbag.

"I noticed that we passed the house where the Curtises live when we went to take that basket this morning," Miss Dimple pointed out. "I saw their names on the mailbox."

Annie frowned. "Who are the Curtises?"

"The couple from Mrs. Hawthorne's church," Miss Dimple reminded her. "They brought supper to Esau Ingram and his wife while we were there the other day. Remember the fried chicken?"

"Ah—of course! But won't it seem kind of strange—our dropping in like this?" Charlie asked.

But Miss Dimple had that covered as well. "They seemed a pleasant sort and I feel certain they might share a few sprays from that lovely holly tree in their yard. Phoebe would like some, I know, and Virginia as well. I would have felt uncomfortable asking them about Mrs. Hawthorne with the Ingrams present and this might offer an opportunity to get an opinion from someone outside the family."

Charlie nodded. "It's all right with me, but I'm afraid I didn't bring any clippers."

Miss Dimple patted her handbag. "My little pocketknife should do fine."

"Well, of course! Please take all you want," Harriet Curtis said when she met them at the door. "We use that holly tree to decorate our church every Christmas and, my goodness, you can hardly tell we've taken any."

"Miss Dimple, Annie and I will do that," Charlie offered, accepting the pocketknife. "I know you must be tired from all our tramping around." She avoided looking at Annie, knowing, as Annie did, that the morning's amount of walking was trifling to Dimple Kilpatrick. It did encourage, however, the invitation they had hoped for.

"Oh, you mustn't wait out here in the cold! Please, come in and get warm. There's coffee on the stove and I'll cut us a nice piece of fruitcake. Stanley can't ever wait until Christmas to get into it so we might as well enjoy some before he eats the whole thing."

Dimple, who had begun to remove her shoes on the doorstep, considered slipping them back on. She simply despised fruitcake and the idea of anyone consuming an entire cake almost made her ill.

"Thank you. Coffee would be most welcome, but I really don't care for—"

"Nonsense!" Harriet Curtis seated Dimple at a small kitchen table covered in bright blue oilcloth and proceeded to pour the coffee. Dimple eyed the tin warily as her hostess pried off the cover. "I really shouldn't . . ." she began as Harriet sliced into the cake . . . "Well, just a *small* piece, please." She hoped it wouldn't have citron in it. Her aunt Ethel had used enough for ten cakes in her recipe and had always brought one along on her annual Christmas visit.

Harriet sliced servings for both of them, and pulled up a chair to join her. Miss Dimple thanked her and picked up her fork. The slice would have been more than enough for three.

"You know, you just can't get the candied fruit

162

like we used to before the war," Harriet said, "but I had plenty of citron left from last year, so I just doubled that and it worked out fine."

Miss Dimple nodded and smiled—or tried to smile. Perhaps if she ate fast and washed each bite down with coffee . . .

"My goodness, you must like fruitcake as much as my Stanley!" Harriet reached for the tin. "I'll cut you a piece to take home."

Realizing that no amount of arguing was going to dissuade her, Dimple thanked her hostess in as gracious a manner as possible, tucked the wax paper–wrapped offering in her handbag, and got down to business.

"I wish I'd had an opportunity to know Mrs. Hawthorne better," she began. "She seemed a lovely person and was certainly kind to me."

"Yes, we're all going to miss her. She didn't come to our church on a regular basis . . . I don't believe she felt comfortable in crowds, but she seemed to feel at home there when she did." Harriet stood and refilled their cups. "It was so sad about Madison, her grandson. You knew he was killed back in May?"

Miss Dimple nodded as sipped her coffee but all she could taste was citron. "She told me all about him. He was planning a medical career."

"Such a shame!" Harriet cradled her cup in both hands. "She commissioned a window in his memory for our little chapel."

Miss Dimple said she thought that was a lovely way to remember him. Perhaps, she thought, Mae Martha had confided in her friend about the paintings Isaac claimed were missing.

"Her paintings—" she began, reaching in her handbag for a handkerchief. *Dear heavens! All that cake was giving her heartburn!*

"Oh, aren't they wonderful? You may have noticed I have one of hers in my living room—the little girls with the kittens."

"If I might trouble you for a little water . . ."

Harriet hovered with a worried frown. "Are you all right?"

Dimple thankfully drank the offered water. "It's my own fault for eating so fast. I bought one of her paintings for my brother," she continued. "Isaac Ingram tells me he thinks some of her work might be missing."

It surprised her when Harriet laughed. "Oh, they aren't missing, Miss Dimple! I know exactly where they are."

CHAPTER FOURTEEN

W hat do you mean?" Miss Dimple asked.
"The paintings . . ." Harriet dribbled milk into her coffee and stirred. "They're in a closet at our church."

Dimple waited impatiently while the woman dropped in saccharine and stirred again.

"But why—?" she began.

"A few months ago Mae Martha asked me if we had space to accommodate several of her paintings. She didn't explain why, only said she wanted them safely stored away. I had a feeling she wanted them protected."

"Protected from what? From someone perhaps?"

Harriet shook her head and frowned. "She didn't say, but I had the feeling it was urgent, and of course I agreed. There's a small room behind the sanctuary. Part of it's used by the choir for storing music and robes, but our choir lost members when the war began." She smiled. "It's mostly a few women now and some of the older men—none of us is anything to brag about, but I reckon we do the best we can. Anyway, we rarely wear those robes anymore and that's where we put the paintings."

"Are there many?"

"I didn't count them, but I'd say at least twenty—maybe more. Stanley and I came over and took them away in our truck, and no one except for the two of us and our minister know they're there. Brother Collins thinks—thought—the world of Mae Martha Hawthorne. As far as I know, nobody goes in that closet anymore.

"I keep meaning to tell the nephews now that she's gone but for some reason I've held off on doing that. I mean, why didn't she ask one of them to store them instead of Stanley and me? But I expect everything will come to them anyway, don't you think?"

Miss Dimple said she thought it probably would but couldn't be certain. "Isaac is the one who markets her paintings and he said he'd taken what was left to a dealer in Atlanta, but from what he told me, I don't believe he's ready to sell them yet."

"Naturally they'll be worth more now that she's gone," Harriet said sadly. "We just learned the authorities are finally releasing her body. Funeral is tomorrow afternoon at Zion."

Miss Dimple made note of that. She certainly intended to be there.

Harriet moved her chair closer. "I understand you spent some time at Mae Martha's when that little girl was lost. What did you think about her companion—that Japanese woman who's disappeared? Of course Mae Martha told us a little about her, but Stanley and I were there several times and she never showed her face."

"Why do *you* think that is?" Dimple asked.

Harriet thought for a minute. "I suppose because she's Japanese." She shrugged. "With all the others to choose from I can't imagine why Madison hired *her.*"

Miss Dimple explained Suzy's situation to Harriet as it had been explained to her. "You can see she's in a difficult situation," she added. "She can't go back to California, and even with her medical degree, who would take a chance on hiring her now?"

Harriet's face was solemn. "I can see she has a problem, but do you think she had anything to do with Mae Martha's death? I heard they found the empty money box in her room, and her prints were—"

"Suzy used that poker several times a day," Dimple said, "and no, I don't believe for one minute that she killed Mae Martha Hawthorne. I do know she saved Peggy Ashcroft's life the night we showed up on their doorstep. That young woman must've been terrified when she discovered Mae Martha's body, and I think she ran away because she knew she'd get the blame."

With her fingers Harriet smoothed the wrinkles in the oilcloth, although there weren't any wrinkles there. "I wonder where she could be? It's been . . . what? Over a week now."

"Somewhere safe, I hope. I suppose she's waiting for the police to find out who's responsible for all this." Dimple gathered up her handbag and thanked Harriet for her hospitality as she rose to go. "I expect my friends are eager to get back as they plan to look for their Christmas tree this afternoon.

"About those paintings," she added before leaving, "I believe it might be best to at least let

Isaac know where they are. If something happened while they were in your possession, your church might be held responsible, and it would at least keep the record straight."

"You're right. I never thought of that.

"You all come back, now!" Harriet called after her. "I'll save you a piece of cake!"

"What cake?" Charlie asked as Dimple slid in beside her. Dimple Kilpatrick waved over her shoulder as they drove away. "You really don't want to know."

"Will you look at all the cedars in that pasture!" Charlie said the next afternoon on the way to Mae Martha's funeral. "And we couldn't find a decent one yesterday. Mama had to sell most of our farm after Daddy died and there's not a lot of land left. I wonder who owns this."

"I expect it belongs to one of the Ingrams," Virginia said as she turned into Zion Chapel's crowded parking lot and found a spot at the end of a row. "They'd probably be glad for you to have one, but I doubt if this is the proper time to ask."

"You're right, and of course I wouldn't think of it, it's just that Delia was so disappointed yesterday when we couldn't find a tree. This will be little Tommy's first Christmas, and naturally we're more excited about it than he is." Her nephew was not quite nine months old and had no idea what all the fuss was about.

"I do wish Suzy could've come with us," Virginia said. "Of course it would've been a disaster, but she really was fond of Mae Martha and it's a shame she couldn't be here. I promised I would give her a full report."

"I'll be curious to see who is here," Miss Dimple said as they filed inside the small sanctuary. The double chapel doors, she noticed, were hung with wreathes of holly and cedar and the scent of it was still fresh on the air. The four of them filed into a pew near the back and she recognized Harriet Curtis and her husband a few seats in front of them. Although Mae Martha hadn't belonged to the little church or lived in the area long, several floral sprays filled the space in front of the altar, and a blanket of tiny white mums, gladiolas, and carnations covered the casket, which, Dimpled noted thankfully, was closed.

The church soon became stifling with so many people packed inside, and the sickly smell of flowers was heavy on the air. Miss Dimple held her handkerchief to her nose and inhaled the lavender sachet. Beside her, Virginia fanned with an old grocery list she'd found in her purse. They rose as the family walked down the aisle while the pianist played the hymn "All Things Bright and Beautiful," which Dimple thought most appropriate to the legacy the artist had left behind. She wondered who had chosen it.

The two nephews looked neat but uncomfortable in suits and ties. Isaac was unaccompanied but Coralee, in a dark winter coat with black velvet collar, clung to Esau's arm and looked suitably distressed. Suzy had told them earlier that the couple's one daughter was married and living somewhere up north. Charlie looked around to see if Bill Pitts was there but couldn't find him in the crowded sanctuary. Maybe, she thought, he had come in later and was sitting in the rear, but as everyone filed out after the brief service, she saw no sign of him.

They had not planned to attend the graveside rites but found themselves hemmed in by other cars and unable to leave, so at Dimple's suggestion, the four trailed behind the others to the cemetery in back of the church. Standing at some distance from the rest, Dimple scanned the group, wondering if the woman named Becky who sold milk and eggs to Mae Martha had come to pay her respects, but of course she had no idea what she looked like. A brisk wind picked up as the minister said his final words and people began to leave soon after, obviously making an effort not to seem in too much of a hurry.

Dimple Kilpatrick had no such reservations and began quickly to retrace her steps to the car as the wind swayed slender pine saplings and moaned like a mourner through branches of the studier oaks. She paused to speak briefly with Mae

Martha's nephews, who obviously had the same idea and seemed eager to get out of the cold. Coralee, she noticed, had held back to chat with the minister and several others. At the edge of the parking lot Dimple stopped to clean red mud from her good shoes. She had only two pair, as shoes were rationed because of the war, and if she had thought ahead, she would have worn her others.

"I should've warned you about the mud!" someone called out behind her, and Dimple turned to find Harriet Curtis and her husband, Stanley, hurrying back to their car. "By the way," Harriet added, lowering her voice, "as you suggested, I told Isaac about the paintings stored in the church and he plans to come by and collect them in the next day or so."

"I'm glad," Dimple said, attempting to wipe the bottoms of her shoes on the grass. "I thought the service today was exactly what Mrs. Hawthorne would have wanted—especially the music."

Harriet smiled. "Our minister chose that, and I agree. I think Mae Martha would approve."

"I didn't see Bill Pitts there today," Dimple said, looking about.

"Poor soul! I doubt if anyone thought to tell him. He's an odd one, but I think he really cared about Mae Martha in his way."

Dimple pulled her coat snugly about her. "I understand there was another neighbor, Becky, who furnished Mrs. Hawthorne with milk and eggs on occasion."

Harriet Curtis nodded. "Rebecca keeps to herself. It's a shame, really. She was injured as a child when she pulled a pan of boiling water over on her, and one side of her face was badly burned."

"Harriet, my feet are turning to ice!" Stanley reminded her as he waited, stomping his feet by their car. His trousers, she noticed, were flecked with dried mud.

"Oh, dear! I guess I'd better go." Turning, Harriet noticed Miss Dimple's three companions and called to them. "I hope you found your tree yesterday. I expect you're in a hurry to get home and decorate."

"I'm afraid we didn't have much to choose from," Charlie said. "I guess we'll have to go back today and settle for the lesser of the evils."

"You're welcome to see if you can find one in our pasture," Harriet offered. "It's just across the road over there. We're spending Christmas with our daughter in Milledgeville, so I'm not even going to bother with one this year."

"Oh!" Charlie smiled. "I thought that probably belonged to one of the Ingrams."

"It backs up to Isaac's farm, but his property's mostly wooded. Don't snag yourself, now, on that barbed-wire fence—and please—all of you, take all the cedars you want. There'll be plenty more next year."

"How many trees do you think you can get in your car?" Annie asked Charlie when she telephoned later.

"How many do you need? Besides ours, I promised Miss Bessie and Lottie I'd find one for them."

"It looks like Miss Phoebe's going to be stuck with a couple of us over Christmas," Annie explained. "My folks are spending the holidays with my grandmother in Vermont—she hasn't been well lately—and I can't afford to travel. Miss Dimple usually spends Christmas with her brother at his mountain place, but he's working on some important project for the Bell Bomber plant and won't be able to get away, so she'll be here, too."

Charlie knew Phoebe Chadwick dreaded the holidays because she didn't like being alone. "I'll bet Phoebe's already planning Christmas dinner," she said.

Annie laughed. "She and Odessa are in the kitchen right now going over recipes, but we've decided we need a tree."

"We'll work it out somehow, but you'll have to come and help me. Little Pooh came down with a cold last night and he's so fretful and feverish Delia doesn't want to leave him. We'd better get started, though, or it'll be too dark to see."

"I'm grabbing my coat! Wait for you at the corner."

• • •

Charlie was surprised when she pulled up at the corner a few minutes later to find Annie accompanied by her student and neighbor, Willie Elrod.

"Do you mind if Willie comes, too?" Annie asked, slipping in beside her. "He wants to see if he can find some mistletoe. And he's had a major disappointment," she whispered aside to her. "He's threatening to resign from the Lone Ranger Club."

"I thought you liked the Lone Ranger," Charlie said as Annie made room for him beside her. "What happened?"

"It took forever but I finally got my secret code in the mail yesterday," Willie said, disgusted. "You have to listen to the radio show to get the message and I thought it was going to be something really important—something I could do to help win the war."

"Well, what was it?" Charlie asked. "What did it say?"

Willie Elrod stuck out his lip. "It said, 'Buy delicious, nutritious Merita Bread!'"

Charlie turned away so he wouldn't see her smile. "Well then, I think we can find something more exciting to do than that. Let's go hunt some mistletoe."

"What are you going to do with all that mistletoe, Willie?" Annie asked him.

"I can sell it downtown tomorrow," Willie said.

"I ain't got any money for presents and I want to get Mama something nice."

"Haven't!" Charlie and Annie said together.

"How do you plan to get that mistletoe down?" Charlie asked as they drove the few miles into the country. "You certainly aren't going to shoot it."

"Well, I could if I had a gun, but Mama won't let me. Shoot, I reckon I could knock an acorn off a fencepost at fifty yards!" Willie boasted.

"Fifty?" Annie narrowed her eyes.

"Well, okay. Twenty-five then. But I can poke some down with a long stick or even shinny up a tree if I have to."

They parked on the dirt road beside the Curtises' pasture, ducked under a fence, and walked through a herd of grazing Hereford cattle, who ignored them in favor of the next mouthful of grass. Harriet Curtis hadn't mentioned anything about a bull, and Charlie hoped they wouldn't meet one. The meadow was dotted with cow pies as well as small, fluffy cedars, and Charlie was glad she'd thought to wear her old rubber boots. Thank goodness it didn't take long to find three cedars just the right shape and size that met with their approval because it was getting darker by the minute. Charlie had brought rope, and after shoving one tree in the backseat and one in the trunk, the three managed with much difficulty to tie the third to the roof of the car.

"It's getting late," Charlie said, glancing at the sky. "You'd better hurry, Willie, if you want to find any mistletoe."

"And cold!" Annie shivered. "Come on! Let's see if we can find some in the woods."

"Mrs. Curtis said that property belongs to Isaac Ingram," Charlie pointed out, "but I don't guess he'd mind if we took some mistletoe."

"I don't see any *No trespassing!* signs so it must be okay," Annie said, holding up barbed wire for the others to step under.

Charlie thought of Miss Dimple and little Peggy Ashcroft as they tramped through the winter woods. Today the sun hadn't yet gone down and it was already cold and beginning to be difficult to see what was ahead. She could only imagine how the two of them must have felt when they became lost not very far from here with night quickly descending.

"I haven't seen any mistletoe yet!" Annie called, venturing ahead with Willie. "Usually it seems to be on every tree."

Charlie looked about her, hoping to find the telltale cluster of the green parasite in an other-wise winter bare tree. She hoped Willie would be able to find some to sell, but if they stayed any longer it was going to be too dark to see.

"I'm afraid your mother's going to be worried if we don't—" she began but was interrupted by the little boy's shouting.

"I see some! It's in that big oak—right up ahead, and I think I can reach it!" Willie began to run, and the others followed closely behind him.

When he couldn't dislodge the mistletoe with a long stick, Willie scampered up the tree squirrel-like while the two women waited below, gathering it as it fell. Charlie had already decided that she would be Willie's first customer just in case Will could get a break from advanced flight training and somehow manage to make it to Elderberry. She smiled at the thought. *Of course they wouldn't need mistletoe!* Annie's fiancé, Frazier Duncan, had shipped out with his company a few weeks before and she wasn't even sure where he was.

"All right, Willie, that's enough!" Annie called as the pile grew. "You'll be rich enough to buy out the store if you sell all this!"

"Come on down now!" Charlie shouted, joining in. "Be careful—watch your step."

"I'm coming." Willie reluctantly began his descent but hesitated halfway down the tree.

"Come on, Willie! It's time to go! What are you waiting for?" Annie called.

"Miss Annie, there's . . . somebody down there. . . ." The child spoke haltingly.

"What do you mean?" Annie strained to look about. "Where?"

"Over there—it looks like a man, and he's lying

in the creek!" Willie Elrod came down from the tree swinging like Tarzan from limb to limb and grabbed each of his teachers by the hand. "Oh, lordy! We gotta get outa here! It looks like he's dead!"

CHAPTER FIFTEEN

W illie Elrod, that's not funny!" Annie leaned down to speak to him face-to-face, although as short as she was, she didn't have far to lean.

But Charlie could see by the child's expression he was genuinely frightened and tightened her grip on his hand. "Where is he, Willie? Show us."

"Over there—in the creek." Willie pointed but still hung back.

"He might be hurt," Annie said, moving closer. "We have to make sure."

"Be careful!" Charlie warned, following her. "Willie, you stay right there!"

The man lay facedown with his head and shoulders submerged in the muddy waters of a shallow creek, and Charlie knew as soon as she saw him, he was beyond help.

Annie knelt beside him and pulled at the wet, rough cloth of his jacket. "Oh! I can't . . ." Turning her face away, she tugged once more and with Charlie's help, managed to drag the inert body from the water. The man's dark hair was plastered to his head with mud and water and Charlie hesitated before touching his face, but what if there was a chance he might still be breathing?

He wasn't. The dead man's face was cold and blue, and mud and debris from the creek had become lodged in his nose and mouth. His eyes were open and covered in a bluish film, but even with the distortions of death, Charlie recognized Mae Martha's handyman, Bill Pitts.

"Oh, please, Miss Annie, let's go!" Willie called. "I done got the heebie-jeebies! They's haints around here—I just know it! Everybody knows ole' Raw Head and Bloody Bones hangs around water, and he's probably got his eye on us next. Come on, Miss Charlie! It's almost dark."

"Don't pull that on me, Willie Elrod! You know that's not true." Charlie was familiar with the story of the frightening specter who carried off children who misbehaved, and while she knew it was only a folktale meant as a warning, she didn't like the way darkness was closing around them, either. Bill's face had abrasions from the bottom of the creek bed, where the water was only a foot or so deep. What or *who* had kept him from standing?

Annie was probably thinking the same thing. Without speaking, she called Charlie's attention to a half-empty bottle of whiskey that had been tossed to the side under a nearby tree. Had Bill had too much to drink and then passed out while washing his face in the creek? Surely he hadn't tried to drink water from the same source the Curtises' cattle waded in, drank from, and sometimes even defecated in upstream. And even if he had lost consciousness momentarily, the cold water and frantic need for air would have brought him around. Had something or someone held him down?

Charlie felt a tug at her back. "Miss Charlie? I don't like this!"

"I don't either, Willie." Putting an arm around him, she led him away. "We're leaving right now, but we had first to find out if there was anything we could do to help. I think the poor man must have had a heart attack and fallen into the water."

Oh, please make it so! she thought, but somehow, Charlie felt there was more to it than that. The back of Bill's jacket was streaked with mud although it hadn't been underwater, and a dead tree limb lay in the damp soil nearby.

"Here, Willie, let's gather up your mistletoe and head for the car," Charlie said in an effort to distract him and calm his fears. "We'll tell the sheriff as soon as we get home, and I'm sure he'll be able to find out what happened. Don't forget to save me a sprig of that mistletoe, now. I'll bet my mother will want some to hang in the living room."

Willie Elrod flushed and giggled. "Aw, Miss Charlie, I know good and well it ain't your mama who wants that mistletoe."

Charlie didn't even correct him.

"We'll need to stop by the sheriff's office and report this before we do anything else," Annie said as the three of them crammed into the car where the scent of cedar was almost over-powering.

Charlie admitted her friend was right although she disliked dragging Willie into another murder investigation—if it did turn out to be murder. He had been the first to notice the man lying in the creek, however. She sighed. They must be cursed or something. Why was it they always seemed to stumble into some kind of baffling foul play?

Sheriff Holland shook his head. "Don't tell me you all have come upon another crime!" He meant it as a joke, but his smile faded when he realized they were serious. Quickly he closed his office door and gestured for them to sit down. "Well, what is it this time?"

Charlie didn't want to sit, and neither did the others, but she held to the back of the straight chair as she told him about finding Bill Pitts. "It looks like he might have had a heart attack, and I believe he's been dead for several hours at least."

The sheriff glanced at the clock. "He isn't going anywhere, I reckon, but I'd better notify Doc and get on out there, and one of you will need to come along. As dark as it is, it'll be hard enough to see where we're going."

"I'll come," Charlie said. "But first let me take the others home. It's so late I'm afraid Willie's mother will be worried."

Sheriff Holland reached for the phone. "We can remedy that," he said, and put in a call to Emma Elrod. As soon as he had taken a brief statement from all of them, Charlie delivered her two passengers and one of the trees, which Annie, with Willie's help, wrenched from the backseat.

Minutes later, parking the mud-splashed Studebaker in her driveway, she dashed in to tell her family of the latest development. "Ask Lottie to give you a hand with the trees!" she yelled to Delia just as the sheriff pulled in behind her.

Charlie was glad she had dressed warmly since Sheriff Holland's car was as frigid as an icebox, and even in boots her feet were numb from the cold as they tramped over the now familiar pasture and climbed through the barbed-wire fence to the wooded section belonging to Isaac Ingram.

Doc Morrison had arrived at the same time they did and he and Peewee Cochran, the sheriff's deputy of sorts, followed along behind while Charlie and Sheriff Holland led the way. Another deputy remained behind to wait for Harvey Thompson and his hearse. Flashlights did little to illuminate the woods that had been dark even in daytime, and Charlie hoped she could remember the way they had come. Everything looked different at night.

Catching herself after stumbling over a root, Charlie stood still and cast the beam of her light about. "Are you all right?" Turning, the sheriff took her arm, but Charlie put out a hand to silence him. Dry leaves rustled somewhere just ahead of them. *Someone or something had moved in the underbrush—and it wasn't Bill Pitts!*

Shining his light ahead, the sheriff stepped in front of her. "Is anyone there?"

In the silence that followed Charlie could hear the sluggish sound of icy water forcing its way through stones in the creek and knew they were almost there.

"Probably a possum," Peewee muttered. "Coon, maybe."

Charlie hoped he was right. Both were nocturnal animals common to the area. Her father used to joke that possums were suicidal, throwing themselves under vehicles, as you saw so many flattened on the road.

"There it is! There's the tree," Charlie called out a few minutes later as the large oak where Willie had harvested mistletoe came into view. "He's there by the creek just a little farther on."

"Where? I don't see anything here," the sheriff said, pushing forward.

"There! On the creek bank!" How could he miss anything as large as a man? Charlie was tired, cold, and hungry. Did she have to take him by the hand and lead the way?

"Right over there!" she directed, plunging through winter-bare bushes that snagged at her clothing and clawed at her hair. But the body of Bill Pitts was not where they had left him.

Peewee chuckled. "Are you sure he was dead, ma'am?"

Charlie chose to ignore that. This had to be the right place. She looked closer. *Here. It was right here.* "This is where Annie and I pulled him out of the water. After we were sure he was dead, we didn't move him any farther than this."

Peewee grinned and shook his head but Doc Morrison focused his light on the muddy bank. "Look! I can see where somebody has been dragged along here, but where is he?"

Sheriff Holland stepped to the side and swung his light in a circle. "The last I heard, dead men don't get up and walk, so what's he doing here?"

Charlie looked where he was pointing, and there, propped against a tree with the liquor bottle in his lap, sat the late Bill Pitts looking every bit as dead as he had before.

Doc Morrison knelt beside him. "Hard to say

how long he's been dead in this cold weather but I should be able to tell more tomorrow."

"Footprints everywhere," the sheriff grumbled, "and a lot of them are ours. It'll be impossible to tell anything from all this mess."

Charlie stooped to look closer. She never wanted to see that ghastly face again, but something didn't look right—besides him being dead. Someone had attempted to clean him up!

"Now, why in the world would anybody do such a thing as that?" Peewee wanted to know when she told them what she suspected.

"Probably because they wanted whoever found him to think he died a natural death," Sheriff Holland said. "Now, don't anybody touch him until I've had a chance to get some pictures." With his flash camera he took photographs from several angles before moving in closer to get a better look at the body. "I'll swear, if this don't beat all! It's pretty clear he's been moved here and tidied up." He turned the dead man over just long enough to get a look at his back. "Shine your light here, Doc. . . . Sure enough, there's a streak of mud across there that might've come from being struck or held down by a log. Can't tell much tonight. We'll have to come back in the morning when I'll be able to get a better look at the surroundings, and my wife isn't going to like that one bit! We're supposed to go to her aunt Ora's for an early Christmas dinner."

"Why would whoever killed him leave him in the creek and then come back and move him?" Charlie asked. "Surely, they must have noticed we had already pulled him out of the water."

The sheriff shook his head. "I don't know. Maybe they heard you all coming and didn't have time to get him cleaned up. They're probably hoping nobody will believe you. Isn't this Isaac Ingram's property? This fellow Bill Pitts—he lived around here somewhere, didn't he?"

Nobody had an answer for that, but Doc Morrison suggested one of the Ingrams might know.

Charlie could hardly feel her feet, and even in gloves, her hands were so cold they hurt. She stuck them inside her jacket and stamped her feet. The others seemed impatient, too, and a stiff wind whipping the trees around them made matters even worse.

"What in the devil is keeping Harvey?" Sheriff Holland stormed. "I called him the same time I called you, Doc. If he doesn't get here soon, we'll all be as cold and stiff as poor old Bill there."

Minutes later a light flickered in the darkness and someone called out from the direction they had come.

"Here's Harvey, finally!" Doc went to meet him while Sheriff Holland stayed at the scene. Charlie never thought she would be so glad to see the local funeral director when he arrived with his assistant and the deputy who had stayed behind where they'd left the car.

Fighting her way back through the tangle of trees and underbrush, Charlie tried to stay as close to Doc as possible. He had kindly offered to take her home while the sheriff lingered to talk with those responsible for transporting the body. What a relief at last to duck under the barbed-wire fence that separated the densely wooded area from the Curtises' pasture! In her haste she snagged her sleeve on the wire, but Charlie didn't care. All she could think about was the possibility that someone might have been watching the whole time she and Annie dragged Bill Pitts's body from the water. *And they could be watching them now!*

CHAPTER SIXTEEN

With Christmas only five days away, Phoebe Chadwick could think of nothing else, but even with Miss Dimple and Annie joining her at the table, why, my goodness, the three of them would rattle like peas in a gourd in that big house! Why not invite that new young music teacher, Lottie Nivens, who was staying with Bessie Jenkins? And of course, she would include Bessie as well. Phoebe's cook, Odessa, and her husband, Bob Robert, would be joining relatives for the holidays, but with Odessa's help, Phoebe was preparing as much ahead of time as possible. Odessa had already made corn bread for the dressing, and baked two loaves of her wonderful orange marmalade nut bread to be served later with cream cheese, and Phoebe filled a tin with sugar cookies cut in the shapes of trees, stars and angels.

The tree, however, left something to be desired and sat in the parlor window strung with colored lights and very little else. "I don't know what happened to all my ornaments," Phoebe said, searching her hall closet for the third time. "The few I have left look just plain lonely hanging there. We can't even get icicles anymore because of tinfoil being used in the war, and the ones made out of cellophane aren't worth putting on the tree."

"Why don't we just use popcorn chains and candy canes?" Annie suggested. "I'll be glad to pick up what we need from Mr. Cooper's store."

Phoebe thought that was a fine idea and said that while Annie was there, why not invite that nice Jesse Dean Greeson to Christmas dinner, too, as she'd learned Harris Cooper and his wife were spending the holidays with their daughter in Covington? "And you'd better order another hen as well," she added, as it looked as if one chicken might not stretch for the six of them.

Although agreeable to running an errand, Annie was eager to hear a report from Charlie about the activities of the night before. She had told Miss Dimple about finding the lifeless body of Bill Pitts, but hadn't shared the information with anyone else. She didn't want to destroy Miss Phoebe's Christmas spirit with such a grim tale, and besides, they weren't really sure what had killed him.

Bundling into her warm jacket, Annie started off for town, hoping to avoid her next-door neighbor, Willie Elrod, who she was sure would want to elaborate about their grisly discovery.

So far, so good! Annie thought as she waited at the corner for the light to change. On the other side of the street Lottie Nivens waved to her and waited for her to join her.

"How thoughtful of Phoebe to invite us for Christmas dinner!" Lottie said as they fell into step together. "Miss Bessie and I are looking forward to it and I thought I'd look for a little gift to show our appreciation. Any suggestions?"

Annie laughed. "I'm sure she'd tell you that isn't necessary, but we are a little short of decorations for the tree. I'm on my way to Cooper's for popcorn and candy canes if he has any left."

"That isn't what I had in mind, but our tree could use a little help, too. Maybe he'll have enough for both of us. And isn't there a little gift shop on the corner? It won't hurt to look in there."

Bennie Alexander usually carried gift items in his jewelry store, and although Annie had finished most of her shopping, she did want to look for something for Miss Dimple so they decided to stop there first.

Lottie frowned as they passed Brumlow's Dry Goods. "Why do they have all those posters in the window? I've seen them on every tree and telephone pole. Haven't they found that Japanese woman yet?"

Annie did her best to look nonchalant. "Guess not. Seems to me Emmaline's the only one really serious about looking for her."

"But didn't she kill that woman, the artist she was supposed to be taking care of?"

"As far as I know, the police haven't learned who killed Mrs. Hawthorne." Annie stopped to admire a small picture frame in Bennie's window.

"Then why did she run away?"

Before Annie could answer, Willie Elrod hailed her from across the street and Annie held her breath as she watched him weave through the traffic on Court Street.

"Tell Miss Charlie I saved her my best piece of mistletoe, and it has berries on it, too!" he announced, waving a paper bag with a sprig of the plant inside.

"And I'm sure she'll be happy to get it, but not

at the risk of your getting run over crossing the street! You know you're to cross at the light, Willie Elrod! You just about scared me to death!" Annie accepted the mistletoe for her friend and reached in her pocketbook for change.

"No'me." Willie shook his head and grinned. "That's my Christmas present, and there's something in there for you and Miss Dimple, too. I got 'em at Murphy's with some of my mistletoe money. I sold every bit of it, too. Wish I had some more!"

"Oh, Willie!" Annie swallowed a sob as she opened the bag to find two small pinecone elf ornaments to hang on the tree. "How did you know we needed ornaments? Thank you! I can't think of anything that would please us more." Annie smiled, knowing this simple trinket would always bring to mind this special little boy.

Willie flushed as she hugged him. "That sure was somethin' yesterday, wasn't it, Miss Annie? Finding that dead man and all! Looked Gawd-awful, didn't he? I'm glad I was there so you and Miss Charlie wouldn't be so scared."

Annie laughed and hugged him again. "I'm glad you were there, too, Willie." She watched him as he ran to the corner and waved back at her before crossing at the light. Lottie, she saw, stood admiring a small china angel in the window of the jewelry store.

"This reminds me of one we had when I was

little," Lottie said. "I'd forgotten all about that angel—wonder what happened to it."

"It is beautiful. Why don't we go in and take a look?"

Bennie took the angel out of the window and set her on the glass counter. The figure had yellow hair, blue eyes, and held a tiny stringed instrument close to her breast.

"Oh . . ." Lottie reached out to touch it, then changed her mind. "How much is it, Mr. Alexander?"

He quickly removed a price sticker from the bottom. "Well to tell you the truth, this angel came as part of a pair, but the other one was broken in shipping."

"What a shame!" Annie said, watching his face. "What instrument was the other one playing?"

"Instrument?" The shopkeeper seemed puzzled.

"Yes. This one's playing a lute—or I think it's a lute."

"Oh . . . yes, of course! I believe it was a horn of some kind." He smiled at Lottie. "At any rate, we'll let you have this one for less than half price, which would come to about two dollars."

"Oh, thank you. I'll take it!" Lottie paid for the gift and watched as he carefully laid the figure on a bed of cotton in a small box, wrapped it in silver and blue paper, and added a curl of ribbon.

"Next time you write, be sure and tell that sailor husband of yours we're all pulling for them here at home!" he called after them as they left the store.

"What a kind man," Lottie said, looking back. "How did he know my husband was in the navy?"

"Bennie and his wife have a son in the service, too," Annie told her. "And you might as well know here in Elderberry, there aren't any secrets!" *Except for one,* she thought.

Harris Cooper was busy in the back of the grocery store, but Jesse Dean welcomed them and smiled when Annie told him what they wanted. "Our tree is practically bare, and Lottie tells me the one she and Miss Bessie have looks kind of pitiful, too," Annie explained, introducing Lottie Nivens. "And I'd like to find something for Miss Dimple, but frankly, I've run out of ideas."

"Well, you just happen to be in luck." Jesse Dean reached under the counter and brought out a box of candy canes. "We've plenty of popcorn, but this is the last of the peppermint. It should be enough for two trees if you space them far enough apart.

"As for our Miss Dimple Kilpatrick, I know the very thing—but you'll have to promise you won't tell anyone else."

"What?" Annie leaned over the counter. "Now, Jesse, I am *not* buying any ingredients for her awful Victory Muffins!"

"Not what I had in mind. Back in a minute." Jesse Dean held up a finger before disappearing into a stockroom. Moments later he returned with a cardboard box filled with Hershey bars. "This just came in today, and I can't let you have them all," he said, scooping some into a bag, "but these should last her a few weeks at least."

Annie smiled. She had seen the candy in Miss Dimple's desk drawer but considered the possibility it might have been confiscated from an errant snacker. Here was a secret she wouldn't object to keeping. Miss Dimple Kilpatrick had a dent in her armor!

"And by the way, do you think you can scare up another hen for Miss Phoebe? She's inviting a few people over for Christmas and said to tell you she hoped you'd be able to join us, too."

The young clerk flushed with pleasure, bringing color to his usually pale face. "Oh, that would be so . . . well . . . that would be . . . great!" he stammered. "Please tell her I look forward to it, but only if you'll let me contribute the candy canes and popcorn."

Annie agreed and paid him for the Hershey bars. "What a thoughtful thing to do!" Lottie exclaimed as the two of them left the store with their tree decorations bagged separately. "Is he always so nice?"

Annie laughed. "Well, most of the time. Just don't let him catch you with a light on during an air-raid drill!"

"Tell me about little Peggy," Annie said on the

way home. "I hear she came through her tonsillectomy fine but haven't had a chance to talk with Kate since she came home from the hospital."

"To hear her mother tell it, I believe she's fallen in love," Lottie said with a smile. "She and Max are inseparable, and the cat's so jealous she won't come out from under the dining room table."

"Poor Peaches! What a rude awakening! Maybe she'll come around in time."

"Looks like we'll have our work cut out for us stringing all this popcorn," Annie added as they paused at the corner. "Guess we'd better hurry home and get started."

But Lottie lingered, her gaze fixed on a house across Katherine Street. "Wouldn't it be nice to have a place like that?" she said.

"Like what?" Annie asked.

"The white house on the corner, the one with the big magnolia." Lottie sighed. "It appeals to me somehow. Maybe one of these days when this war is over, Hal and I will have a home like that."

Annie smiled. She knew just what Lottie meant. She liked to think of the home she and Frazier might have someday and children they had planned: a girl they would name for her mother and a little boy called Frazier. In bed at night she tried to imagine them, imagine how it would be when he finally came home, but sometimes Annie couldn't remember his face.

"Maybe you will," she told Lottie, squeezing her hand. "Well, not *that* house, but one like it, right here in Elderberry."

They all had to hold on to dreams because right now that was all they had, Annie thought as she crossed the street. But Christmas was just around the corner, and it was going to be pleasant not to have anything else to do that afternoon but string popcorn for the tree.

But Dimple Kilpatrick had other ideas. "Charlie called awhile ago and something's come up. She wants us to meet her at Virginia's."

Annie took a deep breath and handed over the popcorn and peppermint. "Just give me a minute. The candy canes are for the tree, and I guess we can pop and string the corn later this afternoon." Hurrying upstairs, she put Miss Dimple's Hershey bars on her closet shelf and on her way out hollered to let Phoebe know she was leaving.

Frowning, Odessa poked her head around the kitchen door. "She be in here shelling pecans for you all's Christmas pie. Where you goin' *now?*"

"Oh . . . just some last-minute errands," Annie lied. "Is there anything you need?"

Odessa muttered something that sounded like "a little help in the kitchen," and let the kitchen door swing shut.

"Oh, dear!" Annie sighed to Miss Dimple as they started out for Virginia's. "I'm afraid

Odessa's upset with us for not helping more in the kitchen."

Miss Dimple looked suitably contrite—at least for a moment. "Ah, well, first things, first, I suppose. And I did promise to make some of my Victory Muffins. I expect she's forgotten that."

Charlie met them at Virginia's front door, being careful not to open it too wide. "I don't suppose you ran into the Kilgores? Jerome was lying in wait for me before I got halfway down the street. He pretended to be looking for the mailman, but I know good and well Boyce doesn't deliver that early in the day."

"Oh, dear!" Miss Dimple took off her coat and laid it carefully aside. "What did he say?"

"Wanted to know if Virginia was all right. I guess he wonders why I'm here while she's at the library." Charlie smiled. "I told him I was helping her with some new curtains."

"But now he'll expect to see them—" Annie began.

"For the bedroom!" Charlie continued, looking sly.

Miss Dimple looked at Annie and laughed. "What's our excuse?

"Seriously, we're going to have to be more careful. All it would take is one brief careless moment for them to realize Virginia's not alone.

"Now," she said, turning to Charlie. "Tell us about last night. Was the sheriff able to learn

197

anything about the way the Pitts fellow died?"

"Well, he knows it wasn't natural," Charlie said. "Doc had Harvey bring in the body, and Sheriff Holland planned to go back out there this morning to get a look at the place in daylight. But wait until you hear this: Someone had moved the body! Had it propped against a tree with that liquor bottle in his lap just as pretty as you please!"

A gasp came from both Annie and Suzy, who stood in the hallway behind them.

"And that's not all," Charlie continued. "I phoned Harriet Curtis this morning to thank her for the trees and to let her know about finding Bill Pitts—twice. After all, we did have to tramp all over their property last night."

"That must've been a shock," Annie said, taking a quick peek through the draperies to see if they were being watched.

"Not only that," Charlie told them. "Harriet said when Isaac Ingram came to their church to collect his aunt's paintings, several of them appeared to be missing."

"Did he think someone took them from the church?" Suzy asked.

"No, because Harriet's husband got a list from Mae Martha and every one of them—all twenty-nine—was accounted for."

"Then Isaac Ingram is obviously mistaken," Miss Dimple said, but Charlie shook her head.

"He mentioned several specific paintings—said there should be at least eight or more that weren't there."

"Maybe she sold them," Annie suggested. "The way she did for us."

"Or somebody might have taken them," Charlie said, thinking aloud. "Maybe that's why she asked the Curtises to keep the others at their church."

"With her grandson killed in the war, I can't imagine why Isaac—Esau, either—would go to that kind of trouble," Miss Dimple said as they moved into Virginia's small kitchen to sit around her familiar table. "I don't think there's much doubt they'll inherit everything from their aunt's estate."

Suzy shook her head. "Not necessarily," she said. "I believe she may have had other plans."

CHAPTER SEVENTEEN

"What do you mean?" Miss Dimple asked as she put on a kettle for tea.

Standing on tiptoe, Suzy reached into the cabinet for cups. "She mentioned once that she was considering establishing a scholarship fund in Madison's memory at Emory. It would go to help students working toward a medical degree."

"I can't think of a better way to remember him," Annie said. "Do you know if she ever finalized the plans?"

Suzy shook her head. "I can't be sure, but I wouldn't be surprised. When Miss Mae Martha made up her mind to do something, she usually didn't waste any time."

"Do you know if she mentioned this to anyone else?" Miss Dimple asked.

"I would think she'd say something to Isaac, as he usually handled her business affairs, because if I remember right, she planned to contribute most of her future earnings to that endowment."

"And when was this?" Miss Dimple pried the lid from the tea canister and set it aside, her expression grave.

"Sometime back in the fall," Suzy said. "Around September, I believe."

"About the time hickory nuts begin to fall," Dimple said.

Charlie had been playing with a saltshaker on the table, moving it about like a chess piece on the checkered tablecloth. Now she set it down with a thump. "Do you think somebody deliberately put them where they would cause her to fall?"

Annie spoke up. "Obviously, they did. She could've broken a leg, a hip, or worse."

"They didn't get there by themselves," Miss Dimple reminded them. She poured scalding water into the teapot. "It seems to me that Mrs.

Hawthorne's life was in danger as soon as she made a decision about that bequest."

"That's a legal matter," Charlie said. "Do you know who represented her?" she asked Suzy.

Suzy leaned against the sink looking troubled and vulnerable and very, very small. "That would be another question for Isaac. If she saw an attorney, it's likely he would have taken her there, and the two of them did go into town—or I assume it was into town—on occasion."

"Isn't it time for the reading of the will?" Annie asked. "And shouldn't something be in the *Eagle*?"

Miss Dimple nodded. "A notice to creditors. I'll admit I don't usually read that kind of thing. Has anyone seen it?"

No one had. "I imagine the will is going through the probate process," she said, "but it shouldn't be difficult to learn if Mrs. Hawthorne did, indeed, leave the proceeds from her paintings to a scholarship fund."

"Isaac certainly didn't waste any time getting his aunt's paintings to a dealer after she died," Charlie pointed out. "He seems to be making sure every one of them is accounted for."

"And it looks like they aren't," Suzy said. "And now there's this unexpected predicament with the death of Bill Pitts. Does the sheriff believe he was murdered?"

"I think it's obvious he was." Charlie told them

about the abrasions on the man's face and hands. "And then they came back and tried to clean him up so it would look like he died from some other cause."

Annie shuddered. " 'Alas, poor Yorick!' Charlie, has it occurred to you that we might have interrupted whoever killed him? Somebody could've been hiding right there in the bushes watching us while we dragged that man out of the creek."

Charlie made a face. She had, of course. "That's a comforting thought, but I choose to think otherwise."

Annie laughed. "Well, so would I, but that doesn't make it so."

"No, really, I'm serious." Charlie held up a hand. "Just think about it. We didn't manage to pull Bill Pitts very far out of the water—just far enough to know there was nothing we could do. I believe the person who killed him left him there intending to come back and move him later. I'm not sure he—or she—would notice he wasn't in exactly the same place."

"Perhaps not," Miss Dimple said, pouring tea all around, "but wouldn't they put him there to begin with? Why wait and come back to do it?"

Charlie thought for a minute. "I don't know . . . they might've heard somebody coming— probably us. Or maybe they had to be somewhere and were running late."

"Like a funeral?" Miss Dimple said.

"Oh my goodness!" Annie looked at them over her cup. "We looked for Bill Pitts at the funeral Sunday. Remember?"

"Well, I suppose he had a perfectly good excuse for not being there," Charlie pointed out. "He was probably already dead."

"Or soon to be," Annie added. "But why would anybody want to kill him? The man made me feel uneasy, I'll admit, but I can't imagine why someone would want him dead."

Suzy spoke quietly. "He knew things."

Charlie frowned. "What do you mean?"

Suzy shrugged. "Bill seemed to be everywhere. You never knew when he would show up, and I'm sure he knew everything that was going on around there."

"Like what?" Annie asked.

"If I knew that, I would probably know who killed Mrs. Hawthorne," Suzy said.

Miss Dimple, noticing the young woman's attempt to keep back the tears, reached for her hand. "We know how difficult this must be for you," she assured her, "this living in fear that someone will find you, accuse you, but I promise we'll see this through together. I don't think it will be long until whoever killed Mrs. Hawthorne, and probably Bill Pitts, as well, makes one last mistake."

The others nodded in agreement, and Charlie

quietly went to stand behind Suzy and placed a hand on her shoulder.

"But you *don't* know!" Covering her face, Suzy broke down in tears. "How could you possibly know?" Silently she accepted the lace-trimmed handkerchief Miss Dimple placed in her hand. "Any mail I get from my family comes through neighbors back in California. I worry about my parents . . . their business was just taken from them with no promise they'll get it back." Suzy looked from Annie to Charlie. "You talk about your brothers and all the men you love in the armed forces and how you worry about them and miss them! Well, I miss Kentaro, too! My brother— we call him Ken—wasn't able to enlist until this year. I guess because the government wasn't sure they could trust him and others like him."

"Suzy . . ." Annie spoke softly. "I'm so sorry. I didn't even know you had a brother."

"Ken signed up in February, soon after the army began allowing Nisei volunteers . . . that means second-generation Americans whose parents came here from Japan," she explained. "He's in Italy now with the 442nd Infantry, and I don't know of a more loyal and courageous group of men. Many have given their lives and several in Ken's platoon have been decorated."

"You must be very proud," Miss Dimple said.

"Of course I'm proud! We all want to do our part as much as you do—as much as anyone does.

I would gladly volunteer to serve in the Medical Corps, but there's no way they would take me. If I tried to practice medicine now, I would probably earn less than a fourth of what other doctors receive—that is, *if* I were allowed. That's one reason I agreed to come here and live with Miss Mae Martha." She shook her head. "Poor Madison! He thought he was doing us both a favor."

Miss Dimple spoke softly. "Mae Martha Hawthorne thought the world of you. I don't know what she would've done without you, especially after Madison was killed."

Suzy wiped her eyes and smiled. "I don't want you—any of you—to think I haven't been grateful for all you've done for me, but I'm putting you all in a dangerous situation. It will be only a matter of time before the neighbors across the street find out I'm here. Already I understand there's a woman in town circulating a campaign of vicious rumors about me. I honestly don't know what those people might do."

"I think most people here would take anything the Kilgores say with a grain of salt," Charlie said.

"And as for that other woman you spoke of, I haven't noticed a large enrollment in the Select Society of Emmaline," Miss Dimple said.

Annie giggled. "I doubt if she even serves refreshments."

"They probably earn badges, though." Charlie spoke with a straight face.

That brought a laugh, even from Suzy. "I know you mean well, but I think it's time I turned myself in. Your sheriff seems fair, and they must realize they don't have any evidence against me."

The others exchanged silent glances sending a clear warning. "I don't think you want to take that chance," Miss Dimple said. "Not yet, at least. I want you to promise me you'll give this a little more time. I think we're closer than you might suspect to getting to the bottom of this."

Virginia arrived soon after that and the others left for home and their midday meal. During the holidays Charlie didn't eat at Phoebe Chadwick's and she missed the good food as well as the company. Her mother usually worked three days a week at the munitions plant in nearby Milledgeville, but due to a temporary lull in the manufacturing process, Josephine Carr had spent that morning rolling bandages for the Red Cross instead.

"I hope Delia remembers to warm up that leftover vegetable soup," Charlie said as the three paused in front of Phoebe's. "I'm starved and I know Mama will be hungry when she gets home."

Annie smiled. Everybody knew Charlie's mother disliked cooking and until Delia had finally started pitching in, it had been up to

Charlie to take care of most of the meal preparation. "I almost forgot we have to pop and string that popcorn," she said, "and with the mood Odessa's in, I sure don't want to get in her way."

"Why not pop it at our house?" Charlie offered. "Aunt Lou gave us an electric popper a couple of years ago. All you have to do is turn the handle."

"I'll lend them a hand polishing the silver," Miss Dimple said. "Perhaps that will smooth things a little. I know how Phoebe dreads it, and Odessa doesn't have time, but I find it oddly restful."

And so soon after lunchtime, Annie showed up at the Carrs' house, popcorn in hand. Jo Carr greeted her and went back to writing the social news for the following week's issue of the *Elderberry Eagle*. She found Charlie washing dishes while her sister put little Tommy down for his nap upstairs. To save precious coal, the family had put their tree in the sitting room this year instead of heating the larger living room, and Annie thought it looked festive in the corner by the window while across the room a low fire burned cheerfully in the grate.

Charlie rummaged in the pantry until she found the popper and it took only minutes to pop enough to string garlands for several trees. Sitting at the kitchen table, the two munched as the snowy ropes grew longer and longer.

"I wonder . . ." Charlie began as she slid the fragrant corn along her thread.

"Wonder what?"

"I wonder what Miss Dimple knows that we don't," Charlie said. "She seems to think it won't be long before we know who killed Mae Martha Hawthorne. I hate to admit it, but I thought it might've been Bill—poor thing!"

"You're right. He didn't seem very likeable, but it's beginning to look like this all hinges on those missing paintings—"

"And Mae Martha's decision to leave her money for a scholarship fund," Charlie added. "Isaac said several of her paintings went missing earlier and that was why he took the others to a dealer for safekeeping right after she died." She paused. "So how do we know he's telling the truth?"

"Both the nephews seemed genuinely fond of her," Annie admitted. "Even Bill Pitts, from what I've been told."

Charlie looked up. "Suzy thinks he knew something—or *saw* something. But what?"

"Do you think he might've found out where the paintings are being stored?"

"*Hidden,* you mean." Charlie tied off her popcorn chain and eased it into a paper bag. "He was killed on Isaac Ingram's property. I suppose they could be in an outbuilding somewhere."

"And don't forget about the Curtises," Annie

reminded her. "Their land backs right up to Isaac's. Maybe they know more than they're telling about those eight paintings Isaac claims are missing . . . but they seem so *nice,* don't they? Of course, you never know."

"What about Rebecca, the milk and egg lady?" Charlie asked. "Maybe we should try and talk to her."

"Maybe. Let's wait and see what Miss Dimple says.

"Ouch!" Annie stuck her finger and popped her thumb in her mouth. "And don't forget," she said. "Esau has outbuildings, too."

In the hallway on the other side of the closed kitchen door, Jo Carr quietly picked up the telephone receiver. "Florence," she whispered. "Ring Lou for me, would you, please? If she doesn't answer, just keep on ringing. I need to talk with her right away."

CHAPTER EIGHTEEN

They're up to something, Louise. I just know it!" Josephine Carr sat in her sister's sunny yellow kitchen while Lou peeled and sliced sweet potatoes for supper. She didn't risk talking about what she suspected over the phone, as everyone knew Florence McCrary at the telephone company listened in on any conversation she found interesting.

"Who's up to something?" Lou didn't look up.

"My daughter and *your* niece. Charlie, that's who! Annie Gardner, too, and frankly, I'm getting curious."

"Really? About what?" Lou's smile lit up her whole face. There was nothing she liked better than a hearty taste of adventure.

Jo told her what she had overheard in the hallway. "They've been finding some excuse to go out there where that artist woman lived ever since the night Miss Dimple found little Peggy Ashcroft. And Miss Dimple's in on it, too!"

"Now, really, Josephine!" Louise paused, knife in hand, with a half-peeled potato. "What do you suppose they're doing?"

Jo helped herself to a couple of grapes from the bowl on the table. "I'm not sure, but it has something to do with the Hawthorne woman's death. They went to her funeral, you know—Charlie and Annie, and of course Miss Dimple, too.

"And right after that they found that man's body in the creek." She shuddered. "Charlie won't say much about it, but I'm telling you, Louise, there's something peculiar going on out there and I'm . . . well . . . I'm uneasy about it."

Lou slid the sliced potatoes into a bowl of

salted water to keep them from turning brown and washed her hands at the sink. "Have they found out how that man died?"

Her sister shook her head. "I don't know for sure, but from what I've heard, it sounds like murder."

"I wonder . . ." Lou absently dried her hands on her apron. "That Japanese woman—what's her name? I wonder if she had anything to do with it. They haven't been able to find her yet so she must be hiding somewhere. Maybe this man threatened to tell, and—"

Jo ate another grape and helped herself to a few gingersnaps from the cookie jar. Unlike her sister, who seemed to put on pounds at the very thought of food, Jo's metabolism allowed her to eat as much as she wanted without gaining weight. This was sometimes a source of friction between them. "I can't be sure," she said, "but it's beginning to look to me like those three might *know* something."

"About the Japanese woman, you mean? How could they possibly know anything about that?" Lou rinsed a small chicken at the sink, slammed it onto a cutting board and, with a large knife, cut it into pieces for frying while Jo watched in fascination. She had never learned to cut up a chicken properly.

Jo lowered her voice, although there was no one around to overhear. "Louise, I'm sure I heard them say something about Suzy! That is her name, isn't it?"

"Well, for heaven's sake, Jo, she's not the only Suzy around."

"No, but they're always going over to Virginia's—even when she's not at home. Charlie said they were working on some kind of project for school, but school's out for the holidays, Lou! Delia told me they'd been over there all morning."

"Well, my goodness, Jo, why don't you just ask her?" Lou put the salted chicken in a bowl, covered it, and set it in the refrigerator, shutting the door with a nudge of her hip.

"I've tried, believe me, but you know how stubborn Charlie can be."

Lou tossed off her apron and smiled. "And loyal to a fault. She must have a very good reason for keeping quiet about whatever's going on. I feel better, though, knowing Dimple Kilpatrick is involved. She's as sensible as that old umbrella she carries around. I can't see Miss Dimple leading anyone into danger."

Jo's eyes widened. "Then you have a short memory," she said, and reminded her sister of the teacher's recent narrow escapes.

"Oh, dear! I suppose you're right. She has such a proper demeanor, it tends to make one forget her inclination to delve into risky detective work." Lou laughed. "But then who am I to talk?"

Jo Carr sighed. "At least it's keeping Charlie occupied so she doesn't have as much time to worry about her brother and Will."

"What do you hear from Fain, Jo?"

"Nothing recently. We know he's *somewhere* in Italy but when we do get a letter it's been censored so much it's hard to tell much of anything." She shrugged. "Not that I care if it keeps them safe. Delia's Ned's over there, too. We shipped packages to them for Christmas weeks ago but God knows when they'll get them—or even if they'll get them."

Lou Willingham linked an arm in Jo's. "Come on, let's go and sit by the living room fire awhile and think up some devilment to get into. It sounds to me like Charlie and that bunch could use a little help. What else did you *overhear* in the hallway?"

Jo, momentarily relieved to have her mind off her soldier son, spoke before thinking. "It seems to have something to do with some missing paintings," she said.

"Really?" Lou gave the wood fire a hearty poke. "Where do you suppose they might be?"

"They were talking about some outbuildings near where Mrs. Hawthorne lived."

"Whose outbuildings? I know her nephews live somewhere close by."

"They mentioned them," Jo said. "And some-body named Rebecca."

Lou frowned. "I wonder who that could be."

"And . . . oh, yes, those people who let us cut down a Christmas tree—the Curtises." Jo stretched her feet to the fire. "I do hope it doesn't turn out they had anything to do with it. It's really a beautiful tree."

Lou was quiet as she watched the logs crackle and blaze. "Oh, Jo, wouldn't it be fun if *we* could find them?" she said finally.

"I wouldn't know where to begin." Jo Carr tried to ignore the warning bells going off in her head.

"You just said they might be in an outbuilding. We could start with one of the nephews, or see what we can find on the Curtis property."

"I suppose we could look there," Jo said, rising to her feet. "Charlie said they weren't going to cut down a tree because they were leaving town for the holidays. We should be able to look around all we want and nobody will be there to see us.

"But, Lou . . ." Josephine Carr forced her sister to meet her gaze. "We are *not* going to take any silly chances. Do you understand? This will be a quick—what do they call it in the army? *Reconnaissance!* We'll go there only to scout out the area, and then come home—that's all!"

"Well, of course, Josephine, I don't know why you would assume I'd do otherwise."

Lou's offended demeanor seemed to have no effect on her sister, who continued to drive home her case. "I mean it, Lou! Don't tell me you've already forgotten that horrendous night you got the car stuck in—"

"And a good thing I did, too," Lou reminded her, "or we never would've found what we did." She gave the fire a final poke and replaced the poker with a clang. "You'll have to admit it, Jo, the police never would've figured out that one if it hadn't been for us."

"And Miss Dimple," Jo said, smiling. "Don't forget Miss Dimple."

"Theee holly and theee ivee, when they are both full grooown . . ." Jo sang, making herself comfortable beside Lou in the Willinghams' car the next morning as they drove through the streets of Elderberry. "Remind me to look for some holly while we're out there, will you, Lou?"

"Is that what you told Charlie and Delia we were doing this morning?" Lou stole a glance at the brick building on the corner where her husband practiced dentistry and hoped he wouldn't be glancing out the upstairs window overlooking the street. It wasn't that Ed Willingham minded her using the family car as long as she left gas in the tank, but whenever Lou and her sister went on one of their rambling adventures, he sprouted additional gray hairs on his head and the car ended up being more worse for the wear than before.

"I had to tell them something," Jo admitted. "And I don't mind stretching the truth one bit after all Charlie's hush-hush goings-on."

This close to Christmas most people had completed their holiday shopping but a few shoppers looked for last-minute items at Brumlow's Dry Goods, Murphy's Five and Ten, or Bennie Alexander's Jewelry and Gifts. Although many goods were in short supply, store windows, decorated for the season, displayed what they could offer, and as they passed the post office, Jo noticed that someone had tied a pine branch to the recruiting sign out front with a bright red ribbon.

The sun had been playing peek-a-boo since breakfast but by mid-morning seemed to have used up most of its light and the day turned gray and dreary. Both women wore warm—although worn—jackets, and, having learned from past experiences, had brought along hats and gloves as well.

"Looks like you're in luck about the holly," Lou observed later as they approached the Curtis farm. "There's a huge tree right in their yard. I wonder if they'd mind—"

"Of course! Charlie brought some home the other day. This must be where they got it." Jo tugged on her galoshes as she spoke. "She said the people told them they could take all they wanted.

"Don't stop yet, Lou! First we have to be sure nobody's there. Just slow down a little."

"I don't want to risk turning around in the road. I'll just pull in their driveway and pretend we're turning around. Look, now, Jo, and see if you see a car."

"The garage is empty," Jo said, stuffing salt-and-pepper curls under her hat. "Looks like we can pull around and park in that grove of trees behind it. Might look suspicious if we were seen from the road."

Lou thought it probably looked suspicious anyway but she kept that to herself. "Oh, lordy, Jo! What if there's a *dog?*"

"Charlie didn't mention one." Still, Jo stepped cautiously out of the car and looked about. "There's a barn back there. Do you think the paintings might be stored in there?"

"We'll never know if we don't look." Louise stopped still in her tracks. "Jo, what if somebody's actually at home? What if somebody's watching?"

"Guess we should've thought of that first. One of us will have to go to the door and knock."

"Good idea." Folding her arms, Lou leaned against the car. "Go ahead. I'll wait."

"*You* go ahead! Why do I have to do everything?"

"Oh, all right! We'll both go," Lou grumbled. "We'll have to hurry, though, in case Ed decides to come home for dinner."

"I thought you said he was going to get a grilled cheese today at Lewellyn's."

"He said he probably would, but he might change his mind, and you know he's going want to know where we were."

Leaving her sister behind, Jo marched right up to the door and knocked. Just then, Ed Willingham's dinner was the least of her problems.

After knocking several times, the two waited a few minutes before walking around the house to the barn lot. Chickens, confined to a fenced area behind the barn, squawked wildly before returning to peck at whatever they could find on the ground, and Jo hoped that whoever was responsible for gathering their eggs and feeding them had completed their job for the day.

Closing the gate behind them, she looked around the barn lot. A rough-hewn trough was half filled with water but other than a gray-striped cat, there were no animals in sight. "I think the cattle must stay in the pasture," she said. "Seems empty in here."

"Still smells like horses, though." Lou sniffed as they stepped inside the yawning barn where bridles and farm implements hung on the walls and wisps of hay were scattered underfoot.

"Or mules," Jo said, peering into an empty stall. "I guess Mr. Curtis gave up plowing the old-fashioned way."

"And here's why!" Lou made her way to the

other end of the barn to find a tractor tucked away to one side.

Jo sneezed and dug in her pocket for a handkerchief. "If there are any paintings in here, I don't know where they'd be. Come on, let's get out of here before somebody comes."

"We haven't checked *everywhere* yet," Lou reminded her, looking up.

Jo spied the ladder that led to the loft from a wall of the barn. It didn't seem too sturdy. "Be my guest," she said with a bow.

"All right, I will." Sighing audibly, Lou walked purposely over to the ladder and tugged on a rung. It creaked.

Jo sneezed again. "My hay fever's acting up, Lou. I have to get out of here. That ladder's probably been there for ages. Do you really want to chance a broken leg?"

"For heaven's sake, Jo! All old buildings creak. This ladder is perfectly safe." Lou put one foot on the bottom rung and pulled herself up. "See?" The ladder protested again.

Jo Carr glanced from her pudgy sister to the opening at the top of the ladder and estimated the distance in between. "Oh, all right!" she said, pulling her aside. "I'll take a quick look up there, but I'm not doing more than that, and if I kill myself falling off this ladder, I'll haunt you the rest of your life, Louise Willingham!"

Cautiously and steadily, Jo made her way up the

ladder while Lou stood watch below. *Could their car be seen from the road? And what on earth were they going to say if somebody found them here? Had the chickens already been fed? And who was taking care of the gray cat she'd seen earlier?*

Finally reaching the top, Jo pulled herself through the opening and crawled onto a rough floor thick with dust. "I can't see much of anything up here," she said, coughing.

"Well, *look,* Jo!" her sister insisted. "It would be a perfect place to hide them. We have to be sure. And just think how exciting it would be if *we really did find them!*"

"There's a trunk over there against the wall—or I think it's a trunk." Jo stood and tested the floor with an exploring foot. "There are probably rats up here, and no telling what else."

"I've heard most farmers keep black snakes to keep down the rats." Lou spoke before thinking. "Not that there are any here, of course, and black snakes aren't poisonous anyway."

Jo, who had made her way halfway across the floor, did an about-face. "That does it, Lou! I'm coming down right now!"

"No! No, stay there!"

Jo heard the creaking of the ladder as her sister made her way to the top, and huffing, squirmed through the opening onto the floor of the loft. "Oh, damn!" she hissed. "Quick, Jo! Get down and be quiet. Somebody's coming."

CHAPTER NINETEEN

Don't *you dare sneeze!* Jo held a hand over her mouth and pinched her nose. If someone were to look up from below they would be able to see them, as the loft covered only a portion of the barn. Lou had made her way over to the trunk and knelt beside it and Jo, finding nowhere else to hide, lay facedown on the floor as someone walked below.

"Here, kitty!" a woman called. "I know you're in here somewhere! Come on, now and get your dinner."

Jo didn't recognize the voice, but she did recognize the rat scat that was almost under her nose and forced herself not to jump up and exclaim in disgust. If there *was* a snake in here, it hadn't done its job. Quietly moving her head an inch or so, she found she could see below through a crack in the flooring but her vision was limited, and she had no idea where the woman might be.

On the other side of the loft her sister was making frantic gestures that seemed to have something to do with her foot and the ladder. Naturally the loft had been used in the past for storing hay, and Jo pressed her hand against her mouth and nose to avoid choking on the film of dust and debris. She frowned. What was Louise trying to tell her?

Lou's eyes widened in fear as the footsteps below came nearer, and it was then Jo realized her sister was missing one of her galoshes. She must have lost it in her hurry to get up the ladder.

Jo Carr held her breath and closed her eyes. What if the woman saw it? Would she pursue them into the loft? Heavy footsteps paused beneath them. "Kitty?" the woman called again and sighed. "Oh, well, I guess you'll eat when you're hungry."

Jo squinted through the crack to see a large woman in a brown coat bend over and set a dish on the floor of the barn. She wore a green knitted cap over dark hair streaked with gray that had been gathered into a bun in the back, and looking about once more, plodded out of the barn.

After what seemed an eternity of waiting, Lou crept from behind the trunk and Jo rose and brushed herself off.

"I thought she'd never leave!" Lou said. "Were you able to get a good look?"

Jo finally allowed herself to sneeze. "It wasn't anybody I recognized. Probably a neighbor. We need to get out of here, Louise, before she or somebody else comes back."

"One of my galoshes fell off when I was trying to get up that blasted ladder and I didn't have time to go down and get it. Do you reckon she saw it, Jo?"

"We're lucky she didn't seem to notice it," Jo said, making her way to the ladder. "I know one thing—I'm going to soak in a hot tub as soon as I get home! Let's go!"

"Wait. First I want to see what's in that trunk. For all we know it might be crammed full of expensive paintings." Lou carefully raised the lid of a battered chest of peeling leather that appeared to have been there at least a hundred years, and yelped as a mouse scurried from a hole in the bottom.

"Oh, lordy! That scared me so I nearly wet my pants!" Lou said, letting the lid slam shut with a bang.

"Well, if anybody's still around, they'll know we're up here now." Jo hesitated at the top of the ladder. "Did you see what was in the trunk?"

"Just some old clothes and a lot of rat mess. They'd have to be crazy to store paintings in there." Lou glanced behind her with a shudder. "Hurry up, will you, Jo? And for heaven's sake, don't let me forget that other galosh!"

Jo waited impatiently while her sister retrieved the rubber shoe covering and put it on again. It must be close to noon or even later, as her stomach rumbled in expectation. She was standing near the open door to the barn when she heard someone approaching.

"There's somebody up there, Esau! I just know it!" The woman spoke in a near whisper. "And I think I saw one of those rubber boot–like things at the bottom of the ladder. Now, why would anybody leave that there?"

Heart thumping, Jo turned and dragged her bewildered sister into the closest stall. Lou didn't go willingly. "What are you doing, Jo? Leave me alone! I thought you were ready to get out of here."

"Shh! Be quiet! Somebody's coming." Jo pulled Lou into a nest of hay and hastily threw a smelly moth-eaten blanket over the two of them just before footsteps sounded on the floor nearby.

"I don't see anything under that ladder." A man spoke as the two walked past. "Are you sure you heard something, Coralee?"

"I tell you it was *there!* And now it's gone! They've got to be here somewhere."

Jo's nose itched and Lou's elbow jabbed into her side but she didn't dare move. *Please, oh please, don't let them look in this stall!*

Jo felt her sister's hand reach for hers and she clasped it tightly. How on God's green earth were they going to explain this?

"I reckon you heard that cat," Esau said. "Must've been hungry. Look at him eat."

"How could a cat get up in the loft? I tell you I heard something moving up there!"

"This old barn is probably overrun with rats,

but you're welcome to go up there and look. My back's been acting up all week."

"I don't have a good feeling about this, Esau. I know what I saw." From the sound of her footsteps, Coralee seemed to be walking about the barn.

"Well, if somebody *was* here, they're gone now and no harm done. Come on now. Let's go or I'm gonna miss the farm report on the radio."

Coralee's reply was muffled and the footsteps finally seemed to be fading, but neither Jo nor Lou dared to move. *What if they're just pretending to leave?* Jo thought, because that's what she would do. She squirmed and her sister kicked her. *If only her nose would stop itching!* How long were they going to have to crouch under this suffocating blanket?

"Ugh! I can't stand this any longer!" Lou stood and tossed off the offending blanket. "If we get arrested for trespassing, at least the jail will be more comfortable than this!"

Jo looked at her sister and laughed. Lou had a smudge of dirt on her cheek and straw sticking out of her hair.

"What's so funny?" Lou said.

"I wish you could see yourself, Louise. If you had a straw hat, you'd make a good scarecrow," Jo told her as her stomach rumbled again. "I wonder if they've served dinner yet at the jail?"

Fortunately, no one came but they waited a few minutes longer just to be sure before bolting for the car. "Good thing we parked here in the trees," Lou said as they made their escape. "I guess they weren't looking for a car."

Jo looked behind them as they turned into the road. "I hope they didn't see us leave." She pulled off her hat and gloves and crammed them into her coat pocket. "Wonder what time it is. I'm famished."

Lou groaned. "I hope Ed ate at the drugstore. He'll take one look at me and know I've been up to something. And we forgot all about getting that holly. We'll have to think of *something,* Jo."

Her sister agreed. Before the war it was perfectly natural to go pleasure riding, but with gas rationing that was unacceptable if not impossible. "We're not too far from our little patch of land," she reminded her, speaking of what was left of the family farm. "It shouldn't take long to grab a few branches of pine."

It didn't, and they were soon on their way again, the car smelling strongly of mule sweat and pine rosin. Jo rubbed her hands together in an effort to remove the sticky smears. "Well, at least we know where the paintings *aren't,*" she said.

Lou turned down Katherine Street. "That was a close shave, Jo! I think I lost a year off my life back there. I'll swear, I don't know how I let you talk me into all these crazy things!"

"You know, Virginia, I could be happy living right here in this library," Dimple said, looking around at the book-lined room where a wood fire leaped in the stone fireplace and evergreens festooned the mantel. She stooped to stroke Cattus, the rotten spoiled library cat who slept on the braided rug before the fire. Cattus twitched and ignored her. "If there's such a thing as reincarnation," she said, laughing, "I'd like to come back as Cattus the Second."

Virginia stepped down from the stool she used in reshelving books. "I suppose you finished decorating the tree at Phoebe's last night."

"With Annie and Charlie helping, it didn't take long. They strung so much popcorn we even decorated a small tree outside for the birds." She sighed. "Phoebe mentioned inviting you for Christmas dinner and I do wish you could come, but I didn't know what to tell her."

"Tell her I appreciate the invitation but I'm expecting a visit from my cousin."

"Which cousin?" Dimple asked.

Virginia shrugged. "I have several. Let's see, how about my cousin Roberta? I always liked her. Unfortunately she died several years ago.

"Really, Dimple, Suzy would be most upset if she thought her being there was depriving me in any way," Virginia said with a frown. "But as much as I would love to accept, I just couldn't bring myself to leave her—not on Christmas Day. I hope she doesn't learn of this, Dimple."

"We'll just have to make sure she doesn't."

Dimple joined Virginia at the window where afternoon shadows spread a splotchy cloak across the lawn. "Isn't that Annie coming now? And Charlie, too."

Virginia glanced at her watch. "And just in time if they want a book. I was thinking of closing a little early today. I have several errands to run and Jesse Dean's holding a few things for me at Cooper's."

"Well, they know." Charlie stood in the doorway with Annie standing behind her.

"Know what? And who is *they?*" Virginia wanted to know.

"My mother, that's who!" Charlie announced, flinging herself onto the old cracked leather chaise longue. "And Aunt Lou, naturally. I'm pretty sure they know we've been looking into what happened to Mae Martha Hawthorne."

Miss Dimple took a deep breath and straightened her shoulders. "And Suzy? Do they know about Suzy?"

"I'm not sure, but they might suspect," Charlie said. "And knowing those two, it won't be long before they do."

Virginia calmly collected the pencils and pens on her desk and put them into a can a young reader had decorated for the season. "You could be jumping to conclusions, you know."

"I hope you're right, but they came back from

some excursion this morning they *said* to collect greenery for the church altar and all they had was a puny little bucket full of pine boughs."

Miss Dimple nodded. "Pine is lovely at Christmastime and so fragrant, too."

"But it shouldn't take all morning to collect it— especially since we have a good-size tree in our own backyard. Mama tried to sneak in the back door, too, so we wouldn't notice how she looked—all dusty and grimy with straw sticking to her. No telling where she'd been."

Virginia shrugged. "Certainly not Christmas shopping. So . . . what should we do?"

Annie, who had been standing by quietly, spoke up. "I think we should tell them—not about Suzy—not yet, but we might as well take them into our confidence and share what we've learned about Mrs. Hawthorne. After all, we can use all the help we can get, can't we?"

"You're right," Miss Dimple said. "They might know something we don't, and frankly, I'd be glad of their assistance."

Virginia nodded. "I agree. Christmas is almost upon us, and the longer this drags on, the less chance we have of finding out who's responsible for all this grief. It stands to reason that whoever took the paintings is the one who killed Mrs. Hawthorne, and probably that fellow, Bill, as well."

"Which means we'll have to find the paintings," Annie said. "So, where do we start?"

"I can tell you where *not* to look," Louise Willingham told them when they stopped by her house later that day. "You won't find them in the Curtises' barn!" And she told them about their narrow escape. "Esau Ingram and his wife must've been asked to feed the cat and chickens while the Curtises were out of town and unfortunately, we happened to show up at the same time."

Charlie frowned. "Are you sure they didn't see you?"

Her aunt gave a dismissive wave of her hand. "I haven't been sure of anything since that awful day the Japanese bombed Pearl Harbor and turned our lives upside down, but I don't believe they saw us."

"Did you notice any other outbuildings where the paintings might've been stored?" Miss Dimple asked, and Lou thought for a minute. "Well . . . there was a garage, and the chicken house, but I can't imagine them being stored there. And it seems there might've been a woodshed or something like that."

"How do we know they aren't being kept in someone's house?" Annie said.

Charlie shrugged. "We don't, but I don't want to be arrested for breaking and entering. Besides, from what Isaac said, quite a few are missing. I'd think they'd need a lot of space."

"It shouldn't take long to check out the woodshed," Dimple said, "but I really don't believe Harriet and Stanley Curtis had anything to do with taking those paintings. Mae Martha trusted them enough to ask them to keep some of her artwork in their church, but still . . ."

"Still, what, Dimple?" Virginia asked.

"Oh, it's nothing—nothing worth worrying about. First, I think we should see what we can find on the nephews' properties and, of course, there's the woman who sold milk and eggs."

Lou, who had been hemming a dress she was making for Delia's Christmas present, set her sewing aside. "I haven't heard about her. What makes you think she had anything to do with all this?"

A warning glance from Virginia alerted Dimple she had probably shared more than was wise. "Mrs. Hawthorne happened to mention her when I was there," she explained quickly. "She's one of the few neighbors who live nearby—close enough for Suzy to walk there and collect what they needed from the springhouse."

"It doesn't seem likely either of the nephews would be bold enough to try to conceal those paintings on their property," Virginia said. "They must be visiting back and forth all the time and it would be taking quite a risk, don't you think?"

Dimple admitted that was true, but it was also a risk to take someone's life. "We must be very, very careful," she reminded them, setting aside the cup of tea Lou had served. "I learned today from Doctor Morrison that the man Charlie found in the creek, was indeed drowned, murdered. I fear we've been staring evil in the face."

"But whose face?" Annie asked.

CHAPTER TWENTY

W e can't go prowling around somebody's property in broad open daylight," Charlie said.

"Well, your mother and I are both working at the ordnance plant tomorrow, so we won't be able to prowl anyway," her aunt said.

Virginia smiled. "I thought you might take a few days off around the holidays," she said, but Lou Willingham shook her head. "War doesn't take a holiday," she said. "I wish it would, but we do have Christmas Eve and Christmas Day."

"Now that we know about what time Esau and his wife feed the Curtises' animals, we might be able to examine their place in the morning if we do it quickly," Miss Dimple suggested.

"And if we're caught, it might be a good idea to pretend we're calling on the bereaved," Annie said. "We could bring a jar of jam or something."

"We've already been there once," Charlie reminded her, thinking selfishly about the two remaining jars of peach preserves on the pantry shelf.

"But we didn't *bring* anything, and we don't have to give it to them unless they show up," Annie insisted.

Lou laughed. "Don't worry. I can spare a jar of chow-chow."

"What about the other nephew—the blacksmith?" Virginia asked.

"He has plenty of places out there to store paintings or anything else," Charlie told her, remembering the buildings scattered about, "but why would he call attention to the paintings being missing if he took them himself?"

Dimple polished her glasses with a purple-bordered hankie. "I imagine he has a list of them. And his brother probably has one, too. Even if he doesn't, surely he and his wife would know Isaac was keeping an account."

Lou bit off a thread and folded the finished skirt. "But wouldn't the two of them inherit anyway?"

Dimple dared not look at the others. "That's something we don't know for sure," she said.

"I wouldn't be a bit surprised if that Japanese woman wasn't hiding out there," Lou informed them as they started to leave. "She has to be somewhere, and she's probably already killed once—maybe twice. Promise me you'll be careful now—please!"

"Oh, dear!" Miss Dimple sighed as they walked down Katherine Street for home. "This is getting most complicated. It bothers me so when people assume Suzy is responsible."

"What if you had to put up with Emmaline Brumlow?" Virginia said. "She keeps putting up those silly signs at the library and I keep taking them down." She laughed. "Now she thinks Suzy herself is sneaking around under cover of darkness to dispose of them."

"Poor Suzy! What a dilemma!" Miss Dimple slowed her pace to match the others. "We couldn't mention Mrs. Hawthorne's leaving her estate to the university as we aren't supposed to know that."

Charlie paused to relieve Virginia of some of her groceries. "Do you want to check out Esau's place tomorrow? Aunt Lou said she thought they fed the Curtises' chickens about mid-morning."

"I'm ready with the chow-chow just in case," Annie said, holding up the jar Lou had given them.

"I think we'd better take advantage of the situation," Miss Dimple advised as they waited for the light at the corner. "I'll take care of the gas if you'll drive," she said to Charlie.

"Wouldn't you know it would be raining?" Charlie grumbled the next morning when she stopped for the others at Phoebe Chadwick's. Virginia was working at the library and couldn't accompany them.

"It's not supposed to last, or at least that's what they said on the radio this morning." Miss Dimple placed her umbrella on the floorboard beside her. "When we were there earlier I noticed a place a short distance from the Curtises' where we might watch unobserved. As soon as the Ingrams arrive to feed the animals, it should be safe to take a quick look at their property."

Annie shivered and tugged a jaunty red beret over her ears. "Maybe it will stop raining by then. I think it's turning colder."

"Some detectives we are!" Charlie said as they drove through the outskirts of town. "We're bound to leave footprints all over the place."

The parking spot Miss Dimple had suggested was sheltered from the road by underbrush and pines but they found if they leaned in just the right direction they were able to see the Curtises' driveway through the trees.

"I think my foot's asleep," Charlie said after they had been there awhile. "Seems like they should've been here by now."

"Let's give it a bit longer," Miss Dimple suggested. "Look. I believe the rain's clearing up."

"Ah! 'What light through yonder window breaks!'" Annie quoted as the sun suddenly came through the clouds. "And it looks like that car's slowing . . . it's turning in at the Curtises'! Is that the Ingrams' truck?"

The three waited until they saw two figures emerge and walk toward the back before they felt it was safe to proceed, and Charlie drove carefully to Esau Ingram's farm over the narrow two lane road, now slick with red mud.

Turning into the graveled drive, Charlie froze as a large dog raced out to greet them, barking nonstop. "Oh, lordy! I hope he's had breakfast," she said.

"But not dessert!" Annie laughed, but she didn't try to get out of the car.

Dimple Kilpatrick had no such qualms. "He's a nice boy," she said in a calming voice, and held out a hand for the dog to sniff. "He knows we aren't going to hurt him, don't you, fella?"

Still, Charlie gripped the steering wheel. "But does he know we plan to snoop around with ill intent?"

"It's only ill if we find the paintings," Dimple told her. "Now, come on, you two. We don't have time to dawdle. See, he's wagging his tail."

No one came to the door when they gave it a cursory knock, although Annie had remembered to bring along the chow-chow just in case. Setting it aside, she followed the others to look at the outbuildings. The dog, befriended by Miss Dimple, trotted happily along beside them.

Aside from the usual farm equipment, the small barn sheltered a mule, a couple of hogs, and several cats, but no paintings, and hens frittered away their time in the fenced chicken yard nearby. The ruling rooster pranced and huffed about to let everyone know he was in charge, and Charlie paused at the henhouse door. "Do you really think they would hide paintings in here?" she asked, holding her nose, and to her relief the others agreed that would be unlikely.

The only other buildings were a toolshed and smokehouse, the latter, empty of everything but hams suspended from the ceiling. Charlie inhaled deeply and reluctantly shut the door, thinking of the delectable prospect of a country ham breakfast with grits and red-eye gravy.

In the toolshed they discovered only the things you might expect to find there. A lean-to on the other side sheltered the family's supply of firewood from the elements. "You'd think they would have locks on the doors if something valuable is stored inside," Annie said finally. "Unless the paintings are in the house, it looks like we're wasting our time here."

"I believe you may be right," Miss Dimple said, and began picking her way back across the muddied property using her furled umbrella for balance. They had almost reached the place where they had left the car when Esau Ingram's faded blue truck turned into the driveway.

Annie, who was in the lead, froze in her tracks. "Oh, no! Is it too late to hide? We could make a dash for the woodshed."

"Nonsense!" Miss Dimple raised her hand in greeting, noting the dog had already alerted his owners of their uninvited visitors. "Just try to appear calm. After all, we haven't done anything wrong.

"Ah, so there you are!" she called, hurrying to meet the couple as they climbed out of the truck. "We thought we might find you out in the barn and were so afraid we'd missed you." Smiling, Miss Dimple extended her hand and reintroduced all of them. "My friends and I have been sent on a mission to round up a few eggs, and we were hoping you might have some to spare. It's so difficult to find things now with all this wartime rationing."

Charlie and Annie nodded in agreement, muttering something about running out of eggs for their Christmas baking.

"We plan to pay you, of course," Miss Dimple continued, stooping to pet the dog.

Coralee shook her head. "I wish I could help you, but our hens have been off a bit lately and I'm afraid I'll need the few I collected this morning." She darted a look at her husband and lowered her voice. "My Esau does love my cake!"

Dimple, remembering Mae Martha's comments on the woman's culinary efforts, restrained a knowing smile. "I understand," she said, turning to go. "And I hope we haven't inconvenienced you."

"You might try Rebecca Wyatt down the road," Esau told them. "She sometimes has extra to sell." He paused to scratch his head. "She's kinda peculiar, though. Never can tell if she'll take to you or not."

"I guess we'll *have* to go there now," Charlie said once they were back in the car.

"We'd better ask her if she'll sell us some eggs," Annie said, "in case Coralee or Esau mentions it."

"A few extra eggs always come in handy, and we wanted to see that place anyway," Miss Dimple reminded them. "Perhaps this will give us a chance to look around. Mr. Ingram said it was only a few miles down the road—not very far from his brother's place. It shouldn't be too hard to find."

"Are you sure you turned the right way back there?" Annie asked Charlie after they had driven for what seemed like ages.

"He said turn right after we passed that abandoned barn with *See Rock City* on the roof," Charlie said. "That was the only one I saw."

239

"I believe we might have missed it." Miss Dimple concentrated on her side of the road. "There should be a mailbox and some sort of driveway along here somewhere. Maybe we should turn back."

"No, no! Not yet! I think I see it. Slow down." Annie pointed to a narrow trail leading off into the grass and brambles just ahead of them.

"That doesn't look like a driveway to me," Charlie said, coming to a stop. "The ruts are a foot deep and it looks like a jungle growing in the median. I'm not driving up there."

"Look, there's a mailbox." Annie brought their attention to a rusty metal box on a tilted wooden post. She narrowed her eyes to read the name. "I can barely make it out, but it looks like *Wyatt.* This has to be Rebecca."

Charlie turned into the overgrown trail and parked. "I hope you're up for a hike because it looks like we're walking from here."

This was no inconvenience to Dimple Kilpatrick, as she walked almost every morning and the others had thought to wear sturdy boots. The tall grass and underbrush from either side snagged at them as they trudged along, side-stepping to avoid puddles.

"Aunt Lou said she was sure the Ingrams didn't get a look at them yesterday at the Curtis farm," Charlie said, "but what if they did? What if Coralee connects our being there this morning to her suspicions about somebody hiding in the Curtises' barn?"

"I doubt if either of them would know your aunt or your mother," Dimple assured her. "What reason would they have to link the two incidents?"

"Oh, dear!" Pausing, Annie turned to face the others. "That might not be completely true."

"What do you mean?" Miss Dimple asked.

"I left the jar of chow-chow on their porch. It has your aunt's name on the label."

Charlie shrugged. "Oh, well, I think we should let Miss Dimple handle the situation," she suggested, holding aside a clawing limb. "You certainly thought fast back there when the Ingrams suddenly showed up."

Miss Dimple poked at a briar with her umbrella. "I dislike telling falsehoods as a rule, but there are times when a person has to do what she deems necessary."

"This Rebecca sounds like a recluse," Annie said. "I hope she doesn't have a shotgun."

"I expect she's just shy because of her scarred face," Miss Dimple told her. "At any rate, we should find out in a minute."

The small house sat in a grassy area bordered by trees on one side and a fenced garden on the other. A weathered barn sat behind the house, and to the rear of that, the rolling hills of a pasture. The garden was barren now, but a tangle of brown bean vines still clung to the remaining skeletons of cornstalks and it looked as if the withered leaves of melons or pumpkins had been gathered into piles at one end. At one time the house had been painted white but it was sorely in need of another coat, and orange-red berries on nandina bushes on either side of the steps gave the only color to a drab setting.

Miss Dimple walked boldly up to the front door and knocked but it appeared that either the woman wasn't at home, or didn't welcome company.

"I don't see a light inside," Annie said, peering in a window. "Maybe she isn't here."

"She has to be somewhere unless she knows how to fly," Charlie said. "There's no way a car could make it down that driveway."

"Perhaps she's somewhere out back," Miss Dimple suggested, noticing a plump calico cat inside on a chair by the window. "Surely she can't have gone far."

"Maybe we should try the back door," Annie said, leading the way around the side of the house. But although a glance through the window revealed a tidy kitchen with yellow dishes lining a green-painted cupboard and a potted red geranium on a table, the house seemed empty and silent.

"Suzy said Mrs. Hawthorne's milk and eggs were always left in the springhouse," Miss

Dimple recalled, looking about. "I expect it's in that stone building over there under the oak.

"Mrs. Wyatt!" she called, not wanting to startle the woman as they approached the small, ivy-covered springhouse. She repeated the greeting as they drew nearer, but no one answered.

"Wow! It's even colder in here than it is outside," Charlie said, shivering as they stooped under the low door and stepped down into the earthy chill of the springhouse, where a stream of clear water flowed through a wooden trough in the center of the building. Crocks of milk and butter were keeping cold in the water along with a wire basket of eggs. Shelves along the sides of the walls held jars of canned vegetables, probably from Rebecca's garden, as well as baskets of onions and potatoes. A dipper hung from a shelf near the spring.

The evasive Rebecca was obviously industrious, Dimple thought, and probably wouldn't welcome their prying about. "This woman, it seems, is an extremely private person," she said. "I don't have a good feeling about this. I believe we should leave right now."

"Suits me!" Charlie said, following her up the narrow steps.

"Ah! 'How poor are they that have not patience!'" Annie quoted. "We're here now. Why pass up the opportunity? Let's at least take a quick look in the barn. Maybe we'll get lucky."

The usual chickens roamed about the barnyard, but the three stalls inside the building were empty except for obvious evidence of resident cows that had most likely been turned out to pasture. Annie scampered up the ladder for a hasty glance into the loft to report it revealed nothing but hay, while Dimple inspected a storage room in the rear.

"Okay, we looked," Charlie said, stepping outside where a blast of cold wind whipped bare branches of the lone tree in the barn lot, causing her to turn up her collar. "I couldn't see any place in there where paintings might be stored, could you?"

Miss Dimple shook her head. "Nor could I. Let's head on back, shall we?" She didn't want to say anything to the others, but Dimple was almost certain she'd seen something in there that seemed out of place, and she had an uneasy feeling that the sooner they left, the better.

CHAPTER TWENTY-ONE

It was almost impossible to hurry as they made their way across Rebecca Wyatt's soggy backyard but Dimple Kilpatrick picked up her feet and set the pace. Once they reached the car, she could begin to relax, but she wouldn't feel completely at ease until they were surrounded by the dear, familiar town of Elderberry.

"Golly, Miss Dimple!" Annie protested, panting. "Are we going to a fire or something? I can't keep up with you." They jumped as the sharp crack of a rifle shot rang out that seemed to come from the other side of the house.

"What's *that?*" Charlie asked, pausing.

"Probably just somebody hunting," Annie said, catching up with her.

"Don't stop!" Quickly Miss Dimple reached back to hook the crook of her umbrella on Charlie's arm and gave her an unceremonious tug.

Good heavens! What's come over our Miss Dimple? Charlie glanced at her old teacher in concern but she didn't have time to do anything else before a second shot zinged nearby, sounding much too close for comfort.

"Run!" Miss Dimple shouted, giving the umbrella, and Charlie along with it, another tug.

But where? The house was probably locked, and even if it wasn't, chances were, the person shooting was Rebecca Wyatt herself. Dimple looked about. The closest building was a small shed at the edge of the now-spent garden. "This way!" she commanded, and took off in that direction.

Good heavens, was she leading them from the frying pan into the fire? Dimple wondered as she slid off the metal bar that kept the door closed. Together they wrenched open the door and stepped inside a tiny, foul-smelling room less than half the size of Phoebe Chadwick's garage, and since there was no window, it took awhile for their eyes to become adjusted to the darkness.

"We're going to be sitting ducks in here!" Annie said, attempting to hold the door shut behind them. "What's to keep whoever that is from coming in here after us? We can't even lock the door."

A narrow opening between the walls and the roof let in just enough light for Charlie to make out an assortment of garden tools lining the walls, and a cold December sun crept between gaps in the weathered boards to stripe the dingy floor. "Maybe we can tie it shut," she said, looking frantically about. "See if you can find a rope."

"What about a belt?" Annie hurriedly unbuckled the narrow leather belt around her waist. Thank goodness she'd worn dungarees! "We can loop it around the door handle."

"But there's nothing to tie it to." Charlie dug in her heels and tugged on the handle. What chance would they have if somebody really wanted to pull open that door?

"Yes, there is. Quickly, Annie, give me that hoe," Miss Dimple demanded. Taking the hoe, she positioned it across the door, and while Annie held it in place, tightly secured it to the metal handle.

"And if that doesn't keep them out, this oughta help," Charlie said, snatching up a garden rake with sharp metal prongs. "Here," she added, passing a shovel to Miss Dimple and a pickax to Annie. "We'll clobber him if we have to."

"If he—or she—doesn't get to us first," Annie said under her breath.

Now, armed and with the door fastened as best they could manage, they waited, quietly listening for the gunfire to continue.

"Do you think it could be Rebecca?" Annie asked Miss Dimple. "I thought you said she was *shy!*"

"Maybe she didn't see us come in here," Charlie said, hoping. "What if she thinks we've gone?" But Miss Dimple quietly put a restraining hand on her arm. "Listen," she whispered.

Charlie found it hard to listen over the pounding of her heart, but as the three of them stood, unmoving, she heard not gunfire, but something just as threatening: the sound of footsteps approaching. She gripped the rake, poised to strike if he attempted to force open the door. Were they all going to be killed in this horrible shed that smelled of something dead? She thought of Will, her wonderful, witty, lovable Will, and their plans for a future together. Not a day went by that she didn't worry about him training to become a fighter pilot where he would risk his life confronting the enemy with nothing but space between himself and the blessed ground. *Oh, Will! I'm so sorry I got myself into this mess!* she thought, longing to hold him once more. Beside her, she was sure Annie was thinking much the same about her Frazier.

Dimple Kilpatrick had no such thoughts. She had been in tight spots before, but this time was different. It had been *her* idea to spend the morning investigating the area near where Mae Martha Hawthorne had lived—and died; her idea to take shelter in the garden shed instead of taking a chance on making it to the car. If this crazy person managed to open the door and fire at them they would be like fish in a barrel. There was no way she could escape being shot, but first she would do as much damage with her shovel as possible and give the others a chance to escape. A pity, she thought, hoping a better solution would soon present itself, as she did look forward to the beautiful Christmas Eve service at her church and a pleasant dinner with friends on Christmas Day. And then, of course, there was Suzy. What was to become of her?

Whoever was out there made no effort to be quiet but tramped around on the muddy ground, seemingly circling the shed. Well, why should he be quiet? Dimple thought. He was the one with the gun. At least, she thought, he hadn't tried to burst open the door.

The three clung together in the middle of the shed as the person outside stomped right up to the door and slid the metal bar back into place.

He's barricading us inside! Miss Dimple turned to face the others and knew they were all thinking alike. *Well, it's no secret now that we're in here, so what's to lose?* she thought, and began to make her displeasure known.

She was joined in shouting by Annie and Charlie, but whoever was outside remained ominously silent.

"Hey!" Annie shouted, thinking whoever locked them inside might not realize what they'd done. "We're in here! Let us out!"

Still nothing.

Did he intend to leave them there until they died of exposure or starvation? Dimple wondered. Would Rebecca Wyatt sit inside by her warm stove with her warm cat while three people died in her garden shed?

Of course they weren't going to die! Rebecca must have occasional visitors, although from the appearance of the driveway, they were few and far between. And Esau and his wife knew they were going there. When they didn't return, Lou and her sister would surely trace them here. Wouldn't they? *Except they were working that day at the munitions plant!*

"You're taking this rather poorly, don't you think?" Charlie shouted. "We only came to buy a few eggs!" Still no response from their captor except for the sound of muffled footsteps in the grass.

"I'm freezing," Annie muttered through chattering teeth, and then wished she hadn't because through the cracks of the old wooden shed came the distinct smell of smoke, and gray wisps began to curl through the crevices and waft toward the ceiling, consuming the air around them. Whoever was out there had set fire to the tall grass and dried underbrush surrounding the shed!

Somebody screamed. It was Annie, Charlie thought. No, it was her. It was both of them. "Save your breath!" Miss Dimple told them. "Get down on the floor, quickly!"

Charlie obeyed, remembering from her first aid training that smoke rises. She covered her mouth and nose with an arm and saw the others doing the same, but how long could they stay here? Already the walls were growing warm.

Beside her Annie began to cough. "Ugh! Dead rat!" she yelled, and turned her face away.

So, that was what smelled so bad, Charlie thought, but the rat was nothing compared to the realization that they could be burned alive if they weren't first overcome by smoke. She coughed in an effort to breathe through the choking fumes and was aware of Miss Dimple doing the same. *I would rather be shot than be roasted alive,* she thought. They had to get out of here!

"Kick!" Miss Dimple shouted hoarsely, inching her way toward the wall. "We have to try!"

Charlie, eyeing cracks between the weathered boards in the shed's wall, began to squirm along beside her, and together they kicked the loose boards as hard as they could. Some, she saw, had rotted at the bottom and would, she hoped, be easier to break. Annie, struggling to breathe through the suffocating smoke, wormed her way to join them and they were soon rewarded with a brief but precious gulp of fresh air as a splinter of the plank creaked and gave way.

"Harder!" Dimple Kilpatrick compelled them, pummeling the wall with her feet. All those morning walks were paying off. If only she could get enough air to continue! The wall felt hot through her heavy shoes and even the floor was becoming uncomfortably warm. *Was the maniac with the rifle waiting out there to shoot them if they managed to escape?*

But it was not a question of choice. "All together now!" she told them in a voice foggy with smoke, and the board cracked and gave way, creating an opening big enough for a small animal to crawl through—but not one of them.

"Wait a minute!" Annie said and, gasping, crawled toward the door, eyes shut against the suffocating smoke, to feel in the darkness until her hand came in touch with the pickax she knew was there. "Stand back!" she warned them, and slammed it against the side. It thudded and bounced away.

"Give me something to pry off this board! Hurry!" A woman's voice screamed at them from outside while at the same time they were soaked with a deluge of icy water. "Pass it through the opening and stand back."

No one hesitated to comply. If this woman meant to kill them, why would she dash them with water? Quickly Annie thrust the pickax through the opening and they all held their breath as with a wonderful splitting noise, enough of the wall came away to permit them to crawl out into the cold, clear air, coughing and sputtering and thankful to be alive.

Miss Dimple, who was last to emerge, gratefully grasped the hand offered and was pulled to her feet. Scrambling to move away from the smoke and breathe, she opened her eyes to see the woman who had helped them. Rebecca Wyatt wore a man's gray tweed overcoat over a baggy pair of overalls. A blue knitted shawl covered her head and part of her face. Annie and Charlie sat on the cold ground nearby, coughing and gasping until color finally returned to their faces. "Thank you," Charlie said weakly, looking up. Behind them, one side of the garden shed, which had apparently been doused from a barrel of rain-water, still smoked and steamed but the flames had been extinguished.

"Who did this?" Dimple demanded when she could speak. "Why would somebody want to kill us?" She shivered, realizing her skirt was drenching wet. The others, too, were showing signs of being chilled. "We have to get dry," she said, looking about, but Rebecca seemed to be alone. *Dear, God, please don't let this be the person who set that shed on fire!*

"Yes. Yes, of course. Come to the house. I'll get blankets," Rebecca said.

The strange woman hurried inside ahead of them, leaving them to follow. The front of the shed, Dimple noticed, had been almost completely charred by the fire, which was probably why Rebecca chose to guide them out through the back. She looked around for a gun but all she saw were a hammer and some other tools lying on the grass. Of course she might've hidden it somewhere, but at this point, Dimple was willing to take that chance.

"What should we do?" Charlie whispered, taking Miss Dimple's arm.

Dimple Kilpatrick sneezed. "I suggest we dry off, get warm, and go home," she told her, "*after* we call the sheriff, of course."

In the snug kitchen Rebecca built up a fire in the woodstove and doled out rough blankets smelling of mothballs. "This is terrible! I can't imagine how it happened," she said, putting a pot of coffee on the stove. "Are you sure you're all right? Do you think you might need a doctor?"

"No, we're *not* all right, and the person we *need* right now is the sheriff," Dimple told her, moving closer to the stove with the others. Most of her skirt was wet, and Annie's dungarees were steaming, but the water had hit Charlie full force. Although she had removed her jacket, her dress clung to her body, and sooty water dripped on the floor. "Surely you must have some idea who's responsible for this," Dimple continued, looking carefully about in case the person who wanted to kill them returned.

"Where were you?" Charlie's voice trembled. "You must've noticed what was going on—not that we aren't grateful for what you did—but somebody just tried to burn us alive!"

Rebecca busied herself taking mugs from her cupboard before answering. She kept one side of her face averted, Charlie noticed, probably because of the ugly red scar that marred the lower part of her face. "I was down at the pasture mending the fence. One of my cows got out awhile ago and had almost reached the road before I found her. Can't have that happening again." She poured cream into a brown pitcher and set it on the table with a small bowl of sugar.

"I didn't see the smoke until I got back to the barn lot."

Annie sighed. "Thank heavens for that! Did you see anyone? The person who set the fire—was he still there?"

Rebecca shook her head and turned back to the stove. "No. No, I told you, whoever did it was gone. Maybe somebody followed you here." She poured steaming coffee into four mugs and carried them to the table. "Do you know anybody who might want to hurt you?"

Charlie sneezed. "Of course not!" she said. But obviously someone did.

"You should get out of that wet dress," Rebecca told her. "I'm not as tall as you are, but I think I have something that will do, at least until you get home."

"No thanks. I'll be okay." Charlie sneezed again. That coffee looked like heaven but she was afraid to drink any until she saw Rebecca stir sugar into hers and take a couple of swallows.

"For goodness sake, Charlie, do change into something dry," Miss Dimple said, sipping from her steaming mug. "You don't want to be sick here at Christmas. Meanwhile," she added, addressing Rebecca, "we need to call Sheriff Holland. Whoever locked us in that shed is probably gone by now, but he might be able to trace his footprints in this wet ground."

Rebecca shook her head. "I'm sorry. I don't

have a telephone, but you should be able to call from Esau and Coralee's place down the road."

While Rebecca went to look for dry clothing, Charlie stepped out of her dress and wrapped the blanket around her. "We'll leave as soon as I'm dressed," she told them. "I'm not staying in this place one minute longer than I have to!"

"We can't get out of here soon enough for me, but what if he's still out there?" Annie reminded her. "The man with the gun? He could shoot us before we get to the car."

Rebecca stood in the doorway with a dress over her arm. "I'll walk there with you if you think it'll help, but whoever did that is probably long gone by now."

"Perhaps it might be a good idea if you accompanied us to the road," Dimple told her. If Rebecca Wyatt had been the one who tried to kill them, at least they would be able to keep an eye on her until they reached the car.

"I think Rebecca was just as eager for us to leave as we were," Charlie said as they at last drove back down the narrow country road. She tugged at the sleeves of the blue plaid dress that was tight under her arms. "That story about the cows and the fence . . . how do we know that's true?"

"I'm sure Sheriff Holland will look into that," Dimple said. "I don't believe the woman tried to kill us, but something is definitely not right, and I think it's best that we not stop to telephone from the Ingrams'. For all we know, it might have been one of them who set fire to that shed."

"You're right," Charlie said. "They were the only ones who knew we were going there. We can stop by the sheriff's office when we get to town."

"We seem to be getting too close to something," Annie said. "And you must be psychic, Miss Dimple—you tried to rush us away from there even before we heard the gunfire."

Dimple's laugh was fragile. "Hocus-pocus had nothing to do with it, dear. I became suspicious because of something I saw in that storage room in the barn. There was a whole shelf stacked with canvases."

Charlie frowned. "Canvases?"

"Blank canvases. The kind an artist uses for oil paintings," Miss Dimple explained.

Annie leaned back against the seat and closed her eyes. "Well, I'm sure of one thing. I'm never going to go looking to buy eggs from anybody again!"

CHAPTER TWENTY-TWO

"C harlie," Delia said, "Sheriff Holland's here
to talk to you." She frowned. "What's going
on?"

"It's a long story! Tell you later—I promise."
Charlie paused to listen. "Do I hear Pooh waking
up from his nap?"

After her sister hurried upstairs to check on her
baby, Charlie dressed hastily in warm corduroy
slacks and a sweater and towel-dried her hair. No
matter how many times she'd shampooed, it still
seemed to smell of smoke. They had gone
directly to the sheriff's office on the way home to
explain what had happened at Rebecca Wyatt's,
and after only a brief period of questioning, Sheriff
Holland and two of his deputies had left to
investigate.

She hadn't told her sister about the experience
as she didn't want to frighten her, and their
mother hadn't returned from the ordnance plant
in nearby Milledgeville. All Charlie wanted to do
was lie in a tub of warm water and wash the dirt,
smoke, and fear away. One out of three was the
best she could do.

With grim face the sheriff stood waiting in the
living room. "This isn't good," he told her,

shaking his head. "I don't mind telling you, Charlie. It doesn't look good at all."

I could've told you that! Charlie thought. *It wasn't looking all that grand when we were almost barbecued in that garden shed, either.*

He refused to sit down and had twisted and mangled his hat until it had no shape at all. "You saw the shed?" she said.

He nodded, his face taut. "I've investigated a lot of crime scenes over the years, but never— *never* have I heard of anybody with such evil intent. *Miss Dimple!* My God, *Miss Dimple!* All three of you would've died in that shed."

Charlie felt a tremor that left her weak. She didn't need to be reminded. "Did you speak to Rebecca Wyatt?"

"That's another thing. Couldn't find her." Sighing, he paced to the window as if the elusive woman might be standing outside on the front porch.

"But she was there when we left. Where else could she be? She has no car and no phone, and her cows have to be milked. She can't be gone long. Did you check with the neighbors?"

He nodded, and finally but reluctantly took a seat in the gold brocaded Victorian chair that had belonged to Charlie's grandmother. "Isaac Ingram wasn't there, and his brother—what's his name . . . ?"

"Esau," Charlie told him.

"Right. Well, Esau had gone into town, his wife said, but according to her, neither of them had seen Rebecca Wyatt." He shifted in an attempt to get comfortable in a chair intended, no doubt, for brief visits, and finally perched on the edge of the seat. "And Stanley Curtis and his wife, I understand, have gone to their daughter's for Christmas."

"I suppose you asked Coralee Ingram if they told anybody we planned to stop by Rebecca Wyatt's. Her husband was the one who suggested we might buy eggs there." Not that they cared a whit about eggs, Charlie thought, but she wasn't ready to share that with the sheriff.

"Of course I did," he said, giving up on the chair to stand. "And she vowed they hadn't mentioned it to a soul. The woman was all broken up when I told her what had happened . . . or at least she appeared to be. Said she couldn't imagine anybody doing a thing like that.

"I left Peewee and another deputy out at Rebecca Wyatt's. They'll be waiting when she finally does show up, and I'll talk to Esau and his brother soon as I can track 'em down."

"Speaking of tracks," Charlie began. "Were you able to tell anything from the footprints out there?"

Sheriff Holland almost smiled. "*Whose* prints? It's almost impossible to get a cast in all that stirred-up mud. We've got footprints on top of footprints out there, but I do want to take a look at each of your shoes—Rebecca's, too. At least we might find out if there were others involved."

The sheriff was a large man, and when he stepped in front of someone, as he was doing now, it was hard to look anywhere else. "Now, listen here, I don't know what you three were doing out there, but if you have reason to suspect what's going on, you need to tell me *now*. I don't think I have to remind you that you're dealing with an extremely dangerous person, and one who would just as soon kill you as step on a cockroach."

Sighing, he leaned on the mantel where Jo Carr had arranged a bowl of holly and pyracantha berries and where baby Tommy's stocking would soon hang. "Is there anything you want to talk about, Charlie?"

Charlie wandered over to the Christmas tree in the window and touched the celluloid angel ornament her Sunday school teacher had given her when she was six. The smell of cedar permeated the room; brightly wrapped presents were piled beneath. It was almost Christmas. Wasn't it enough that they were mired in this horrible war? And now they were being forced to deal with a lunatic!

"I suppose you've spoken with Miss Dimple and Annie," she said.

He nodded. "And now I'm speaking with you."

What had the others told him? She would have to be careful what she said.

"We didn't intend to get mixed up in all this, Sheriff. I can't explain why we always seem to be the ones who stumble onto murder scenes, but, believe me, we didn't plan it that way! Obviously they're connected: Mae Martha Hawthorne's murder; that awful thing that happened to Bill Pitts; and the fire today in Rebecca Wyatt's toolshed. I can't imagine why somebody tried to kill us unless whoever did it thinks we know something."

"And do you?"

"If I did, I'd tell you," Charlie said, and meant it. At least she was sure Suzy had nothing to do with it, and there was nothing to gain by exposing her to danger.

"I wonder . . ." Sheriff Holland turned to go.

"Wonder what?"

"If Rebecca Wyatt started that fire and then had second thoughts and put it out," he said.

"Huh! If she did, she sure took her sweet time doing it!" Charlie told him.

Emmaline Brumlow tucked three hefty books under her arm and planted her feet in front of Virginia's desk. "Well, Virginia," she said. "I hope *now* you'll believe that Japanese woman is dangerous! I doubt if you and Dimple will make light of my little warnings anymore. Why, none of us is safe with that sneaky little Jap on the loose!"

Virginia drew in her breath to answer, but Dimple, who had stopped in earlier, thought it best to ignore the comment. "I see you're reading Mark Twain," she said, peering at the titles. "I do so enjoy him. His stories never get old, do they?"

"Oh, these are for Hugh." Emmaline stroked the cover of *A Connecticut Yankee in King Arthur's Court* as one might caress a loved one. "I never have time to read, but Hugh asked for these especially."

It amazed Dimple how quickly the woman's expression changed from downright hateful to Christmas-morning happy. "You know he's coming home tomorrow," Emmaline said, "and Arden and I are trying to cook everything he likes—or at least as much as rationing will allow. I'm going home now to bake that jam cake he loves so. Marjorie Mote, bless her heart, insisted I take her last jar of blackberry jam."

Marjorie knew how important that jam was, Dimple thought, after losing one son earlier in the war and with another serving somewhere in the European Theater. "I can imagine how excited you must be," Dimple told her. "I'm so pleased that Hugh will be here in time for Christmas and I hope to see him after he's had a chance to settle in." Dimple Kilpatrick had known and admired Hugh Brumlow since she taught him back in the first grade, and she, as well as others who had watched him grow up in Elderberry, was grateful he was coming home at last after losing a leg serving as a navy corpsman. And, as many others did, she often wondered how grumpy Emmaline had given birth to two such delightful offspring as Arden and Hugh.

"We've moved his bedroom to that little study downstairs," Emmaline continued, "but as soon as he's fitted with a prosthetic leg and learns to walk with it, my brave boy plans to apply for medical school, so we won't get to have him long."

Dimple smiled. "He'll make a wonderful doctor," she said, and meant it.

Virginia agreed. "Please give him our love, Emmaline, and do let me know if he'd like more books and I'll be happy to drop them by."

Virginia sighed as Emmaline left, balancing books under one arm and her huge purse, the other. Dimple hurried to close the door behind her. "Well, that's a relief!" Virginia said. "Thank goodness Hugh will be here to keep that dreadful woman occupied for a while." Frowning, she moved around her desk to face her friend. "Dimple, is it true what she just told me? Good heavens, you smell like you've walked through a forest fire!" Locking the door, she led Dimple to a comfortable chair. "Please, sit down now and tell me what happened out there yesterday."

Dimple permitted her friend to seat her. Although she was reluctant to admit it, she did feel a bit unstable on her feet. "I don't see why we even need telephones or newspapers," she said. "Emmaline Brumlow seems to know everything as soon as it happens. I wonder how she does that! I was hoping to tell you about it before the news got around, but it took longer than I thought to wash away all that smoke and grime."

Virginia poured coffee from her Thermos and opened a tin of molasses cookies Lou Willingham had brought her, and Dimple allowed herself to relax at least for a little while as she told Virginia what had happened at Rebecca's Wyatt's.

"Somebody must think we know more than we do," Virginia said. "I wonder if it's one of the Ingrams? Esau suggested you go there for eggs, didn't he? And his brother lives nearby."

"Don't forget about Coralee," Dimple reminded her. "She could've recognized Lou yesterday at the Curtises' and her name was on that jar of chow-chow Annie left. Whatever they're trying to cover up must be something terrible to make them set fire to that shed with us in it!"

Virginia nodded solemnly. "And I think we all know what that is."

"I'm hoping Rebecca Wyatt will be able to help clear this up," Dimple said, deciding one more cookie wouldn't hurt just this once. "I can't imagine where she might be, and frankly, I'm afraid she might be in danger herself."

"I imagine she'll turn up soon," Virginia assured her.

Although later that afternoon when Dimple spoke with Sheriff Holland, he still hadn't been able to locate the missing woman.

"Someone has to be looking after her animals," Dimple said. "Cows have to be milked, chickens fed, and then there's the cat. I can't see her going off and leaving them."

"The Fuller boy is taking care of that, I understand. Abbott Fuller, lives about a mile or so on the other side of the hill. Esau Ingram said he helps out at the Wyatt place on a regular basis and the boy's mother told me Rebecca had left a note in the barn asking him if he'd see to the animals for a few days."

"What about the Ingram brothers? I assume you've spoken with Esau."

"Said he was at the barber's and then picked up a couple of things from Clyde Jefferies at the Feed and Seed, and his alibi checks out. Still haven't been able to find Isaac, but his brother said he thought he went into Atlanta to see a customer about a wrought-iron gate."

"I see," Dimple said, but of course she didn't.

"When we learn anything more, we'll keep you posted. Meanwhile, I want you ladies to promise

266

you won't go roaming around where you don't belong." Sheriff Holland paused. "I mean that, Miss Dimple. I'd have to find me another job if I let anything happen to you!"

"My goodness, the sheriff sounded rather short with me," Miss Dimple told Annie after relating the conversation. "You'd think he would welcome our help."

Annie finished wrapping a teapot for Odessa and slipped it under the tree. No kitchen should be without one, Odessa claimed. This one was dark blue with yellow flowers and Annie knew she'd been admiring it at Murphy's Five and Ten. Tomorrow would be Christmas Eve and everyone had been saving their ration stamps to buy sugar for fudge, and she and Charlie, with some of the other teachers, planned to go caroling after the evening church service. For a couple of days, at least, Annie Gardner didn't even want to think about the fact that somebody wanted them dead.

"It's a shame Virginia and Suzy won't be able to have Christmas dinner with the rest of you at Phoebe's tomorrow," Charlie said as she and Annie walked home together after caroling the following night.

Annie agreed. "Virginia's planning on having a baked hen with dressing and cranberry sauce, and Phoebe sent one of Odessa's sweet potato pies, so at least they'll be able to enjoy a traditional dinner, even if it's just the two of them." She knew it wouldn't be the same, though, and hoped Suzy would never learn Virginia had turned down an invitation to be with friends.

The two had stopped at Virginia's after caroling and stayed long enough to enjoy a mug of mulled cider. Earlier they had delivered small gifts of chocolates for Virginia and a colorful scarf for Suzy. Dimple had also left a package under the tree so the young doctor would have something to open Christmas Day.

"Do you think it's safe to walk home?" Virginia asked as they prepared to leave, the other carolers having gone their separate ways earlier. "I never thought I'd feel unsafe in Elderberry, but after that dreadful thing that happened the other day, I don't know what to believe."

"It's only a couple of blocks and if we see anybody suspicious, we'll just run in somebody's house." Charlie smiled when she said it, but as they began walking down the dark street, she was tempted to look over her shoulder. "Just think, Annie!" she said, in an effort to think happy thoughts, "This time next year Will and Frazier might be with us. As soon as I get home I'm going to sit by our lighted tree and write Will a long, long letter. Oh, I wish they could be here for Christmas!"

As soon as she said it, Charlie regretted the

words because Annie hadn't heard from Frazier in several weeks and only knew he was on his way to *somewhere.*

But that didn't stop her from writing. "I wrote Frazier this afternoon," she said. "Of course I have no idea when he'll get it."

"You didn't tell him what happened yesterday?" Charlie asked.

"Absolutely not! What good would that do?"

Charlie agreed. "They don't need that worry on top of everything else, but it's going to be hard to pretend everything's all right."

"I guess that's what they have to do all the time," Annie said.

CHAPTER TWENTY-THREE

Phoebe Chadwick looked around her table and, beaming, raised a glass of blackberry wine. "Thank you all for being a part of my Christmas! I do dislike an empty table, and with three of our guests away, Odessa and I wouldn't have known how to prepare for the few of us remaining."

"I propose a toast to the cook," Lottie Nivens said, raising her glass. "Where is Odessa?"

"Spending Christmas with her family," Phoebe explained, "but she did some of the baking ahead and left me *detailed* instructions on how to deal with the rest." She smiled. "With help, of course, from Miss Dimple and Annie. But let's first drink a toast to our brave men and women in the service of our country," she added with a catch in her voice. Everyone knew her grandson, Harrison, was just completing his training at Fort Benning.

"And to victory and an end to this horrible war," Miss Dimple added, and everyone echoed, "Amen."

The wine, musky and sweet with an essence of summer, came from Phoebe's own cellar from berries picked before the war, and everyone drained their glass—even Bessie, who went to the Baptist church and claimed to be a teetotaler.

After a brief blessing from Phoebe, the diners helped themselves to baked hen with corn-bread dressing and cranberry sauce—and, of course, rice and gravy. Bessie had brought yeast rolls made earlier that morning and everyone bragged on how light they were, although Dimple didn't think they were nearly as good as Odessa's. Jesse Dean contributed a jar of olives from Mr. Cooper's store, and Lottie, a sweet potato pie— her first attempt, she said.

In the parlor behind them a fire burned low in the grate, and lights on the tree reflected in the window while from the radio in the kitchen a program of carols played softly in the background. Dimple Kilpatrick served herself green beans canned last summer from Phoebe's victory garden, admiring as usual the familiar violet-patterned china, and smiled at Jesse Dean across the table. The two had become good friends during a frightening experience the year before and she was glad to see him looking well and strong after a recent accident.

"I imagine you've been busy at the store these last few weeks, Jesse Dean," she said. "You must be ready to relax."

Usually good-natured, it was surprising to see him scowl. "We had to hide things from Mrs. Brumlow or there wouldn't be anything left on the shelves," he said, shaking his head. "I can understand why she wanted everything perfect for Hugh, but for goodness sake, a few other people live here, too! If I hadn't put away those olives, there wouldn't be a jar to be had."

Lottie laughed. "I'm glad you did. I've always loved olives. They say most people have to develop a taste for them, but I don't remember not liking them."

"Me, either!" Jesse Dean said. "I was told my mother craved them when she was . . . well . . . when I was on the way." His face turned pink and he suddenly concentrated on helping himself to the cranberry sauce.

"I'm surprised Emmaline Brumlow has time to shop, she's been so busy passing out flyers," Annie muttered.

Bessie looked up from buttering a roll. "Dimple, do you believe that Japanese woman they've been looking for had anything to do with that fire? My goodness, what a fright that must've been! Thank goodness you were all able to escape!"

Miss Dimple, with a knowing glance at Annie, admitted she was kind of glad of it, too. "Right now we just don't know who's responsible, but the sheriff's working on it, and if the woman is a suspect, he hasn't said anything about it."

"Then where is she?" Lottie asked. "She simply seemed to disappear after that artist was killed. If she didn't have anything to do with it, why doesn't she come forward?"

"I imagine she's afraid to," Phoebe said. "After all, it seems there are those who're ready to lynch her, guilty or not."

Thank you! Dimple thought, and smiled at her friend. *Did Phoebe suspect?* "And how is our little Peggy?" she asked, turning to Lottie. "Have you spoken with Kate Ashcroft recently?"

Lottie Nivens smiled. "From what I hear, they're having a hard time keeping her still, and she simply adores that dog! Kate says he follows her everywhere and they've had to move everything breakable because of his constantly wagging tail."

"Max is a gentle soul," Miss Dimple said. "I had a feeling those two would become friends."

"I expect Peggy will be ready to come back to school after the holidays, but Kate has asked me to stay on for a few more weeks while she takes a brief leave of absence."

"She's lucky you were available," Annie said. "You are staying, aren't you?"

"If Miss Bessie will have me." Lottie looked around the table and smiled. "I enjoy working with the children, of course, and my cousin Thelma lived here a few years back and she's talked about it so much, I feel right at home. There's something about . . ."

"About what?" Jesse Dean asked, spearing another olive.

Lottie shrugged. "Oh, I don't know. I can't exactly put it into words, but the other night the Ashcrofts invited me over to have supper and help decorate their tree, and Peggy brought out her doll—"

"Lucy," Miss Dimple said. "Odessa made it for her soon after her mother died."

"I had a rag doll named Lucy, too," Lottie said, toying with a stalk of celery. "She had yellow yarn hair and wore a red-and-blue-striped dress." She shook her head. "I wonder whatever happened to her."

"My favorite doll was named Dorothy," Bessie mused. "Her body was stuffed with sawdust but she had a china head. I made the mistake of letting my cousin play with her and she tried to give her a bath." She shook her head. "Poor Dorothy!"

Everyone laughed but Jesse Dean. "Your doll," he said to Lottie, "I wonder if that particular kind was made in the thousands—you know—like Raggedy Ann."

Lottie shrugged. "I don't know. It could be, but I don't think I've ever seen another."

"What do you hear from your husband?" Miss Dimple asked her, and Lottie Nivens frowned. "Not much lately. I know Hal's on a ship somewhere and when he does write, he has to be careful not to give anything away. He usually writes about his shipmates and the crazy things they do to entertain themselves—and the food, of course. I think they eat a lot of dehydrated stuff. I sent him a box with some of his favorite things for Christmas and I hope he's received it."

"I'm sure it will be welcome whenever it gets there," Bessie said, "and you'll be welcome in my home, too, for as long as you'd like to stay."

Phoebe asked about Lottie's cousin Thelma and discovered they had once worked together on the same committee in the Woman's Club.

"She's really Hal's cousin," Lottie admitted, "but I feel as if I've known her all my life."

During the remainder of the meal the discussion continued on reports from friends and loved ones in the armed services. Annie's brother, Joel, would soon complete his flight training, along with Charlie's fiancé, Will. Annie's Frazier was already on his way overseas, and Phoebe's adored Harrison soon would be. Jesse Dean, Miss Dimple realized, became unusually quiet and ate little of his dessert although they had a choice of three kinds. Jesse Dean only nibbled on his sugar cookie while Dimple and Phoebe did themselves well with Lottie's gingery sweet potato pie, and the others chose Phoebe's rich molasses pecan pie with dollops of whipped cream.

Dimple knew that the young man suffered emotionally from being turned down by the draft board because of his poor eyesight, but he had become a dedicated air-raid warden and served in many other areas to help in the war effort. "Well, Jesse Dean," she began, in an effort to draw him out of his doldrums, "I imagine you'll be in charge of the store until the Coopers return from their visit. When do you expect them back?"

"Not until the middle of next week," Jesse Dean answered. He concentrated on his angel cookie, breaking it in two and nibbling on a wing.

"That's a lot of responsibility!" Bessie said, apparently realizing the situation. "Harris Cooper is fortunate to have someone he can rely on." Jesse Dean smiled as the others all agreed but still had little to say.

"I'm sorry Virginia couldn't join us today," Phoebe said, replenishing Bessie's coffee, "but I

275

can understand why she wants to spend time with her cousin—Roberta, isn't it?"

"Who?" Annie looked up from her pie, noticing, belatedly, a warning look from Miss Dimple.

"Her cousin is visiting from out of town," Phoebe explained. "I can't remember where . . . somewhere far away, I believe."

"*Very* far," Miss Dimple said.

"I told Virginia her cousin would be welcome as well, but I think they planned on spending a quiet day together," Phoebe continued.

Dimple was relieved when Lottie made everyone laugh with a story about her young students rehearsing for the school assembly program. "They were supposed to enter singing and circle the tree on the stage," she told them, "but instead of walking, they *ran,* and the poor tree was in danger of toppling."

"What did you do?" Phoebe asked, laughing.

"I decided on a slower carol," Lottie said. "And speaking of trees, I almost forgot. I brought an ornament for yours, Miss Phoebe. I believe I left it on the hall table."

"Why, this is lovely, Lottie! Thank you," Phoebe said later as she unwrapped the small gift. "As you may have noticed, our tree could use a few more ornaments. I don't know what happened to all the ones I put away."

"It seemed to call to me from the gift shop

window," Lottie admitted. "Reminds me of one we had when I was very small. There's something about its face."

"What a dainty little angel," Bessie said as Phoebe passed the china ornament around. "You should place her near the top, Phoebe."

"Jesse Dean's the tallest," Phoebe suggested. "Why don't you do the honors?"

Lanky Jesse Dean didn't even have to stand on tiptoe to reach a higher branch and soon the fragile angel dangled on a feathery limb near the star.

Annie and Lottie insisted on clearing the table while the older women relaxed by the fire, and Jesse Dean pitched in to help as well. "I'm not accustomed to sitting around doing nothing," he admitted, stacking a tray with dishes.

"I'll wash if you two will dry," Annie said, and tying an apron around her waist, she filled the sink with hot water. It didn't take long with three of them helping to have the table cleared and the dishes dried and put away. Soon after that, Jesse Dean expressed his thanks and left, saying he had to go home to feed his dog.

"Well," Annie said, putting leftovers in the refrigerator, "I'll bet I know what we'll have for supper tomorrow."

"Sounds good to me," Lottie said, hanging up her damp dish towel. "It's always better the second time." She looked out the window at the bare branches of the old apple tree by the back steps. "Annie, what's the matter with Jesse Dean?"

"What do you mean?" Annie said, thinking she was referring to the young man's peculiar lack of coloring and thick glasses.

"Have I said something to upset him? I tried to engage him in conversation but he didn't have much to say. I don't think he likes me."

"I'm sure that's not it," Annie said, rubbing Honey and Almond Cream into her hands. "Jesse Dean's shy, but he was unusually quiet today. I noticed it, too. Maybe he isn't feeling well or he might be concerned about being left in charge of the store. I wouldn't worry about it."

"I think I need to walk off some of that dinner," Dimple said after Bessie and Lottie had left, and from the look Dimple gave her, Annie knew she expected her to go along, too.

"Good idea! Mind some company?" she suggested.

"My goodness, it's already dark out," Phoebe said, "and turning colder, too. Why, it was positively freezing when I went out to feed the birds awhile ago."

Dimple laughed. "It's supposed to be cold at Christmas. We'll bundle up and walk fast."

"And enjoy the tree lights in all the windows," Annie told her, hoping she would be able to keep up with Miss Dimple's no-nonsense pace.

"I hate to bring this up on Christmas Day," Miss Dimple began when they reached the corner, "but I'm concerned about Rebecca Wyatt. Sheriff Holland said he would let me know after he talked with her and I haven't heard from him yet."

"I'm sure he's enjoying Christmas with his family," Annie said, tugging her snug beret over her ears. "You'll probably hear from him tomorrow."

But Miss Dimple wasn't having any part of it. "Whoever tried to kill us the other day isn't going to take Christmas off. I'm sure the sheriff is aware of that. I think that woman is being held somewhere or she's hiding in fear for her life."

Unless she's already dead, Annie thought, hurrying to keep in step. "Maybe we should call him when we get back."

However, the sheriff wasn't there when they called his office, and Dimple was told he would return her call as soon as he came in. Her brother phoned a little later to wish her a merry Christmas, but when everyone finally went to bed after listening to a radio production of *A Christmas Carol*, she had yet to hear from the sheriff.

The telephone was ringing when they returned from church the next day and when Phoebe answered, Dimple hoped it would be Sheriff

Holland calling to let her know he had spoken with Rebecca Wyatt.

"I think it's Virginia," Phoebe whispered, handing her the receiver, "and she sounds upset."

Dimple hung up her coat before answering. Her friend had seemed fine when she'd spoken to her after church only minutes before. "Virginia, dear, is anything wrong? Are you ill?" she asked.

"It's not about me. It's Suzy! Dimple, she's not here. Suzy's gone!"

CHAPTER TWENTY-FOUR

I'll be right over," Dimple said, hanging up the receiver, and Annie knew by her expression that something was terribly wrong. "I'll come with you," she said, her hand on the doorknob.

Phoebe Chadwick sighed. "You might as well tell me what's going on. I'm not deaf and blind, you know. It has something to do with that young Japanese doctor, doesn't it?"

Dimple, reaching for her coat, darted a questioning look at Annie, and Annie, feeling as though they had nothing to lose, nodded.

"Better grab your coat, dear," Miss Dimple said to her old friend. "We'll tell you all about it on the way. And just to put things straight, she happens to be American."

• • •

Annie was breathless by the time they arrived at Virginia's little gray bungalow on Myrtle Street, and Phoebe, she noticed, had difficulty keeping up with their hurried pace. Miss Dimple, however, although noticeably distressed, seemed as fit and hardy as usual.

Virginia, obviously agitated, threw open the door before they could knock. "It's all that Mavis Kilgore's fault!" she said, darting a loathing look at the house across the street. "If she would just tend to her own business, this would never have happened."

Dimple ushered everyone inside as calmly as she could and closed the door behind them. "First, we need to sit down and collect our thoughts. Annie and I have explained the situation to Phoebe, who, as you know, is the soul of discretion, and understands our difficulties."

Looking completely perplexed, Phoebe nodded. "Well . . . as much as possible," she added.

"Tea, I think," Miss Dimple said, leading the way to the kitchen. "It won't do to rush pell-mell into this without putting some thought behind it.

"Now," she said, as the water came to a boil, "exactly what has Mavis done, and what does it have to do with Suzy?"

Virginia poured water into the pot to warm it, her mouth a grim line. "Came over here last

281

night with those blasted cookies—horrible things—hard as rocks with no taste whatsoever!"

Everyone jumped back as she splashed in boiling water, then tea. "We've never exchanged Christmas gifts before so I knew good and well she was just being nosy. Said she'd love to see my new bedroom curtains, but I told her they weren't finished yet, and thank goodness Suzy was able to stay out of sight, so I'm sure she didn't see her."

"Then why—" Annie began.

"Suzy was in her room writing to her family when Mavis came, and even though she couldn't be seen, I'm sure she could hear every word," Virginia continued. " 'I was hoping to meet your cousin,' Mavis said, and of course butter wouldn't melt in her mouth. 'Phoebe told me she'd invited you for Christmas dinner but you weren't able to come because you were expecting your cousin. Has she left already?' "

"Oh, dear! What did you say?" Phoebe asked.

"I told her my cousin was flushed and running a high temperature and that I was very much afraid it might be scarlet fever," Virginia said with a trace of a smile. "She couldn't get out of here fast enough. Told me not to bother to return the plate."

"And you think Suzy left because of that?" Dimple asked after the laughter subsided.

"Well, it certainly didn't help. She left this."

Virginia brought a sheet of folded paper from the drawer behind her and gave it to Dimple to read.

My dear friends,
It becomes more evident every day that I am not only creating a problem in your day-to-day living, but might even be putting your lives in danger. You have sacrificed too much for me already and I just couldn't bear it if you were to suffer unpleasantness—or worse—because of me.

I have a little money and am going to try to get a bus to Atlanta, where I can contact some of my friends from Emory. I'm sure they'll be able to help me until the authorities straighten out this most unfortunate situation. Please *do not* try to find me!

I will be forever grateful for your kindness.

Suzy

Miss Dimple took out her Sunday lace handkerchief and slowly wiped her glasses, which had become all fogged up—probably because of steam from her tea, she explained, although everyone knew better.

"Did she really think she could board a bus in

Elderberry without being recognized?" Annie said. "Somebody's sure to question her."

"It *is* the day after Christmas," Dimple pointed out. "I'm hoping everybody's still filled with the spirit—you know—peace and goodwill, and all that."

"Don't count on it," Virginia said.

"Did she take any luggage with her?" Phoebe asked.

"What little clothing she had is gone, and her warm coat and hat, thank goodness!" Virginia sat at the table and put her head in her hands. "She took that pretty scarf you girls gave her for Christmas, and those nice new gloves from you, Dimple, but she must've packed everything in some sort of bag. She didn't have a suitcase."

"She probably left soon after church began, when few people would be on the streets," Dimple said. "We need to find out the bus schedule for Atlanta."

"It leaves from Clyde Jefferies Feed and Seed," Phoebe pointed out, "and the store would be closed on Sunday, so I suppose she'd have to buy her ticket directly from the driver."

"They post the bus schedule in the store window." Annie spoke from experience, as she had relied on that transportation several times to meet Frazier in Columbus or Atlanta. "I can walk downtown and see."

Virginia jumped to her feet, almost knocking

over her chair. "We don't have time for that. Come on, we'll take my car."

No one waited in front of the Feed and Seed when they drew up minutes later, and Annie hurried to read the sign in the window, returning with a mournful face.

"The first bus to Atlanta left at seven this morning and there's not another until five this afternoon." She looked around them at the empty street. "Where do you suppose she went?"

Virginia frowned. "We had breakfast together this morning and she was there when I left for church. I can't imagine where else she might go."

"Probably to the only place she knows." Dimple looked from one to the other. "I believe she'd go back to Mae Martha Hawthorne's."

Phoebe shook her head. "But that's so *far!* And how would she get in?"

"It's not *that* far," Miss Dimple reminded her, "and I imagine she'd still have a key."

"Suzy wouldn't be able to use the fireplace, as somebody might see the smoke, but it's not that cold today," Annie pointed out, "and I'm sure there are canned goods on hand, so she wouldn't go hungry." Her stomach growled at the thought, reminding her she hadn't eaten since a hurried bowl of oatmeal at breakfast.

"Then I think we should go out there and bring her right back!" Virginia was in such a hurry to start the car she flooded her engine and had to wait to try again.

Miss Dimple was relieved at the delay. "We can't all go traipsing out there, Virginia. The neighbors might get suspicious and we'd frighten the poor woman to death. I suggest we drive as far as the turnoff and if we don't see any signs of Suzy on the road, then it's safe to assume she made it back to Mrs. Hawthorne's. If she doesn't show up for the five o'clock bus, *then* we can decide what to do next."

Virginia reluctantly agreed, and Phoebe, who was expecting her grandson, Harrison, to call from Fort Benning that afternoon, was eager to get back home.

Although they drove so slowly a car behind them blew the horn and passed in a cloud of red dust, they saw no sign of Suzu Amaya on the road that led to Mae Martha Hawthorne's.

"Oh, dear!" Virginia moaned as she turned for home. "I forgot I'm supposed to have supper for the young people at Epworth League tonight! I agreed to do it weeks ago and it's too late to find anyone to take my place. I'm afraid I won't be able to go with you to the bus station at five."

Once a preacher's wife, always a preacher's wife, Miss Dimple thought, although Virginia's Albert had been dead for years. "I would imagine they've all eaten so much Christmas candy, they wouldn't be hungry," she said.

"I'll go with you, Miss Dimple," Annie volunteered, "and Charlie should know about this, too. I'll call her when we get home."

"This doesn't sound good," Charlie said when Annie told her what had happened. "Poor Suzy! I could just smack Mavis Kilgore! We've got to find her, Annie, before something terrible happens."

"Overhearing what Mavis said, probably had something to do with it, but I think it's more complicated than that. It's more than likely Suzy's been thinking about this for a while."

"If she's not at the bus station this afternoon, then what?" Charlie asked.

"I'm hoping we can find her *before* she gets there," Annie said. "She'll have to walk and we can keep an eye on the road between Mae Martha's place and town. Maybe we can convince her to wait."

But Suzy didn't turn up at the Feed and Seed, and they didn't see her walking along the road, although Charlie scouted the area in the family car until it got too dark to see.

"Your mother's not going to be happy when she finds out how much gas we've used," Annie reminded her. Charlie only laughed. "My mother will be unhappy all right, but only because we didn't let her in on the reason we were using it."

Phoebe had decided to remain behind,

explaining that too many people would slow them down, and her presence might alarm Suzy, and Virginia was tied up serving hotdogs and baked beans to the young people at the Methodist church, so only Dimple and the two younger teachers kept watch across the street from Clyde Jefferies Feed and Seed.

"Well, so much for that," Annie said as the bus pulled away without Suzy. She turned to Miss Dimple. "Should we take a chance on driving out to the Hawthorne place?"

Dimple sighed and adjusted her purple velvet hat. "I don't see that we have any other option. It might be best, though, if we could drive without lights when we pass Esau Ingram's place. I'd rather not be seen."

"The Curtises must be back from their Christmas visit," Charlie observed as they drove past their house. "I see lights on in the living room."

"Have you thought they might have had something to do with our being locked in that shed?" Annie asked. "It would be easy for them to *claim* they were out of town when they were at home all the time."

"I've wondered about that, too," Miss Dimple said, "especially since I noticed mud stains on Stanley Curtis's trousers on the day of Mrs. Hawthorne's funeral. If you'll remember, it was the same day Bill Pitts was killed."

"But the mud was awful everywhere that day," Charlie reminded her. "I almost ruined a good pair of shoes in the churchyard. And remember, Esau Ingram and his wife were feeding the Curtises' animals, so they must've been away for a while at least."

"Have you heard anything from the sheriff?" Annie asked Miss Dimple. "I wonder if he's been able to locate Rebecca."

"No word yet," Dimple told her, "and I'll admit, that concerns me. Too, I would think Isaac Ingram would surely be back by now from Atlanta, or wherever it was he went."

"Well I hope we don't run into any of them," Charlie said as she turned onto the road leading to the Ingrams' and dutifully switched off her headlights. "It's a good thing there's a moon tonight or we'd be in the ditch by now," she added driving slowly.

"That's all we need—to get stuck in a ditch!" Frowning, Annie leaned forward to see ahead. "Looks like Esau and Coralee are at home. There's a light on in the back. . . . Oh, lordy, Charlie! Watch out for that possum, or raccoon, or whatever it was. You almost ran over it."

"I think there's a flashlight somewhere under the seat if you want to sit on the front fender and light the way," Charlie snapped. Gripping the steering wheel, she squinted to see the road. "I'm driving in the dark, you know."

Miss Dimple spoke calmly. "The road leading to the Hawthorne house is just ahead to your left. As soon as you turn, I believe it would be safe to turn on your lights."

Thank God! Charlie thought as the car bumped over ruts and fallen debris in the road, and they all gasped as the tires hit a slick spot, bringing them perilously close to the edge before the car righted itself.

It's a good thing Virginia and Phoebe know where we are! Charlie thought, and knew the others were probably thinking the same as they crept, rumbling, to the top of the hill. If Suzy had found refuge in Mae Martha's cabin, she would surely hear them coming.

"I don't see any light inside," Annie observed, "but the electricity has probably been turned off."

"In Suzy's situation, I doubt if she would take a chance on using it, even if it weren't," Dimple reminded her. "The poor child's probably terrified. Perhaps we should call out to her to let her know we're here."

Charlie pulled to a stop in the graveled area behind the house, and it was not until she stepped from the car that she realized she'd been holding her breath. The others joined her at the foot of the steps and they approached the back door together.

"Suzy!" Charlie called. "Please don't be afraid . . . we're friends!" She tried the door and wasn't surprised to find it locked.

"Suzy!" Miss Dimple peered in the window glass. "Please open the door and let us in. All we want to do is talk."

Charlie recognized the authority in her former teacher's voice and knew that if she were in Suzy's place she wouldn't hesitate to come running. "Somebody's been here," she said. "I can see a pan on the stove, and it looks like the remains of a meal on the table." *Good heavens! This sounded familiar. Would the three bears soon wander in from their walk in the woods?*

"Wait a minute!" Annie shouted. "I see someone coming."

The three stepped back and waited as a dark figure emerged from a back room and approached them. Charlie closed her eyes. *Please, God, let it be Suzy!*

*C*HAPTER *T*WENTY-FIVE

C harlie was surprised when the door opened and a figure wrapped in some sort of blanket hurled herself at Miss Dimple in a most un-Suzy-like show of emotion.

"Oh, thank goodness it's you!" Suzy shouted. "It's freezing in here, and dark . . . and I don't know what to do!"

"That's exactly why we're here," Miss Dimple

said, and with a worried look examined the young woman's tense face. "Why, Suzy, you're trembling. Here, let's sit down for a minute, then we'll gather your things and take you back to Virginia's." Putting an arm around Suzy's shoulders, she led her to a chair at the kitchen table and took a seat beside her. It was not like the competent young doctor to let her emotions get the better of her. There had to be another reason.

"It seems to be a little warmer in here," Annie said, touching the stove. "Does the oven work? I see you've been using the burners."

Suzy nodded, teeth chattering. "It's liquid petroleum—comes in a tank, but it was getting low when Miss Mae Martha died and I don't know how much is left."

Miss Dimple patted her shoulder. "When we get back to Virginia's we'll warm you with a nice hot bowl of soup and some of my ginger mint tea."

She was surprised when Suzy stubbornly shook her head. "I can't do that, Miss Dimple. I've made up my mind now and I'm not going to change it. It wasn't dark enough to walk into town to the bus station this afternoon, but I plan to try again in the morning before it gets light, and if things don't work out for me in Atlanta, I'll just have to take my chances with the police."

"Then why not come back with us," Annie suggested, "and if you still want to go, we'll take you to the bus station in the morning?"

It was obvious to Dimple that the suggestion appealed to Suzy, as she seemed to brighten momentarily but continued to insist that she remain where she was. Branches scraped the side of the house in a sudden gust of wind and Suzy jumped at the noise and looked nervously over her shoulder.

"It's all right," Miss Dimple assured her calmly. "It's only the wind." She paused, and spoke softly. "What is it, Suzy? What's frightening you?"

Suzy lowered her gaze, making fists of her fingers. "It's nothing. . . . I'm just tired. I'll be fine, really." She refused to look at Miss Dimple, who continued to watch her in silence. "Something else is troubling you, dear," she said. "Won't you tell us what it is?"

Suzy was quiet for a moment and when she looked up, tears filled her eyes and made glistening pathways down her cheeks. "I think there's somebody here," she whispered. "They were here before I came—I could tell—and they haven't left. I can hear them."

"Where?" Miss Dimple rose quickly to her feet. "Where do you hear them? Show us."

Suzy looked at the floor and shuddered. "Down there. I think someone's down there . . . in the basement."

"I wasn't aware there was a basement," Miss Dimple said. "Is there access from inside the house?"

"There are stairs at the end of the hallway between the two bedrooms, but I never went down there as there wasn't any need." Suzy dried her eyes on Miss Dimple's handkerchief and tugged the blanket closer around her. "I noticed some dishes left out on the table but I thought they might've been left there by one of the nephews or Coralee when they came to pack up some of Mrs. Hawthorne's things." She paused in an attempt to regain her composure. "It's so bleak here without her—so lonely! Miss Mae Martha . . . she made everything come alive in real life as much as she did in her paintings. What kind of person would do that to her?"

"A greedy one, I think," Miss Dimple said, "and obviously someone without much of a conscience. I believe you might be in real danger here, Suzy. I wouldn't advise you to stay in this house alone."

"I think we should notify the police," Annie said with an eye on the door to the hallway. "It might just be a tramp or somebody who knew the house was vacant, but you certainly can't stay here like this."

"But I can't tell the police! You know I can't." Suzy stood, casting aside the blanket.

"Then you might be the next victim." Miss Dimple's voice was even. "Is that the chance you want to take? Come back with us, Suzy, and let's talk about this."

"Wait a minute," Charlie whispered, listening for any noise below. "I think I know who that is down there." She looked from Miss Dimple to Annie. "Rebecca Wyatt hasn't been seen since that fire in her shed. Do you think she might've come here?"

Suzy frowned. "Why would she do that?"

"I believe she's afraid," Miss Dimple said.

"Well, that makes two of us! Do you know if she was wearing a shawl?" Suzy asked, moving into the next room. She held up a blue knitted shawl that had been draped across a chair by the fireplace. "Does this look familiar?"

Annie glanced at Miss Dimple. "It looks like the one she had on, but I'm not sure."

"This is Rebecca's," Miss Dimple said, examining the shawl. "I remember the green-striped trim."

"I know it wasn't here the day I left to gather greenery," Suzy said, "the day Miss Mae Martha was killed . . . If only I'd come back sooner!"

"Suzy." Miss Dimple's voice was kind but firm. "Don't allow 'if onlies' into your life. They do no good and they'll smother you if you let them.

"Now, how do you suppose Rebecca got inside? There must be an entrance to the basement from the outside."

Suzy nodded. "There's a door around the side near the porch, and I doubt if it was ever locked.

She must've gotten in that way and entered the house through the basement stairs."

Annie glanced at the stand on the hearth that had once held the poker that became a weapon. "Do you think Rebecca was the one who killed Mrs. Hawthorne?" she asked Suzy.

"I don't know but I can't imagine why. I didn't know Rebecca—never even saw her." Suzy shivered as the wind swept dry twigs and leaves across the porch behind her. "It seems so desolate here without Miss Mae Martha!"

"If Rebecca killed Mrs. Hawthorne, she probably set fire to that shed with us in it," Charlie said.

Miss Dimple shook her head. "I've thought about that, but I don't believe she did. When Rebecca helped us out of that burning shed I noticed some tools tossed aside on the grass that hadn't been there before—the kind of tools one might use to repair a barbed-wire fence."

"That's right," Charlie said. "I remember her saying something about finding it broken and going down in the pasture to mend it."

"That doesn't mean she didn't lock us in and start the fire," Annie pointed out. "She might've been there all the time . . . watching us . . . waiting."

"Then why would she have fence-mending tools with her?" Miss Dimple asked. "I think she must have dropped them there in order to run to the barrel for water." She raised her voice as she stood in the door of the hallway. "*And* I believe she's afraid for her life.

"Suzy, I urge you to come with us *now*. It's not safe to remain here any longer." Dimple turned and started for the door.

"We can't get out of here soon enough for me!" Annie said.

"Or me!" Charlie echoed. "Suzy?" She paused to look over her shoulder. And Suzy folded the blanket she'd been wearing, laid it over the back of the sofa, and silently followed the others.

The four of them filed through the kitchen and had almost reached the back door when someone called, "Wait!" and they turned to see Rebecca Wyatt behind them.

She stood trembling in the open door to the hallway, hugging herself for warmth. "Please, I'd like to come with you. I can't stay here any longer."

Suzy quickly snatched the blanket she'd just shed and wrapped it around Rebecca. "We have to get something warm in her now!" she said, seeming her confident self once again. "Her lips are turning blue. There should be enough fuel in that stove to heat a kettle of water."

Minutes later they hovered around the kitchen table as Rebecca, her color slowly returning, sipped from a large mug of tea. "I want you to know I had nothing to do with setting fire to that shed," she told them when her chattering subsided. "I'm just glad I got back in time to see the smoke."

"So are we!" Charlie told her. "But you know who did it, don't you, Rebecca?"

Rebecca twined thin fingers around the mug and took a long, slow swallow. It seemed she was about to answer when the yellow glare of headlights suddenly illuminated the room.

Annie ran to the window. "Oh, my gosh! Somebody's here. What are we going to do?"

"Can you tell who it is?" Miss Dimple asked.

Charlie frowned as she joined her friend at the window. "It looks like . . . it is! It's Esau and Coralee. We have to get Suzy out of sight!"

"I'm afraid you'll have to go to the basement," Miss Dimple directed. "Quickly, before they see you!" She glanced at Rebecca, who jumped to her feet, shoving her mug aside. "I'll go with her," Rebecca said. "We can leave by the outside door. There's a shortcut to my place."

"I remember." Suzy nodded, following her. "Here! Don't forget your shawl," she reminded her, plucking it from the chair on the way out.

"What are we going to tell the Ingrams?" Annie asked Miss Dimple as they heard the basement door close behind them and the sound of feet descending the stairs.

"Don't worry. I'll think of something,"

Dimple's voice was calm, but Annie noticed a flicker of alarm in her eyes.

"Coralee thought she heard a car." Esau Ingram stood in the open kitchen doorway, the light from his headlights glinting off the barrel of the shotgun in his hands. "What are you doing here?"

Dimple Kilpatrick sank sighing onto a chair at the kitchen table and rested her head in her hands. "I'm so terribly sorry about this, Mr. Ingram, but you're aware, I know, of what happened to us at Rebecca Wyatt's a few days ago." Her voice trembled as she searched for a handkerchief and, finding it, dabbed at her eyes. Behind her, Charlie and Annie exchanged glances and wondered what trick the older teacher would come up with now.

Esau lowered his gun but stood his ground. "Just how did you manage to get in?" he demanded. "And for God's sake, woman, *why?*"

Miss Dimple stiffened. She was not accustomed to hearing someone take the Lord's name in vain, but it gave her time to think. "Why, we came through the basement. That door was unlocked, you know, and I thought we might find Rebecca Wyatt here. She hasn't been seen since that unfortunate incident when the three of us were almost incinerated." Miss Dimple allowed her voice to shake a little as she explained further. "I thought perhaps she might have come here."

Esau tilted his head and frowned. "I don't understand," he began. "Why—"

Dimple straightened and looked him full in the face. "Why? Because the woman's terrified, Mr. Ingram. She's afraid for her life—just as the three of us were when someone locked us in and set fire to that shed." Dimple Kilpatrick would never look or speak to a child in the manner she addressed Esau Ingram. She was either challenging the man or calling him a fool. Possibly both. Charlie took a deep breath and edged closer to Annie.

Esau leaned the gun against the wall and took a step forward. "Surely you don't think I had anything to do with that? And everybody knows Rebecca's a bit . . . well . . . addled. There's no telling where she might be. Why, she's probably holed up in her house until all this excitement dies down. As far as I know, the Fuller boy's still taking care of her livestock."

"Esau? What's going on here?" Coralee Ingram stood in the doorway behind her husband and took in the scene, looking as if she had just come upon Hirohito himself.

"That's what I'm trying to find out," her husband told her with a weary sigh. "These ladies seem to think they'd find Rebecca Wyatt here, although why they'd want her, I don't know. If I was you," he added, addressing Miss Dimple, "I'd steer clear of that one."

Coralee didn't answer and Charlie got the idea the woman might not agree with her husband. "Look, I'm sorry if we alarmed you," Charlie said, speaking directly to Coralee, "but we're worried about Rebecca. The police haven't been able to find her, and we're afraid she might be in danger."

"Do you still think she might be here?" Coralee asked, stepping inside.

"If she was, she's gone now," Annie said, hoping the woman wouldn't notice Rebecca's empty mug on the table. "We've checked every room."

"We'll have another look at any rate," Esau said, making his way into the room. "And I don't reckon you all meant any harm, but if I was you, I'd stay away from other folks' property, especially when nobody's home."

"We certainly will, thank you, and again, we apologize for any distress we might've caused you." Miss Dimple spoke primly, as if she had only stepped on somebody's foot or accidentally bumped into a person on the street. The three of them walked sedately to the car and didn't speak until they had reached the bottom of the hill.

"Whew!" Annie sighed. "What do you think he meant by that?"

"By what?" Charlie slowed to maneuver a curve in the narrow road.

"That comment about staying away when

301

nobody's at home. Do you think he *knows* we've been poking about the outbuildings around here?"

"I don't doubt that he does for a minute," Dimple said. "I'd just like to find out what else he might know."

"I hope Suzy and Rebecca have had time to get to Rebecca's place." Charlie turned the car in that direction and groaned, remembering the terrible condition of the woman's driveway. "I'll park the car on the side of the road, and Miss Dimple, you can wait there while Annie and I walk up to the house to get the others. There's no need for all of us sliding around in the dark."

Dimple Kilpatrick only laughed. "Oh come now, surely you don't think I'm going to let you two have all the excitement. Of course I'm going with you!"

CHAPTER TWENTY-SIX

Lottie Nivens had looked at the big magnolia tree on the Sullivans' lawn every morning when she walked to school and again when she took her noon meal with Phoebe Chadwick across the street. She noticed the tree when she walked to town or to church and passed it again on her return.

"Do you remember who used to live in the Sullivans' house on the corner?" she asked Bessie Jenkins at breakfast one morning. It was the day after Christmas and the two had skipped church after sleeping later than usual and were enjoying a leisurely breakfast of fresh oranges, coffee, and applesauce muffins hot from the oven. Lottie's aunt Agnes, who had raised her, had seldom allowed her to help with the cooking and she was slowly learning her way around a kitchen. Wouldn't Hal be surprised when he came home after the war?

Bessie broke open a muffin and added a dab of margarine, smiling as she inhaled the spicy fragrance. "The Overtons lived there for a good while until he took a job in Atlanta, I believe, and they sold the place to the Sullivans." Bessie washed down her first bite of muffin with coffee. "I do believe these are even better than the ones you baked before, Lottie."

"But before the Overtons?" Lottie persisted. "Who lived there then?"

Bessie frowned. "Oh, goodness! Let me see . . . that must've been the Greesons—Jesse Dean's folks. Such a tragedy that was! The whole town was just torn up by it!"

"By what?" Lottie picked up her muffin and put it down again. Suddenly she wasn't so hungry.

"Jesse Dean's older sister, little Cassie, disappeared during a picnic that summer and we

303

never did know what happened to her. Some say she drowned in Etowah Pond, but most believe she was kidnapped. Jesse Dean was born a few months later and his mama—Eugenia—well, she didn't live long after that."

"What about the father?"

"Sanford? He left here after Jesse Dean was born and nobody ever saw him again. Something happened to Sanford over there during the war and he just never seemed right when he got back. Old Addie Montgomery, Jesse Dean's grand-mamma, raised him. Tried to turn him into a girl—to replace the one who was lost, I guess. She was a strange one, Addie was. It's a wonder he's turned out so well."

The china tea set was white with pink and blue flowers and a green border. It had been a present from Santa and she was not supposed to play with it outside. But her mama never looked under the sweeping limbs of the big magnolia and no one could see her there. She only took enough plates and cups for the two of them, and in her secret place under the big tree she served dark mud pies decorated with the glossy red seeds from the tree. Only her rag doll, Lucy, was invited to feast off the dainty flowered china. That day, however, the person she knew as Mama called to her in a hurry to go somewhere. The summer afternoon was sweltering and her mama was cross, but it was cool under the tree and Lottie didn't want to leave. *I'll come back tomorrow,* she thought, and she left the tiny dishes hidden away in her secret place in the roots of the big magnolia.

How do you ask someone for permission to dig underneath their tree? Lottie Nivens couldn't think of a suitable explanation and so she waited until she saw Clarissa Sullivan start for town the next day, wheeling her baby wrapped like a blue cocoon in his carriage.

Was anyone looking? The streets seemed deserted as Lottie parted the heavy branches and ducked beneath them to the musky, dusky shade of the tree. Even in late December it smelled of mud and summer and black, sooty bark, and brittle leaves rattled under her feet. Lottie took the small trowel she had borrowed from Miss Bessie's toolshed and began to scrape near the base of the tree. *Which side had she hidden them on? There should be an indentation in the roots somewhere . . . but what if this wasn't the right tree? There were countless magnolia trees in countless Southern towns.*

On her hands and knees she crawled around the base of the magnolia, scraping away the surface of the soil. Years of dirt, twigs, stones, and leaves had filled in the crevices but Lottie, now resorting to her fingers, carefully swept them away. *This must be how an archeologist works,* she thought, smiling at the comparison.

But when her fingers felt the dirt-encrusted surface of the tiny china cup, Cassie Greeson Nivens knew she was finally home.

"I don't see a light. They must not have gotten here yet," Charlie said as the three women made their way up the mud-slicked driveway that led to Rebecca Wyatt's. The beam from her flashlight sent a pale sliver through the dark night, briefly revealing the scorched shed by the garden where the smell of burned wood lingered, reminding them of their close brush with death.

"I hope they're all right," Miss Dimple said. "They had to make their way through the woods with no light, and Rebecca didn't look at all well."

"I guess all we can do is wait," Annie said. "They should be here soon, but it's freezing out here and I'm sure the house is locked."

"The barn isn't," Charlie reminded her. "At least we'll be out of the wind and we should be able to see the house from there."

Later, Dimple Kilpatrick would tell herself she had a *feeling* something wasn't right as the three of them hurried to the barn that cold December night, but then things had seemed topsy-turvy all evening long, not unlike their world since this dreadful war began. It was good to be out of the

306

frigid night air, and the barn smelled as barns should: of animals, manure, leather, and fodder. The only sound she heard was an occasional lowing of a cow, the chickens having long gone to sleep.

Dimple was the first to notice the canvases were gone. The small storage room still held an assortment of tools and implements, but the art materials that had been there before had been moved. "I wonder if Rebecca put them somewhere else," she said.

Annie frowned. "When would she have time?"

"You're right. She wouldn't," a voice said behind them, and they turned to find Isaac Ingram in the doorway with a gun.

Suzy gripped Rebecca's hand as they stumbled over the rough terrain, feeling their way in the dark. "I can't see a thing!" she said, tripping on a fallen limb.

"Just hang on to me," Rebecca said. "I've come this way plenty of times before. I should be able to get us there before long."

Rebecca had thrown her shawl over her head and was still bundled in the blanket Suzy had wrapped around her. It dragged the ground as she walked and now and then she had to stop and cough, holding on to a tree until the spasm passed. Suzy frowned at the sound of it, hoping they didn't have much farther to walk. Rebecca needed dry clothing, warmth, and steam for that worrisome rattle in her chest, and the sooner, the better.

"How much farther?" Suzy asked, shoving aside a limb. "We need to get you out of this cold." She could tell earlier by Rebecca's flushed face that the woman was probably feverish.

"Not too far now." Rebecca coughed again. "Just watch out for that ditch ahead, then there're a couple of hills and we should come out near the barn lot."

Suzy shivered, wishing she had worn warmer clothing. She had left her belongings in a paper bag in the small closet in her old room at Mrs. Hawthorne's and hoped Esau and his wife wouldn't notice it if they decided to search the house. She couldn't imagine what Miss Dimple had told the couple to explain their presence there, but Suzy had known Dimple Kilpatrick long enough to believe she would come up with something credible. After all, who would *not* believe Miss Dimple Kilpatrick?

They had reached the top of the second hill when Rebecca suddenly stopped.

"What's the matter?" Suzy held on to a slender pine sapling, eager to go on. "Are you all right?"

Rebecca held out an arm in the darkness. "Shh! Wait. I think I see somebody moving about down there."

"It's probably Miss Dimple and the others. They said they would meet us here."

Still, Rebecca held back. "Let's get a little closer to be sure, but that looks like a truck parked behind my barn."

"Whose truck?" Suzy whispered as they edged closer.

Rebecca crouched behind a clump of cedars and urged Suzy to do the same. "It belongs to Isaac Ingram, and we can't let him find us here. He's the reason I hid at Mae Martha's, and if he sees us—"

"But Miss Dimple and the others should be there by now. What do you think he might do?" Suzy peered through the feathery boughs to see a stocky figure standing in the open doorway of the barn. "Is there some way we can warn them?"

Suddenly a shout rang out sounding almost like a scream. *Charlie!* Suzy recognized the voice and it was coming from inside the barn. Charlie was trying to warn them.

"What do you want? Get out of my way!" It sounded like . . . it *was! Miss Dimple, of course.*

Suzy gripped Rebecca's arm. "We have to go for help!"

Rebecca nodded. "There's a path up the hill to the left that leads back to the road," she whispered. "We'll have to stay close to—" Her words were interrupted by a harsh spell of coughing and a bright beam of light immediately lit the ground in front of them.

"I know you're up there," Isaac Ingram shouted, "so I'd advise you to come on down now. I don't think you want me taking potshots at those bushes, do you?"

With one arm, Rebecca shoved Suzy to the ground. "Stay low and be still," she whispered. "He thinks I'm alone. Wait here and then go back to the road for help." She stood, still coughing, and made her way slowly down the hillside to where the man with the gun stood waiting.

Suzy held her breath as she lay facedown on the damp ground. *What had happened to Miss Dimple, Charlie, and Annie? In all likelihood Isaac Ingram had killed two people and had tried to kill three others. Could she get help before he added to the list?*

ℭHAPTER 𝒯WENTY-SEVEN

S omething wasn't right. Phoebe tried Virginia's number again. Still no answer. Probably cleaning up at the church after feeding all those young people. It had been much too long since Dimple and the others had left to find Suzy, and they should've been back by now. Phoebe paced the back hallway, wishing Odessa were there. She would know what to do. She could always rely on Odessa for good common sense, but her cook was spending the Christmas holidays with her family.

She would telephone the Carrs. She didn't have to tell Jo anything about them looking for Suzy. Maybe she had heard something from Charlie.

"Three of us will be better than two," Jo assured Phoebe when she and her sister stopped by for her a short while later. "Safety in numbers, you know." *Besides, she knew the wrath she would endure if she didn't include Lou on any would-be adventure.* Jo was relieved when Phoebe had called as she, too, had expected her daughter back sooner. What were the three of them doing out there anyway at this time of night? The unpaved roads could be treacherous, especially in the dark, and everybody knew those artificial rubber tires weren't worth a tinker's damn.

"Maybe we should phone the police or the sheriff or somebody," Phoebe suggested as they drove through the deserted streets of town. After all, if the women were in some kind of trouble, what could they do?

Lou drove, bumping over the railroad tracks as she spoke. "If it turns out to be nothing, I'm not crazy about getting that Sheriff Holland all riled up. You may have noticed we weren't on his Christmas card list this year. Let's drive out and see what's going on. I don't understand why they took a notion to go out there anyway. Maybe we'll meet them on their way back."

But most people, it seemed, had decided to stay at home on the day after Christmas, as they didn't meet a single car on the way to the turnoff for the Hawthorne place. "That's Esau's house just up ahead," Jo pointed out. "Maybe we should stop and ask if they've seen them."

"I don't see a light," Lou said. "Looks like they've already gone to bed. Do you think we ought to wake them?"

"I suppose we could try Mrs. Hawthorne's first, although I can't imagine why they would've gone there," Jo said, looking ahead for the turn. "It's just at the top of this hill."

"Stop! Wait a minute!" Phoebe, in the backseat, rolled down her window. "I hear somebody calling—there's somebody in the road behind us! Maybe it's Charlie or Annie. Quick, Lou, turn the car around so we can see who it is."

Lou made a sudden turn in Esau Ingram's driveway and managed to face the other direction. "Oh, sweet Jesus!" she exclaimed, getting a look at Suzy's frantic face. "We're being ambushed by the Japanese!"

After a few minutes of explanations from Phoebe, Lou and her sister eventually grew calm enough to listen to what Suzy was trying to tell them. "You mean *Isaac Ingram* is holding Charlie and the others at gunpoint in somebody's barn?" Jo gasped. "We have to call the sheriff *now!*"

"We can use the phone here at Esau's," Lou suggested, stepping from the car. "I'll go pound on the door and wake them."

"No, wait, please! This is Isaac's brother, remember!" Suzy put a hand on her shoulder. "How do we know he doesn't have something to do with this?"

"You're right. Then who's the closest neighbor? The Curtises, of course!" Lou answered her own question. "Get in, then—we have to hurry!"

Suzy didn't hesitate a second before sliding onto the backseat beside Phoebe.

"Where do you think he's gone?" Annie asked Rebecca as the four of them huddled together in the crude storage room in Rebecca Wyatt's barn. Earlier Isaac Ingram had held Annie roughly aside and forced the other two to enter by threatening to shoot her if they resisted. As soon as Charlie and Dimple were inside, he had shoved her in to join them. Not long after that, he'd thrust Rebecca in with the others and padlocked the door behind her. Their jail, they found, was of solid boards at least an inch thick and the door was securely bolted. They could scream all they liked, but who would hear them?

The others had made Rebecca as comfortable as possible with a feed bag for a pillow and covered her the best they could with her shawl and mud-spattered blanket. "He'll be back," Rebecca said. "You can be sure of that. I expect he's gone to his place to load up all the paintings he's been hoarding."

"And then what?" Charlie asked, although she wasn't sure she really wanted to know.

Rebecca's coughing caused her to shudder. "Let's hope your friend Suzy gets help here in time," she told them.

Isaac Ingram had set fire to the garden shed with the three of them inside, and he wouldn't hesitate to do the same to the barn. Miss Dimple closed her eyes and spoke to her Creator. *I know you're aware of our situation and that it's in your power to help, but if it's all the same to you, sooner would be a whole lot better than later!*

Rebecca's face was almost gray, and the two younger teachers were trying to maintain their composure, but it was hard to ignore the white knuckles on their linked hands. *How long had it been since Suzy left Rebecca to go for help? Twenty minutes? Thirty? An hour? How far would Suzy have to go to find it? And she would— of course she would!* Dimple wouldn't even allow herself consider the alternative.

"How does Isaac think he's going to sell those paintings after everybody knows what he's done?" Annie asked after a long silence.

"Unfortunately, there are all kinds of unethical

314

dealers in the art world, just as everywhere else," Miss Dimple told her. "I'm sure he has connections. I wouldn't be surprised if he hasn't already found a buyer."

"But *we* know what he's done," Charlie pointed out, and gasped when she realized what she'd said.

Miss Dimple patted her arm. "Perhaps he plans to leave here and go somewhere else to begin anew with all the money he'll be getting. Locking us in here would give him time to be far away before we're discovered."

Charlie smiled in spite of herself. Miss Dimple was becoming quite an accomplished liar. "Virginia knows where we've gone," she said, to assure herself as well as the others. "And Phoebe, too. I'm sure they'll send someone to look for us if we don't come back soon."

"What about your mother?" Annie asked her. "She must be curious about where you've gone."

"I told her I'd probably just have a sandwich with you at Miss Phoebe's, so she isn't expecting me for supper," Charlie said. "Does anybody have a watch? I have no idea what time it is."

But no one answered, and Miss Dimple thought of the timepiece she usually wore pinned to her blouse. Earlier, assuming she wouldn't need it, she had left it on the dresser in her room. Dimple thought fondly of her small room at Phoebe Chadwick's, with its comfortable bed covered with

315

the colorful patchwork quilt that had belonged to her for as long as she could remember; the cheerful rag rug beside it, and the small oak desk by the window. Would she ever see it again?

"The cows!" Charlie said suddenly. "Cows have to be milked. Isn't there someone who has been doing that for you?" she asked Rebecca.

"Abbott Fuller. He usually comes early in the morning and sets the milk in the springhouse, although I told him to sell it if he could." Rebecca paused. "He's only fourteen, but such a great help. I don't know what I'd do without him."

"Then he's sure to come in the morning," Annie said, brightening.

"I almost hope he doesn't. If Isaac were to . . . If anything happened to that boy . . ." Rebecca turned her face away. "Oh, this is all my fault! I should've known what Isaac was doing, but he promised me a chance for a brand-new face—a better life, and by the time I knew what had been going on, it was too late."

Isaac had seen samples of Rebecca's artwork several years before, she told them, and had approached her about painting scenes much like the ones Mrs. Hawthorne created. He could sell them, he told her, and she could invest the money. When she had enough, he assured her that he knew of a plastic surgeon in Atlanta who could give her the kind of face she had before she was scarred in the accident.

"I didn't know he was using Mrs. Hawthorne's signature on my work until I'd been painting them for some time," Rebecca told them. "And then he convinced me that I was even guiltier than he was and could be sent to prison for what I'd done. And, of course, he demanded I turn out more."

"Did he ever pay you?" Annie asked, and Rebecca nodded, pausing again to cough. "Oh, yes, I made sure of that in the very beginning. The money was deposited in a savings account—not enough for the surgery I need . . ." She shrugged. "But I had hoped that someday . . ."

"I don't understand why Mrs. Hawthorne wasn't aware of what was going on," Charlie said. "Didn't she know these paintings were being sold with her signature?"

"Mae Martha was a very private person—extremely shy, and too modest for her own good," Rebecca said. "Her nephews ran most of her errands, so you seldom saw her out, and then, of course, Isaac sold enough of her paintings so that she had sufficient income."

"She must have begun to suspect things weren't as they should be," Miss Dimple reminded them. "That's probably why she asked the Curtises to store several of her paintings in their church."

Charlie groaned. "And that rat Isaac ended up getting them back after all!"

"But why kill the goose that laid the golden eggs?" Annie asked.

"Mrs. Hawthorne changed her will after her grandson was killed. Any paintings that remained, or the proceeds from them, are to go to the university." Miss Dimple shivered in spite of herself and turned up the collar on her coat. "It looks like Isaac planned to make sure there weren't many left."

Annie burrowed into a sparse mound of straw and hugged herself for warmth. "I can't imagine *anyone* being cruel enough to do what he did to someone as kind as she was—and his own aunt, at that!"

"He killed Bill Pitts, too, I'm sure of it," Rebecca told them. "I had Bill mend a railing on my back porch a few weeks ago, and forgot he'd be able to see the room where I do my painting through the window there. He must've mentioned it to Isaac. Poor soul! How was he to know?" Rebecca buried her face in her hands.

"What about Esau?" Charlie asked. "Is he in on this, too?"

"I don't think so," Rebecca said. "Esau loved his aunt—checked on her almost every day, and I think Coralee was fond of her, too. She was the one who told me Esau took his aunt to see a lawyer about changing her will after Madison died."

Rebecca closed her eyes. Her chest rattled ominously when she breathed, and Miss Dimple touched her forehead with the back of her hand

and found it scorching hot. Silently she signaled the others to move closer to provide extra warmth, and snuggled together, everyone grew quiet.

Waiting . . . waiting . . . but waiting for what and for whom?

Dimple bolted upright at the sound of footsteps outside and a slant of light sliced through a crack between the rough boards behind them and wavered on the wall. She'd closed her eyes but hadn't been able to sleep, and neither had Charlie nor Annie, who had continued to whisper spasmodically to one another. Rebecca slept fitfully, coughing in her sleep.

Aching in places she didn't even know she had from sitting in a cramped position, Dimple Kilpatrick gathered her wits about her, ready and willing to fight—but how could you fight smoke and fire? Prepared to kick, claw, climb— whatever it took, she jumped to her feet.

"Miss Dimple?" someone called. "Charlie? Annie? Are you in there? Are you all right?" A man's voice. *Sheriff Holland—at last!*

And once again, Dimple Kilpatrick addressed her Creator. *Well, it wouldn't have hurt if it had been a little sooner. But I'm not complaining, you understand. I'm not complaining!* And, with the two younger teachers, she began to shout her answer.

CHAPTER TWENTY-EIGHT

L ottie Nivens stood on the front porch and raised her hand to ring the bell. What if this was all a coincidence? He might think she had made it up. What if Jesse Dean wasn't her brother after all? He would think she was crazy. She paused by the door until her feet felt as if they were encased in ice and her breath came in clouds. *For heaven's sake, silly, you'll never know if you don't ask!*

Lottie closed her eyes, held her breath, and rang the bell.

Jesse Dean seemed puzzled, but he smiled and invited her inside. "It's nice of you to drop by. You look cold. Can I get you something hot to drink? I've just put on some coffee."

She could tell he was surprised to see her there and was only being polite. Lottie said coffee would be nice and followed him into the kitchen, where a large brown-and-white dog lifted its head from where he was napping by the stove.

"This is Jake," Jesse Dean said, rumpling the dog's shaggy fur. "He won't hurt you—he's a friendly soul, and besides, he's too lazy to move." He took two cups and saucers from a cabinet and set them on the table. "We can go in the living room, but it's warmer in here."

Lottie sank gratefully onto a kitchen chair and clenched her hands together to keep them from shaking. "Miss Bessie said you had a doll," she began. "Or, I mean your sister had a doll, and that your grandmother kept it."

He nodded. "Lucy."

"Do you mind if I see it, please?"

Jesse Dean poured coffee and set the cups on the table. "I don't have any cream, but there's milk and sugar." He hesitated, still standing. "It's packed away—the doll is—in my grand-mother's cedar chest."

Lottie wrapped her cold hands around the cup and took a swallow, accepting it as it was. "She should have a grease stain on her chest," she told him, "from camphorated oil."

Jesse Dean turned even paler than usual and for a few seconds she thought he might pass out right there on the kitchen floor. "You mean . . . you think . . ."

"Please. I'd like to be sure." Lottie remembered her mother scolding her for what she had done to the doll, but Lucy had a cold, the child had explained; her cough was getting worse, and she was sure she had a fever. Wasn't that what she was supposed to do?

The doll, wrapped in layers of tissue, was about the size of an average newborn and smelled strongly of lavender and cedar. Jesse Dean's hands shook as he unwrapped the paper while Lottie hovered over his shoulder. The red-and-blue cotton dress was buttoned to the neck and Jesse Dean, ever-shy, seemed reluctant to undress it. Lottie gently took the doll from him and slipped the little dress down to expose the chest.

"I don't guess there's any way you can wash camphorated oil from a rag doll," she said, clutching Lucy to her chest. Through her tears, she could see that her brother was crying, too.

"It smells like snow." Charlie glanced at the sky through the mullioned library window. "Looks like it, too."

Virginia stamped a stack of books for Emmaline Brumlow and set them aside. "Wishful thinking," she said with a smile. "You're just hoping there's no school tomorrow, but there is a chill in the air. And the new year is almost a month old already. Wouldn't it be wonderful if 1944 brought an end to this war?"

Charlie thought of her brother, Fain, and of Will, her fiancé, who would soon be flying dangerous missions over enemy territory, and said if it ended tomorrow it wouldn't be soon enough for her.

A wood fire cast a cheerful glow at one end of the room, where Emmaline sat leafing through another book to add to her stack for Hugh. "Isn't that exciting news about little Cassie Greeson?" she said, looking up. "You know, I thought from the very first there was a resemblance between those two."

Charlie turned away so Emmaline wouldn't see her smile. "The woman who took her told Lottie her parents had been killed in an accident. Lottie said they moved around a lot, but she always believed she belonged *somewhere*."

"It's lucky for her that Kate Ashcroft decided to take a leave of absence, or those two might never have found each other," Virginia said.

"Humph! I don't think luck has anything to do with it," Emmaline announced. "I happen to believe in fate."

Charlie wondered if fate could be blamed for the fact that the woman who took Cassie happened to be fishing at Etowah Pond on the day of the picnic. Lottie said her "aunt's" husband and baby had died in the influenza epidemic in the fall of 1918, and she believed the woman must've been looking for a child to take her place. Fate or not, Charlie thought, the two siblings had found each other now, and Lottie (or Cassie) continued to live with Bessie Jenkins and had taken a teaching position at one of the small county schools.

"I'm glad to hear they decided not to prosecute Rebecca Wyatt," Virginia said, dislodging Cattus from her lap to tend the fire. "The poor woman's suffered enough. Why, she was in the hospital for over a week with pneumonia, and Doc Morrison told me himself it was touch-and-go there for a while."

"Well, she can thank our Suzy for pulling her through," Emmaline said. "She nursed that woman day and night and rarely left her side. Hugh tells me Suzy has even put her in touch with a surgeon at Emory who might be able to help her."

Our Suzy? Was this the woman who was ready to round up a posse to have the young doctor tried for treason or worse? With one of the local doctors semiretired and the other in the service, Ben Morrison had welcomed Suzy with open arms and had taken her on as his assistant until she could find a permanent position. Charlie hoped she would decide to stay. She had also been working with Hugh in his preparations for applying to medical school, as well as helping him become adjusted to walking with his new prosthesis.

"I think the people here will accept Suzy when they've had a chance to get to know her," Virginia said, forcing herself not to look at Emmaline. "However, we have to understand there are a lot of bad feelings against anything or anyone associated with Japan, so I expect it might take time."

Emmaline shut her book with a bang. "Well,

they'll just have to get over it. Suzy may come from Japanese heritage, but she's as American as you or I!"

A cold draft swept the room as Miss Dimple stepped inside and parked her purple umbrella by the door, setting aside a small bag of groceries. "Odessa needed a few more onions for tomorrow's soup, so I told her I'd stop at Mr. Cooper's." She warmed her hands at the fire. "Isn't it wonderful about Jesse Dean and his sister? He can't seem to stop smiling."

Virginia joined her in front of the blaze. "It's almost like a miracle."

"And that's not the only one," Dimple said under her breath with a sidelong glance at Charlie. "By the way," she told her, "I know what happened to those missing paintings Isaac was looking for. Coralee told Sheriff Holland Mae Martha had asked her to hide them for her."

"Where?" Charlie asked. "We looked in all the outbuildings there."

Miss Dimple laughed. "But we didn't look under her bed."

Charlie smiled at her old teacher, feeling warmth not only from the fire but also from the closeness she felt with Dimple Kilpatrick. Rebecca had told them later that Isaac Ingram had been alone in her house to collect some of her work when the three of them went there to look for the paintings. Watching from a window, he saw them searching in the barn and knew they had probably seen what was stored there. When they ran inside the shed to escape the gunfire, he quickly slid the bar across the door so they couldn't escape, and left them there after starting the fire. Rebecca saw the smoke as she was returning from mending the pasture fence and rushed to extinguish it, not realizing at first that there was anyone inside.

"Do you really think he meant to burn us alive?" Charlie had asked Rebecca.

"I honestly don't believe he cared," she told her. "But when I found you there and put out that fire, I realized he would be after me next. I knew what he had done to you and suspected he was responsible for killing Mrs. Hawthorne and Bill. He couldn't afford to let me live."

"Why didn't you leave with us? Why not go to the police then?" Charlie asked.

"I was afraid. He had frightened me so about selling those paintings under Mrs. Hawthorne's signature, I didn't feel safe anywhere! Thank goodness he didn't think to look for me at Mae Martha's, or I don't know what he might've done."

Now Emmaline added the book to her stack and bundled herself into her coat, buttoning it to her chin. "I'd best get back and help Arden with supper," she said, waiting for Virginia to stamp the latest addition, and Dimple could see she wanted to say more.

"Suzy tells us you all had been locked in that barn for several hours before she was able to reach a phone and call the sheriff," Emmaline said. "You must've been terrified. What in the world do you think of at a time like that?"

"I thought of what I'd like to do to Isaac Ingram if I ever got my hands on him," Charlie lied. What she'd actually done was compose in her head a long letter to Will—and pray a lot, of course.

"Well, he won't be killing anyone else," Virginia assured them. "The sheriff's men found him loading his truck with Mrs. Hawthorne's paintings—no telling how many he had in there. He'd been selling the ones Rebecca turned out and keeping most of hers for himself. It was obvious he was getting ready to clear out."

Emmaline scooped up her armload of books and started for the door. "I wonder if he meant to come back and set fire to that barn."

"I don't think so," Dimple told her, not daring to look at Charlie. "I believe all that wicked man wanted to do was put distance between us and those paintings."

As she spoke, a stab as sharp and cruel as a hot poker began in her throat and plunged to the pit of her stomach. After Isaac left them in the barn that night she had heard something that filled her with dread, something the others hadn't noticed: *Isaac Ingram had opened the stalls and led the cattle from the barn. He had been a farmer too long to destroy livestock unnecessarily.*

"Oh, look!" she said as Emmaline stepped outside. "I think it's beginning to snow!"